WRAITH

MERE JOYCE

WRAITH

ORACLE OF SENDERS

Wraith
Oracle of Senders Book Three

www.merejoyce.com

Copyright © 2021 Mere Joyce

TO THOSE WHO WAITED.

A BRISK BREEZE WAFTS THROUGH THE AIRPORT'S SLIDING DOORS, THE BARB of cold curling around my neck like the first seeping pinpricks of nearby death.

The thought is melodramatic. But even with the bright sunshine ahead of me, I can't shake the dread it brings. The stale warmth of this terminal is the last blockade between me and the summer I'm about to face. When I leave its mundane shelter, I'll be unable to pretend my long trek from Toronto to Ilulissat has been for any happy reason. The next ten weeks of my life will be devoted to the dead, and the cold prickle on my skin is an early reminder of what I have to look forward to.

Ten weeks. How am I going to survive ten weeks of this?

You're here, Cal. You can't go back now. You might as well shove on.

I hitch my backpack higher on my shoulder and

grab the rest of my luggage. Clinging to the sweeping crescendos of Wagner's "Liebestod" streaming through my headphones, I tamp down my nerves and step into the afternoon sun.

Breathing deep to loosen the tightness in my chest, I push past a busy family straggling near the airport's entrance. The mother of the group offers me a scathing glance as I cut through their slow shuffle. But after an overnight flight to Reykjavik—followed by a five-hour layover and another three and a half hours in the air—I only manage a muffled, insincere apology. I'm not thrilled about the adventures awaiting me beyond this terminal. But now that I've crossed the threshold, I'm ready to finish this tedious journey and get to Camp Wanagi.

The family disappears behind the sliding doors as I survey the concrete parking lot. I expected something more astonishing, some breathtaking view to make me marvel at the incredible fact I've arrived in Greenland. But even if that view did exist, I probably would have ignored it. Instead of peering around to see beyond the airport's perimeter, my eyes roam only to the closest row of parking spots. There, they settle on a tall, billowy figure leaning against a nearby car.

I cross the lot to meet my friend and fellow Shade, trying hard not to stare at the brown frames and magnified lenses of Kornelía Tumisdottir's new myodisc glasses. She hasn't sent any pictures since she got them in December. But although she's had several months to grow accustomed to the spectacles, I know they're still a source of misery. So, I force a smile, ignoring the odd way her irises bulge under the lenses' center rings and clearing my head of unfriendly thoughts.

"They're awful, I know," she says as soon as I'm close, striking down my attempt at oblivious cheer.

I shake my head, ready to assure her she looks fine. But Kornelía doesn't allow me time to respond. Adjusting the frames with a frown, she pushes off the silver car and envelopes me in a hug.

Her thin arms are cool as they wrap around my neck, but her closeness still brings with it a small glint of warmth. After an incredibly long ten months, it's good to at last be with a friend again.

"It's nice to see you," I say, failing to hug her back due to the luggage hanging at my sides. "And I'm glad you're able to see me, even if the glasses are... *different*."

She laughs, stepping back. "It's good to see you too, Cal." Her eyes roam over me, her head tilting to one side like she's going to remark on my appearance— or perhaps mention one of the quiet thoughts she's too good at pulling from my brain. Either way, I'm grateful for an interruption when the car's backseat window rolls down and a voice drifts between us through the crack.

"Hey, Cal," Dylan says from inside the car.

"Hi, Dylan," I reply with a nod I'm not sure he sees. I can't make him out through the open slit or the tinted window frame. I wonder if he's still jet lagged from his arrival, or if he's too lazy to get out of his seat.

Kornelía motions for me to follow her to the trunk so I can store my bag and backpack. I keep hold of my violin case as I move to the vehicle's far side.

"Speaking of *different*," she whispers, nodding towards the car.

I quirk a brow, but she only shrugs one shoulder

before opening the front door and sliding into her seat. I pause, taking another deep breath and pushing down the slight queasiness born from knowing this is the last stretch before camp is officially upon me. Then I open the car door and duck inside.

The hired driver I'm guessing is a local starts the vehicle and heads away from the Ilulissat Airport. I settle into my seat before turning to Dylan—and promptly doing a double-take.

Dylan Benowitz has always had a sickly, sallow complexion. But his skin looks nearly gray in the car's interior light. The bags under his eyes have darkened, and there is a definite yellow tint to the whites. Combined with the disheveled, shaggy state of his dark hair, the discoloration makes him look like he's contracted a fake illness only ever seen in the movies.

"Hey," he says again. His eyes are wary and expectant, like he knows what I'm about to say.

"Are you... okay?" I ask, unable to refrain from posing the question I'm positive he's heard many times since his arrival.

"I'm not dying," he mutters with a sigh. He scrapes his hair back, scratching his scalp. "*Trust me.* Between my mother and my stepmom, I've been to at least a dozen doctors over the last six months. Not to mention consultations with the rabbi. I've taken enough tests, I'm shocked I haven't earned some kind of degree. My blood work checks out, my oxygen levels are ideal, and my liver function is fine." He rolls his eyes. "There's nothing wrong with me."

"Well that's good, I guess," I mumble.

Dylan smiles, dropping his hands to his lap as Kornelía turns in her seat to face us. "I can still function, at least," he says. "Unlike poor Korni."

I shift my gaze forward. "They still haven't figured out what's going on with your eyesight, then?"

"Nope," she says with another shrug. "According to tests, I'm fine too. Except my eyes keep getting worse. I never thought I'd miss my old glasses."

The slight release of tension offered by the open air dissolves as worry coils back around my chest. I didn't expect to see my friends in such a bad state. I've talked to both Dylan and Kornelía over the last ten months, but our conversations didn't prepare me for how they now appear.

From the looks of it, our third summer with the Oracle of Senders isn't off to a smashing start.

"We're all falling apart, aren't we?" I muse.

"Not you," Dylan scoffs. He appraises me, his thick eyebrows lost under his unruly waves of hair. "You look like you haven't slept in a few days but, other than that, you seem great."

My fingers seek the front strands of my hair, ensuring the side-sweep is still in place after my latest flight. Dylan's assessment is wildly inaccurate. For me, sleep has come and gone in swells for far longer than the past few days. A constant swing between total insomnia and heavy oversleep has plagued me since January. But even if sleep deprivation is the only mark against my appearance, it's not the sole reason I haven't had a great ten months at home.

I want to tell Dylan as much. But I keep my mouth shut, knowing it will only sound like whining. My summers at Camp Wanagi are supposed to be a relief from the cold monotony of my non-Sender life. I don't want to start off by bombarding my friends with complaints.

"Why are you guys here, anyway?" I ask instead, swallowing the lump in my throat and trying not to dwell on the months gone by. "I wasn't expecting to meet anyone until I got to camp."

"We were bored," Dylan says.

"*And* we wanted to see you," Kornelía adds.

"Oh sure, that too," Dylan agrees half-heartedly.

Dylan and Kornelía both landed in Greenland a couple days ago. For the first time, I'm arriving on a Saturday—which means a full day and a half is left until the unofficial kick-off of camp starts with the new campers' initiation.

"Is everyone else already here?" I ask, my thoughts selfish until my brain catches up with my mouth. "Everyone who's coming, that is," I add in a rush.

Dylan frowns, staring down at his lap. I wish I'd worded my question better. One member of Camp Wanagi's Shade Sector is still in Guatemala. Even after ten months, Mim Castillo hasn't awakened from her coma.

"No," Kornelía says from the front seat. She eyes me for a moment, then glances at Dylan. "There are still a couple coming tomorrow."

I nod and, after a few seconds, Kornelía faces front as silence settles over the car. We don't know the man who is driving, which makes discussing our reasons for being here risky. But mostly, I suspect we're stuck in our own thoughts. I am, at least. Unlike my first year of nervous uncertainty or last summer's sunny excitement, arriving at Wanagi today leaves me with nothing more than a heavy emptiness. I wallow in its weighty presence as I ponder what's in store over the next couple months.

When I packed my bags a few days ago, I held onto the vague hope that returning to camp and seeing my friends would be an uplifting experience. But neither the company nor the rugged terrain passing outside my window spark anything but creeping dread like the bitter pinch I sampled at the airport. Being at Camp Wanagi means I'll be hard pressed to avoid seeing ghosts. Which would be nothing new except, this year, things have changed.

I turned sixteen in February. And I haven't seen a single spirit since a month before my birthday.

If I came here this summer only to discover that my ability dissipated instead of developed, it'd be a relief. I've never been one to attract good luck, though, and I'm fairly certain the lack of sightings isn't a miraculous change in my nature.

My life at home has narrowed to a tepid routine I work hard not to deviate from. I've learned to avoid the places I know are haunted, and I go through somewhat ridiculous pains to evade travelling anywhere new. Still, as each month has slipped by without a single ghostly sighting, my anxiety's grown. Being here is like stepping onto a minefield. An explosion is imminent, and I don't even know how to anticipate it.

I lean back against the seat and try to ignore all thoughts of possible spirit encounters. Soon enough, I'll be forced to confront whatever ghosts may be waiting for me in this arctic land. For now, I need to keep from obsessing over the shadows lurking around each bend. Because it's not only my fear of what will be waiting that tugs me down with hopeless exhaustion.

The harder reality will be shaking off the specters of what—and who—I won't be seeing anytime soon.

2

"HOW LONG IS THE DRIVE?" I ASK, DESPERATE TO KEEP MY THOUGHTS AT bay.

"Not long," Dylan says. His eyes are fixed out the window, the pane still opened a crack at the top. I'm surprised he's not cold. When I first learned this year's location, I thought I might need heavy boots and a winter coat for the climate. Turns out, the summer months in the south of Greenland are mild rather than frigid. Still, Dylan's only wearing a polo tee. He's got to be at least a little chilly.

He doesn't provide any other details about our commute, so I barrel on with more pointless chitchat. "It was a nice short trip for you, eh Kornelía?"

In the front seat, Kornelía pushes her glasses to the top of her head. "Yes, but why they decided to send me so early I'm not sure," she sighs. "We haven't been allowed to do anything but sit around our house since we arrived."

The town is small and, in the five minutes we've been driving, we've already left what seems like the main portion of the community. Now, the car rumbles along an uneven path, rising and dipping as we travel among the low, rocky hills.

"I guess it's not as easy as last year," I offer. "No beach to play on, at any rate."

"The land's rougher here," Dylan agrees. "They probably don't trust us not to fall over a cliff."

"Maybe," Kornelía says, sounding unconvinced.

Dylan shrugs. "Whatever the case, you're about to be a part of it, Cal."

I look away from my window to his view out the other side of the car. We've approached the coast and, now that I see it, the smallest tingle of appreciation fights against the numbness of my indifference. A grassy slope dotted with stony ridges veers gently down to the water, a shoreline so vastly different from last year's tropical beach it's hard to even call them the same element. The water here is a soothing, steel blue and, even in June, it is full of icy chunks. Hundreds of white peaks spread to the ridge of dark blue water stretching close to the horizon.

I've never seen a landscape like this. Since I assume the small, green-slatted house sitting atop a nearby hill is our current destination, I suppose I'll have ten weeks to enjoy the view. For a moment, the sight is dazzling, and I welcome the interest. But then my gaze settles more firmly on the house, and my brows furrow as I take in its size.

"This is where we're staying?" I ask, looking back at Dylan. "How are we all going to fit?"

The car pulls to a stop, and Dylan throws open the

door as he answers. "We don't," he says, one foot already outside.

I take my violin and exit the vehicle. Kornelía joins me at the car's trunk as I pull out my other bags.

"Camp is separated," she explains once I've gathered my things. "All of the sectors are in different parts of town."

I look at her in surprise. "What? Why?"

"Not a lot of availability in Greenland," another voice says.

As the hired car drives away, I look over to see Alex and Robbie—Shade Sector's leads—approaching from the house. Alex smiles. She has a woolen shawl wrapped around her shoulders.

"We had to take what homes were open to us," she continues. "So, we're split. Every sector has its own abode, with one or two classrooms in each. There's an additional apartment near the town center that's got an extra classroom and the library as well."

She gazes in the direction we've just come from but, when I follow her line of sight, sloping hills of grass, dirt, and rock are the only things visible.

"How are we supposed to get from one class to another?" I ask, turning back. "I take it the other homes aren't within walking distance from here."

"There will be a shuttle service, of sorts," Robbie says in his languid, southern drawl. His mohawk was been trimmed, making its height a few inches shorter than last year. But the hair still fans out, the stiff strands dyed black near the front and back, with a stripe of green in the middle.

"It was either that or set up camp in an abandoned settlement," Alex laughs. She glances at Robbie.

"Which was a serious consideration for a while. I'm glad they changed their minds."

"Would've made quite the story, though, wouldn't it?" Robbie grins. "A whole summer camping in abandoned houses. No electricity or indoor plumbing. It'd be like, I dunno… actual *camping.*"

I'm always up for a few nights of sleeping in a tent, roasting marshmallows, and watching the stars. But I shudder to think of what would have happened if I'd shown up in Greenland with my violin only to be shoved into arctic accommodations without heat or proper shelter from the elements.

"You can hide out in derelict shells on your own time," Alex says with a shake of her head. "For now, let's get Cal inside."

Her words catch me off guard, and the ease of the past minute blows away with the breeze. My eyes drift back to the unimposing house, the beat of my heart slow but hard as I picture the people within. Most of the others have already arrived and are on the other side those walls, ready to say their hellos. But some have yet to reach Greenland, one is unable to—and the last member of our sector won't be arriving at all.

Not every camper chooses to attend Camp Wanagi for four years. Some turn their backs on the Oracle of Senders, deciding instead to live their lives as if spirits don't exist—as if no one else in the world does, either.

I rake in an uneasy breath, my fingers squeezing so hard against the handle of my violin case, my fingers burn as I follow Alex to the house.

If one thing makes returning to camp easier this year, it's the fact that we're in a new location. I brace myself at the front door of the slatted home, prepared for an onslaught of olfactory senses reminding me of happier times. But when I take the first step inside, the ache of nostalgia doesn't rush forward to greet me.

This year's accommodation is not a ramshackle château or a clean island fale. A short hallway leads to the main living room and, while the two sofa set-up is familiar, the rest of the layout is not. White paint and a light wood floor decorate half of the square room, while a wall full of windows and a small porch overlooking the sea makes up the house's front side. Against one of the interior walls, a floor-to-ceiling stone fireplace is alight with burning logs.

I stop short of the rug laid before the fire, surveying the room and the view out the front windows. Continued interest—vague but alive—flickers within me, and I revel in the newness of a setting so strange. I kick off my sneakers and sink into the soft rug, holding onto the sensation for as long as possible. My steps are light as Alex welcomes me inside. But when she leads me to the kitchen, the sight of more sector mates brings bittersweet familiarity tumbling back into place.

Sefa, Reed, and Naasir sit at the round kitchen table playing cards. Sefa throws his hand on the table, cursing Reed's smug smile before giving me a wave.

"Hey, Cal. How was the flight?" he asks.

I haven't been active online for a while, so I haven't kept up to date with Sefa and the others. But I appreciate his casual tone, the easy way he greets me suggesting there's no need for us to become reacquainted.

"It was all right," I say. I give Reed and Naasir nods of greeting as Naasir deals out the next hand of their game. "How have you guys been?"

"Bored," Sefa says with a sideways stare at Robbie

and Alex.

"Sefa thought he'd be hunting ghosts already," Naasir says, his sonorous voice laced with amusement. "He's tired of playing cards."

"You're going to be in for a long summer if you're already done with cards," Reed says with a shake of his head.

Sefa sighs, sitting forward and grabbing the cards he's been dealt. "Maybe I wouldn't be so sick of this game if I got to win every once in a while," he grumbles.

We watch as another hand is dealt but, after Reed has once more claimed victory, Alex and Robbie continue their tour of the house. Kornelía and Dylan stay in the kitchen with the others as I follow our leads through the maze of short, narrow hallways. Alex points out the back quarters where she and Robbie are staying, the dining room that's been converted into a classroom, and the single bathroom all of us are somehow going to share. After we pass the girls' closed door, we reach the last room in the house—the boys' bedroom.

"Take some time to unpack," Robbie says as we approach the open door. "Rest up if you need to. Trust me, you ain't gonna miss much."

"Robbie," Alex scolds. She nudges him in the stomach, no doubt annoyed he's sharing in the campers' opinion of this place being a bore.

"What do you want me to say, that he better get in on the high-stakes action before Reed cleans house?" Robbie's expression is dubious, and Alex can't maintain her remonstrance. She rolls her eyes, but her lips crack into a smile at the same time.

"Take a break if you need to, Cal," she says, turning

her attention back to me. "We don't have any activities planned for the remainder of today. Or, if you'd rather, you can take a walk, or play cards with the others. And let us know if you need anything."

"I will, thanks," I say with a nod.

The two leads leave me alone in the hall. I watch them disappear around a corner, then I swallow hard before venturing through the doorway.

The bedroom is bright. The decor features the same white paint and light wood floor as the rest of the house, and thick curtains frame a wide window that looks over the grassy slopes and coastline to the far left. Beside the window is our black dresser, and our bunk beds line the other three walls.

I place my luggage on the far lower bunk, the same bunk I've used for the past two summers. The motion reminds me of last year, when I had to dig through my luggage to find sunscreen. When I wasn't alone in the room.

I slump onto the bed until I'm sitting across from Dylan's bunk. His pillow is jammed against the wall, and mud-caked running shoes peek out from where his sheets have spilled onto the ground. I let out a breath of a laugh at the familiar, messy sight before my eyes slide to the bunk above his.

The bunk has been neatly made—it's devoid of any folds, creases, or extra blankets stolen for warmth.

Persistence never paid off in regards to Meander Rhoades. After we left Tonga last August, I wrote him a long email promising I would be ready to talk whenever he calmed down enough to realize he was being a fool. He was—is—ludicrous to believe his talent for angering spirits will cause me harm. But his response to my letter was only long enough to tell me he wouldn't change his mind and to urge me to stop writing.

I didn't stop. My letters continued, once a week for months without reply. I took it upon myself to pretend Meander wasn't deleting the messages unseen, and I recapped my weeks as if he were eagerly awaiting the next installment in the less-than-thrilling memoir of my life.

I lower my gaze from his empty bed, tempted to write one of those pointless emails now.

Arrived in Greenland. No dead people on the plane. No one sleeping in your bed.

I pull my phone from my pocket but, this far from the middle of town, there's no reception. Not that it matters. I sent my parents a message when I landed. And the other email would be ignored anyway.

I didn't receive word from Meander from the end of August to almost the end of December. Not until I broke down on Christmas Eve. No longer able to continue our one-sided game, I sent him a pathetically lengthy letter, pouring my heart out and begging him to respond. I'd cringe if I saw the contents of that message now, I'm sure. But in the moment, I was tired and lonely and missed my best friend.

He did respond to that one and, for one moment of elation, I realized he hadn't been deleting my messages after all. But the joy died as soon as I read his irritated reply, consisting of curt sentences that insisted I stop trying to communicate. I read his words three times, willing them to transform into something that didn't hurt so much. When they didn't, I crawled into bed and cried myself to sleep.

It wasn't the last time I heard from Meander. But the pain of that night matches the way seeing his empty bunk feels now. I knew he wouldn't be here this summer. Still, a stupid, incessantly optimistic part of me hoped to find him waiting. Confirming the reality of his absence is like being struck with a totally new kind of silence. I expected seeing his empty bed would be painful, that being around other Shades without him would be like having a black hole forever hanging in my peripheral vision.

But despite what we've been through—or maybe because of it—I never fully appreciated how dark the void would be.

I NAP ON AND OFF THROUGHOUT THE AFTERNOON, KEEPING TO MYSELF UNTIL
Dylan calls me for dinner around seven. Shuffling to
the kitchen, I join the other five members of Shade
who have so far arrived at camp for a miniature feast
of seafood so rich it makes my stomach turn. I'm okay
with fish every once in a while, but waking post-nap to
see steaming bowls of butter-soaked fillets is anything
but appetizing. Still, I take a small portion, forcing
myself to eat to avoid having to explain my distaste.

My sector mates maintain a steady stream of
conversation, talking about the school they are
missing or the friends they've left at home. Reed is
happy he avoided a visit with his annoying cousins,
but the subject makes Kornelía melancholy, since she
had to leave all six of her brothers and sisters behind.
Kornelía is the only female member of Shade present,
except for Alex. She must be lonely sleeping in the
girls' room knowing that, unlike Sabeena and Lu,

Mim is not on her way.

I listen as the others talk and watch as they eat, thankful no one is eager to draw me into the discussion. Once dinner is over, we help clean the dishes, then Dylan retrieves his laptop to put on a movie. I contemplate slumping onto a sofa and zoning out in front of the screen, but it seems wrong to spend so long in a new locale having barely even glanced out the windows. I don't have the energy to go for a walk. So, I sit out on the screened porch instead.

Kornelía follows me outside, her sketchpad tucked under one arm. We settle in chairs, and she flips open her pad. The scratching of her pencil is soon drowned out as I put in my earbuds and turn on Mussorgsky's "Pictures at an Exhibition." I lean back in the wooden chair, watching icebergs floating through the nearby water and wondering why they've put a screen on this porch to obscure the view.

"This place should be comfortable," Kornelía says after a long while.

Her words twist into my music, pulling me from the soothing blankness of watching the ice. "Sorry, what?"

"I mean, I'm closer to home this time," she continues as if she's already got my undivided attention. "It's not like last year, being so far away and in such a different place. But there's an uneasiness here no one is talking about." She pauses, her pencil poised mid-stroke. "Don't you feel it? They won't let us explore, and… Oh, I don't know. Maybe that's not the reason. Maybe we're just uneasy because we're no longer complete."

She gives me a sidelong glance, her expression curious. I can't tell if she's trying to read my mind or if she's deciding whether to share what's on hers.

I shift forward, gripping my knee with one hand and pausing my music with the other. "I'm sure we'll settle into the new routine," I say, my jaw tight.

The false assurance is familiar now, the same lie I've been telling myself for the past month. I knew things would be different this year. But I ignored the yearning to stay home, wrapped in a blanket of bored comfort. Forcing myself to pack and prepare, I pretended that—incomplete sector or not—being with my fellow Shades would bring me a semblance of purpose. I've only been in Greenland for a few hours. But so far, the biggest thing I feel is a desire to get back on a plane and return to Canada. This place isn't a hopeful mystery or a prized vacation. As nice as the calm water and astonishing icebergs are, being so near them is just one more reminder of how skewed my life has become.

"Tomorrow is another day," Kornelía says with a sigh. Her words are light, but I detect a note of pity in them. She has more to say, and the hesitant way her mouth purses before she turns silently back to her sketchbook snaps a flicker of irritation against my chest. She wants to confide something, but she's afraid of upsetting me. Yet as annoying as that truth is, I don't have the will to suffer through her bad news.

"Tomorrow camp begins," I agree, allowing her to retreat.

As I say it, Kornelía's head tilts and she considers her drawing, her attention already back to her task. She brings her face close to the sketchpad, her eyes squinting behind the thick frames.

"Uh-huh," she mumbles, before a *tsk* of frustration escapes her throat. She hastily erases something on the page, her mouth set in a concentrated frown.

"I'm sorry about your eyes," I say.

"They are a bother." She nods, the movement slow and sullen. It's a tragic story to hear of anyone losing their eyesight. But I imagine it's a special sort of hell for an artist like her.

"What about your spirits?" I ask, straining to see something of her sketch. "Are they bothersome, too?"

This time, Kornelía smiles. She turns to me, her magnified eyes momentarily bright. "They're amazing," she breathes. She taps her pencil against the sketchbook. "The one I'm drawing now was so clear to me, I could make out the ringlets in her hair."

Kornelía started seeing ghosts more clearly after our first summer at Camp Wanagi. In the beginning, the change frightened her. But now she talks about the alteration like it's something to be revered.

"It was like she was real, only... transparent? No, that's not right." She thinks for a moment, then smiles again. "Like she was real, inside of a dream. As if she was standing right beside me, only I was dreaming, so everything was a little strange."

"That's great," I say, trying to sound like I mean it. I don't understand the intricacies of Kornelía's talent, so I can't be certain seeing dreamlike versions of dead people is a good thing. But Kornelía beams, which is proof of her belief that it is.

"It's funny," she says with an almost squeaking giggle. "I'd spent most of that morning crying because my brother woke me up but, without my glasses, I couldn't tell *which* brother it was. I thought things were a putrid mess. But then I saw her—" she glances at the sketch that's tilted away from me, "and I realized it's all part of a balance. One sense is failing me, but another is growing stronger. I don't know if they are connected. But if they are, well... I'll take the glasses if it means I can be more helpful to the deceased."

I don't share her confidence, but I do appreciate her ever-positive attitude. The buoyancy of having Kornelía close is the first relieving lightness I've experienced since leaving Toronto.

"You're so open-minded to all of this," I tell her. "You have a very... *calming* presence." I pause and offer her a hint of a grin. "Most of the time. You know, so long as you're not getting me stuck in closets with little ghost girls."

Kornelía laughs, the sound heartier now than it was a moment ago. But then she shakes her head, the warm expression on her face slowly curving back into indecision. She watches me, tucking hair behind her ears and looking poised to speak. I tense, wondering what truth she is going to spill. But my nerves must register, and she must decide to once more let me off the hook. Her eyes stay on mine for a moment, before she turns back to her drawing.

We say no more. When the temperature drops enough I start to shiver, I leave the porch to head back to bed.

4

THE DOZE FROM EARLIER IS ALL I MANAGE AS EVENING TURNS TO NIGHT.
My sector mates filter in sometime after eleven, and
I face the wall while they inch open the thick curtain
to flood the room with brightness from the sun, which
doesn't fully set. For a few hours, I drift in and out.
Near three, I wake in a cold sweat, heart pounding
after a nightmare. Lying on my back, waiting for my
pulse to slow and the lingering shadows of the dream
to dissolve, my eyes drift to the bunk above Dylan's
bed. I stare at the empty space until I finally slip back
into an uneasy sleep.

By the time five a.m. rolls around, I give up on
trying to rest. Returning to the porch, I wrap myself
in a blanket and listen to music until everyone else is
awake. I expect to be alone for a while, but the hour
is still early when I glance through the windows to
see the first campers milling about. Their shuffling feet
and tired eyes are a heartening sight. By eight o'clock,

the little house is bustling with noise and distraction, and I head inside to make myself some breakfast.

The kitchen is small and homey, with l-shaped wood cabinets framing a blue counter. I drop into one of the seats around the table, realizing there are only six available chairs. Last night, everyone crowded into the room to eat. But now that I think about it, Robbie and Alex ate standing at the counter. I wonder what will happen when the other girls arrive later today.

"I forgot to give you this yesterday," Dylan says as he sits across from me. He hands me a bundle of netting, and I lower my cereal spoon to unroll it.

"What the hell is it?" I ask, looking at what appears to be some sort of mesh bag.

"Mosquito head net," Dylan grins. "You'll need it anytime you're outside for long."

"Head net... like, something I'm supposed to wear over my head?" I ask, confounded.

"You're very astute," Sefa says from beside me. He grabs a cereal box and pours his second bowl. "Mosquitoes are killer up here. You'll be bit to no end if you don't wear it."

"Unless you're Naasir," Dylan adds.

Sefa laughs. "Yeah, unless you're him."

"You can't be serious," I say, looking at the netting with dismay. If I'm meant to put the net over my head, it means the flat piece of canvas I thought was the bag's bottom will be resting directly on my hair. My fingers ache for a comb, the thought of squishing my strands under something as tacky as this enough to make me squirm.

"Oh, we definitely are," Sefa says with a sigh. "If you don't believe us, you can experience it for yourself first-hand. But I wouldn't suggest it. Robbie said he tried his first day. If you get up close to him, you can still see the bites. He says it's like having acne all over again."

Dylan laughs, and I cringe. I place the net on the table, hoping it will disappear before I have to make any lengthy trips outside.

Kornelía's glasses are nowhere to be seen when she joins us in the kitchen. Still, even without much sight, she finds Dylan with ease. Her hands slide over his shoulders, and he leans into her touch. She bends forward, and her hair falls down to obscure my view of what I'm shocked—though certain—is a kiss.

I'm still staring when she straightens and, for an awkward moment, the two of them look at me, their expressions shifting from uncertain embarrassment to something more like guilt. Eventually, I lower my eyes to my cereal bowl without speaking. I wouldn't even know where to begin. So, I stay silent while Kornelía walks around the kitchen table and grabs a bottle of water from the fridge.

"They've said I can go to the airport again this morning," she says, pushing through the silence with a convincingly untroubled voice. "Anyone want to join me?"

I glance up to find her watching me, but I shake my head at her questioning gaze. I wasn't impressed by the airport yesterday. The others may be bored, but I'm in no hurry to go back—unless I get to board a plane home while I'm there.

"I'm going into town with Robbie to kill a few hours," Sefa says, stretching his thick arms over his head. "You guys are welcome to come along. At least it's Sunday. New Wraiths arrive tonight, and then onto the initiation. Finally, something to do."

"How long have you been here, Sefa?" I ask.

He groans. "Four days. Every one of them the same."

"That will certainly change soon enough." Kornelía smiles. She turns and missteps, bumping into the back of Sefa's chair.

"Glasses, babe," Dylan mumbles.

Kornelía sighs before she makes her way out of the room. When she's gone, Dylan gives me a knowing smile that fades as soon as he remembers I'm more or less oblivious to him and Kornelía being a thing.

Dylan and I were on shaky ground for a few weeks after we left Tonga. But him not having Mim to talk to and my letters to Meander going unanswered meant our collective company was sparse. Still, even once we came to a quiet truce and continued our normal exchange of sporadic emails, we didn't talk about anything serious. He's never mentioned what changed between him and Kornelía. For all I know, this relationship started before Mim left Camp Wanagi in a comatose state. I never bothered to ask about it, so I can't complain that I haven't been kept in the loop.

Seeing them together is weird, though. My mind travels straight to Mim, and my head swims, wondering how their thoughts aren't constantly turning to her too.

I keep my eyes downcast as I finish my breakfast. When my cereal bowl is empty, I grab my stupid head net and throw it onto my bed before taking my violin to the empty classroom.

The majority of the past year has not been enjoyable. My anxiety has skyrocketed, and neither sitting at school nor wasting time at home do anything to stop the unending cycle of desperate, worrisome thoughts swirling in my head. So, every chance I get, I focus on one of two activities that puts a halt to all of my damned, useless thinking.

I exercise, and I play.

Before last summer, I never would have turned to exercise for comfort. And calling it a comfort now is twisting the truth on its head. I don't find the treadmill in our basement energizing, nor would I classify the push-ups and sit-ups I frequently perform in my room as forms of refreshing release. When I got home last August, I saw the continuation of exercise as a practical step. Our instructor, Althea, made a valid point when she told us that strength was a good way to ward off the draining effects of spiritual encounters.

Plus, I had it in my head that if I could prove I wasn't a pathetic weakling incapable of handling himself around ghosts, Meander might come to his senses. By the time I figured out he was not going to respond to the letters that included less-than-subtle hints about my exercise routine, the process had become habit. Cursing my former instructor for ever introducing me to the concept of Sender Strength was a good way to keep my mind from drifting to more complex targets of frustration.

Still, as often as I exercise, playing the violin takes at least triple the time. Music is the only thing able to ground all my nervous energy, my pent-up fears and anger ebbing with each draw of the bow. In the fall, I even started competing, a task I never strived for but have excelled at anyway. Each challenging new piece of composition provides an excellent excuse to throw myself into my music. Obsessing over individual notes means I don't have to obsess over something else.

Now, I spend an hour lost in those notes before Dylan knocks on the door to tell me Robbie and the other guys are about to leave. The temptation to stay locked inside the room is strong, but I pack away my instrument and join the others as a van pulls up to take us back into Ilulissat.

"What are we going to do in town?" Reed asks from the third row of the van. He sounds uninterested in actually hearing Robbie's response, though it's hard to tell if he's unhappy about coming along on this trip— or if he's just talking in the flat, bored way he favors.

Robbie converses with the driver, ignoring Reed's question as the van starts off. The ocean stretches to our right as we begin a smooth ride past houses and shops. But once we turn onto a road heading east, the car jostles and bumps over rougher terrain. The motion makes me feel vaguely ill, and I rest my forehead against the windowpane until the car rolls to a stop ten minutes later.

"I'm not—strictly speaking—supposed to be doing this," Robbie says once we've climbed out onto the grass. We're standing before a dip in the hills. Below us, a few people I think are fellow campers are busy measuring something in a shallow valley.

"Breaking the rules already?" Dylan laughs. "Nice."

"Just don't tell anyone. Especially Alex," Robbie says. He sweeps a hand forward, and we follow him down the slope.

"What are they doing?" Sefa asks. The figures in the distance look like they're marking a square in the grass. When we get closer, I realize they're Revenant campers, this year's oldest sector. I recognize Ralli and Carrigan, along with their lead Gianna.

"They're setting up for tonight's initiation," Robbie says. He halts when we're still about fifty feet away. We stop by his side, watching the others work.

"This is where we're going?" Dylan asks.

Robbie gives him a sideways glance before he shrugs his shoulders. "They're trying to establish contact beforehand, to make sure there *is* a ghost here," he says.

"So, like, this is a practice round?" Reed asks.

"You can't expect them to just walk into the initiation without even knowing the place is haunted," Sefa says with a roll of his eyes.

"I guess not," Reed reflects. He steps forward, watching the Revenants with far more interest than he showed on our way over here.

"I thought it'd be fun to give you a behind the scenes look," Robbie admits. "Since you'll be in charge of this next year."

"Huh," Dylan says with a nod. "I hadn't thought of that. Hard to believe it's only a year away. So, what are they doing anyway?"

Robbie details the Revenants' process, explaining how they're measuring out where they want to form their circle and testing the air for spikes of energy. The others ask questions about tonight's initiation and what processes Shade might be involved with next year while I hang back. I've seen this kind of examination before—last summer, when Kornelía and I joined a Sender scouting mission.

Besides, the topic isn't one I'm particularly interested in. I'm not planning to mention it, but this might be my last summer with the Oracle. I came back to see my friends and experience spirits in a controlled environment so I can learn what—if anything—has changed since I turned sixteen. But I don't have any interest in furthering my Sender studies after Camp Wanagi is over. One more summer won't make much difference when my current plan is to continue avoiding ghosts as often as possible in the hopes I'll someday have a routine so well-rehearsed no spirits will ever find me.

The guys talk until another distant car arrives, and two more Revenants join the scene. One is the other lead, and the second is a girl named Anna. She lingers on the outskirts of the group. It's not difficult to guess that she's here to get the spirit active.

"Isn't that a Revenant girl?" Sefa asks. "I get why the oldest sector would prep the place. But shouldn't the Wraith leads be interacting with the ghost tonight?"

"Not if they can't make contact," Robbie explains. "We have to work with what's available. If the Wraith leads are unable to establish a connection with the ghost, the Revenants take over. The most important part of setting up the initiation is confirming contact. Doesn't really matter who does it."

"What if no one can see it?" Dylan asks. "Like, no leads, no new kids... what then?"

Robbie shrugs. "If the new leads can't communicate with the ghost, the job of making contact goes to the oldest campers. If they're unsuccessful, the other sectors will be brought in. In dire cases, an instructor might even take part. And if no one from the entire camp can find proof of haunting, we'll try another ghost. That, or tell ghost stories around a campfire all night. Boring, but it helps lure the new kids into a false sense of security."

He grins, and Sefa chuckles. They both fall silent as Anna approaches her sector mates. I hold my breath, nervous about what she's going to do. I haven't been around spirits in a long time.

"Y'all think we should get closer?" Robbie asks.

I want to say no. But Sefa leads a round of agreement, so I trail along with the others as Robbie crosses the field. Before us, Anna steps into the middle of the measured square. Her arms are wrapped tightly over her woolen sweater, a shiver already wracking her limbs.

5

ANNA STEPS INTO THE CENTER OF THE MARKED SPACE AS OUR SMALL congregation reaches the outskirts of the square.

Gianna bounds over to speak with Robbie. She eyes us with annoyance but is unable to wipe the easy grin from his face as he explains why we're here. Their conversation is muted, and I pay it little heed. My attention is focused on Anna.

She bends her white-blonde head, coming to a stop in the middle of the clearing her sector mates marked out. That she's doing this—putting herself through the rigors of being near a ghost for the sole sake of ensuring a good show tonight—is ridiculous. But evidently, confirming the spirit's presence is not enough. The bottom strands of her low-slung ponytail begin to sway, the hair lifting in a heavy breeze the rest of us can't feel. I wait for her to rush to the edge of the marked square, safely out of the ghost's range. But she only lifts her chin, her mouth parting like she's ready to speak.

"Man, I've missed this," Sefa whispers.

He inches closer, his bulky frame blocking most of my view. I take a half-step to the side, curious how long Anna is going to keep this up. She trembles, her legging-clad knees swaying. Still, her lips continue to move and, although I'm glad we're not any closer than the edge of the large square, I wonder what kind of questions she's posing to the invisible mass.

Gianna and Robbie continue their quiet argument while Reed questions why Anna's hair is dancing as if he's trying to find the reason in an optical illusion. On the far side of the square, the other Revenants watch, their eyes calculating as they take note of the spirit's effect. For a hair-raising occurrence, the scene is remarkably casual.

But then Anna's hair shoots straight out, the length of her ponytail straining to one side. As the girl's mouth closes and her eyes widen with surprise, all conversation comes to a stop. The sensation is eerie with everyone standing in stunned silence as we watch Anna reach her hand back and tug at the strands that won't fall against her shoulder. A chill skitters across my skin. Even if I can't see or feel this particular spirit, I blame it for the shiver that makes me hug my arms to my chest.

"Are you okay?" Gianna calls, breaking through the still quiet. Anna raises one arm and waves, signaling she's fine. Still, the Revenant lead looks like she's ready to bolt to the girl's aid. "The reports we have," she explains, the fingernails of one hand coming to her mouth. "They suggest this ghost is…"

Her voice is cut off by a shriek, and the queasiness

of our ride over here reappears as I watch Anna's hair snake around her shoulder and across her collarbone. She yells for the spirit to stop, but the ponytail continues, slithering up the far side of her shoulder before twisting around her neck. Watching her is like viewing a demented magic act as the hair creates a grotesque noose.

Anna grips her hair with both hands, and her choked gargle sends my vision veering off-kilter.

Not her neck. Anything but her neck.

I stagger to one side, kneeling as familiar dread rushes over me. As my ears ring, clouds of black appear at the edges of my vision. Cold sweat beads on my forehead, and my pulse grows erratic as I try to keep balanced. I lower my head and cover my ears, blocking the muffled sound of Anna's struggle. Blocking all thoughts of dead people trying to choke out life.

Ralli and the other Revenants rush forward to pull Anna away. Despite my efforts, I hear their cries, followed by questions and the guttural retch of Anna's gagging. The pulsing point in my neck begins to slow, but I keep my eyes fixed on the ground, working to breathe deep. When Anna's gags turn to harsh sobs and shrill assurances she is fine, I close my eyes and wait for the commotion to fade.

"She's all right," Robbie says, before he notices my position on the ground. "Hey, Cal, you okay?"

I put a hand to my mouth, opening my eyes and willing myself to relax. I haven't been able to keep my calm around a spirit since the major encounter that resulted in Mim's coma and Meander's distance. But I didn't think I'd ever be *this* pathetic near a ghost I can't even see.

Everything slows with the weight of my disappointment. I couldn't have guessed what this spirit would do. But that doesn't make me feel any better. I gambled on coming back to Camp Wanagi this summer—hoped a different environment would give me the courage to face my ability again. It's my second day here. And already I've proved a spectacular failure.

Robbie grabs my shoulder, and I force myself back to my feet. Embarrassment cuts through my sweeping panic, warming my shuddering skin.

"I'm f-fine," I stammer.

"Do you feel the ghost?" he presses.

I shake my head. "No, I don't. I just… I'm fine."

My eyes remain trained on the ground, away from the surely confused stares of my sector mates. I must look like an idiot. No one else seems bothered by what happened to the Revenant. Based on how calm our surroundings now are, I bet even Anna is doing better than me.

"He having some kind of attack?" Reed asks.

"Shut up, Reed," Dylan grumbles. He whacks Reed on the arm before slapping me on the back. "All that altitude, right? Makes you lightheaded."

"Altitude is when you're high off the ground, loser," Sefa laughs.

"Well, we're high up in, you know, the *world*," Dylan reasons. "That has to count for something."

I smirk, raising my eyes and giving Dylan a small nod. "Yeah, it's only the arctic air," I agree.

With an unsteady breath, I glance over at Anna. She's smiling, talking to her friends without a care about what just happened. Her ease makes me angry.

If there weren't others here to pull her away from the spirit, who knows what damage her own hair could have done.

"We should get back to the house, anyway," Robbie says. The van is waiting for us, the driver hopefully far enough away he couldn't see the ghostly incident. "And remember... *No* telling anyone where we went. I don't want to deal with the headache of explaining my disobedience."

"Don't worry," Sefa grins. "We'll act surprised tonight."

Robbie scratches the back of his neck, his head ducking guiltily as he returns to the van.

When we get back to the house, the others prepare for lunch while I excuse myself to unpack the belongings I've barely touched since yesterday's arrival. Alone in the bedroom, I fold and place everything into my drawer, my fingers fighting against the removal of each piece. I feel like a little kid sick on his first day away from home. Unpacking is unpleasant when what I want is to stuff everything back in the bag and hightail it out of here. Maybe coming was a mistake, after all. I'm not sure I can handle a summer full of being freaked out by spirits without any relief to combat the sickening pain.

Still, I do unpack, leaving only a pair of hiking boots and one other outfit I'm still not convinced I should have brought along. I stick the boots under the bed next to my violin. I leave the other clothes in my bag, zipping the duffel and stowing it away with everything else.

When all of my things are stored, I stare at my bed, contemplating what refuge I might seek in sleep. Being alone will give me time to get over my embarrassment. But a nap will do nothing to help me sleep better tonight. I spend a moment stuck in indecision before I force myself to turn away. If I pretend I'm okay, my sector mates will leave me be so I can play some music or maybe deal a few hands of cards.

Crossing back along the room, my eyes sweep its strange-yet-familiar setup. The floor, walls, and even the lighting are new additions, accents unlike any we've had so far at camp. But the bunks are the same, as is the way each one's been claimed. Naasir's bed is neat, while Reed and Dylan's blankets are sloppier than my own. Sefa's got some magazines on his comforter, Dylan's running shoes are on the floor beneath his dangling sheets, and up on Meander's bunk—

I halt mid-step, my gaze shifting back to the bed I've ignored since my middle-of-the-night insomnia. Without realizing it, I'd glanced over the bunk, counting its contents as part of the room's whole. Now, I stare at the bed, swallowing a swell of emotion as my eyes take stock of the object I missed when I first walked into the room.

A thick, worn book.

Placed on Meander's pillow.

MY HEAD CLOUDS AS I TRY TO PLACE THINGS INTO LOGICAL ORDER. MIND spinning, I wonder if the book belongs to Dylan, or if Reed dropped it and some cleaning staff came by and placed it on the sheets. Thoughts whirl, possibilities flicking through my brain at alarming speed. But before I can latch onto any viable explanation for the terrible coincidence of the book's position, a quiet voice in the doorway stops me from thinking at all.

"Hey, Callum."

I swivel around, stomach plunging in perfect rhythm with the hammering uptick of my heart. Meander Rhoades leans against the doorframe, looking less like a confident observer and more like someone afraid he can't support his own weight. The sight of him is surreal. Despite the million things I've imagined saying in a moment like this, for a while, all I can manage is an incredulous stare.

Six months ago, Meander replied to my email and

cracked the last vestige of hope I'd been clinging to since Tonga. His intentions were clear, and his message was finally received.

Except that even he couldn't mantain the pretence of moving on.

On Christmas morning, hours after the response that finally convinced me Meander was serious about keeping away, a text awakened me—the first text he'd sent since the previous summer. The only text I received from him in a year.

I'm sorry. I'm an ass.
Of course I miss you.
Every day. Every hour. Every second.
Of course I miss you, Callum.

Happy Christmas, Long John.

My cheeks wet with tears, I laughed at the nickname. I promised it would make me stop talking to him but, in that moment, it only assured my continued correspondence. The awful night turned into a bright morning, and I spent Christmas Day with my family feeling lighter than I had in months.

Despite his apology, however, Meander's silence did not alter. I continued to write, and he continued to avoid any unnecessary replies. I received a one-sentence message on my birthday asking if I was all right after turning sixteen. He also deigned to offer a short reply when I posed the same question on his birthday two months later. But aside from these minute confirmations of his continued survival, I heard from Meander only once after Christmas Day—a single conversation we shared near the end of April.

I thought he was still in England, his invitation to Camp Wanagi long lost in the depths of some garbage heap. The reality of him standing before me—his mouth drawn, his expression somber—wraps me so tight I've lost the ability to breathe.

He doesn't look good. His pale skin is *too* pale, with no trace of pink in his cheeks and hollows around his eyes from lack of sleep. The scar on his jaw is sharp and defined next to the drained pallor of his skin. His hazel eyes have dulled to the color of mud. Even his golden-brown curls are faded and lanky.

His ill appearance disturbs me. But it doesn't change the fact that he is here. Being this close to Meander is like sinking into the first reverberating notes of my violin at the end of an arduous day. Or—perhaps more accurately—a full, excruciating year.

"I…" my voice catches and, when I work through the stammer, my words are tight with incomprehension. "I didn't expect you to be here."

I take a step and falter, my knees buckling as blood pools in my feet. Keeping upright gives me something to focus on, at least. I stop, hoping I won't make a total idiot of myself by sprawling face forward onto the floor.

Meander is silent as he works out how he's going to respond. My skin buzzes as his lips part and his eyes find mine. Our gazes catch for a short beat, until he looks down and fakes a disinterested smile.

"Yeah, um… Mum. Told me I had to come here or find somewhere else to spend the summer," he mutters.

"Oh."

He's lying. While I'm sure his mother did make

those kinds of threats, her complaints alone would not be enough to send him all the way to Greenland. I know the answer I *want* him to give for why he's made this trip. But I'd settle for any reason, if it were the truth. If my brain could function well enough to do anything more than stand here, I would tell him as much. But I was positive he was not coming to camp, and it's like I've downed a concoction of helium and lead—I don't know if this moment is crushing me, or if I'm seconds away from floating off the floor.

I wish I had a speech prepared, something grandiose to catch him off guard. Hell, I should at least be able to ramble about my trip over here as if I were writing one of my pointless emails. But as my gaze shifts to his gray turtleneck, a jolt of panic prickles down my spine.

"Weather's not bad," I utter, the useless words escaping before I can swallow them.

Meander pushes off the door frame. "Yeah, glad it's not too hot." He nods, his eyes still downcast.

The awkwardness is palpable, like a sharp scythe swinging between us. This conversation isn't going to last long. We can't continue standing here, unsure how to act. And I can't abide restricting our first conversation in months to talking about the weather— even if I was the one to introduce the subject. I have to abandon my half-assed pretence of acting nonchalant. I don't want make a fool of myself, but I'd rather be foolish than pretend the two of us are strangers.

"I'm happy you've come," I sigh. Meander glances only as far up as my chest. I wait a few seconds for a reply that doesn't arrive before I press on. "Even if you *are* going to ignore me the whole summer."

His eyes rise to mine at that, and he shakes his head.

"Don't say—" he starts.

"The truth?" I reply before he can finish. Frustration wells in my chest knowing he's trying to guilt me away from calling him out on his bullshit. I relish the heat of it burning my lungs. Any form of anger is better than the weepy longing of staring at him. "You didn't even tell me you were coming. I asked—*multiple times*—and you couldn't even be bothered to give me a damned 'yes' or 'no'."

"I wasn't sure until the last minute," he mumbles.

I scoff. "Sure."

His lips press together, indecision swimming in his eyes. But then he turns a little, like he's ready to leave the room. I *am* angry now. Angry and upset, struggling to come to grips with how far our relationship has slid since the last time we stood together. I can't let him slink into the shadows so soon after his sudden reappearance.

"You don't have to pretend I don't exist, you know," I start, moving forward in step with his retreat. He doesn't respond, but he does stop, so I scramble to keep words pouring forth. "Y-You can't. Not when we're sharing the same room."

With a half-turn back towards me, Meander shakes his head a second time. "I could never pretend you don't exist," he says with an indistinguishable breath. "You wouldn't let me."

I'm not sure if he says it with amusement or annoyance. Either way, I can't argue against the statement's validity. But I don't like the insinuation I'm a pesky cling-on—mostly because I'm terrified he thinks it's true.

I give him a hard stare, forcing his eyes to again meet

mine as I take another step forward. "Do you want me to go away?" I ask.

The question is blunt, a challenge harkening back to that bleak night in December. He gave up his chance to be rid of me then. For months, his single text acted as proof that his motives for being distant are still only a selfish sort of selflessness. I have no idea how I'll react if he suggests those reasons have now changed.

Everything between us has unraveled. It's like we've been catapulted back to our first summer at Camp Wanagi, when I could never tell what he was thinking— when I had no clue if he enjoyed my company or wished I'd leave him alone. The more acquainted with Meander I became, the better I understood his quiet moods. But now, I can't read his face without fear and hope muddling my interpretation.

"Cal, I..."

He runs both hands through his curls, and I steel myself for his response. But when his arms drop to his sides, he only turns and starts out of the room. Flustered by his movement, I give up all hope of being suave or composed.

"I miss you," I blurt.

Meander halts in the doorway, his head tilting back as he raises his eyes to the ceiling. Silence stretches between us, the pause tediously long before he spares me a quick glance over his shoulder.

"I miss you, too," he admits. Then he walks away.

7

AFTER MEANDER DISAPPEARS FROM VIEW, I HIDE FROM FURTHER confrontation—or lack thereof—in our room. For a while, I pace, my mind reeling with questions I don't have enough evidence to answer. When the parade of torturous possibilities devolves into exhaustion, I give into my earlier temptation and crawl into bed for a nap.

I sleep until after eight. Staring at my phone as I stretch my legs, I'm surprised by the late hour and know I'll pay for the nap with restlessness tonight. But for the time being, my thoughts are focused elsewhere.

After combing my hair before the full-length mirror on the back of the bedroom door, I shuffle out to the living room to find most of the sector present. Meander sits on one of the sofas, his head lowered over a book. I ache to cross the room and sit next to him. But our meeting this afternoon wasn't great and, while I'm not going to let him stay silent all summer, I won't press into his personal space on our first night. So, as much as I want to claim the empty spot beside him, I slump down next to Reed on the adjacent couch instead.

Kornelía's eyes me as I take my seat. I keep my gaze fixed on the fire.

"About time you got up," Dylan says from his place on the floor. "I thought I was going to have to wake you for the initiation."

"Speaking of," Sabeena says, "now that we're all here, does anyone know where we're going tonight? I'm not even sure where the Wraiths are staying."

I glance away from the fire and take a furtive survey of the room. Eight of us are here, which means Sabeena is wrong in her declaration. Mim cannot attend Camp Wanagi with us. But that still leaves one missing Shade.

"Where's Lu?" I ask no one in particular, although my eyes slide to Sabeena since she's the first to look my way.

"You didn't hear?" she asks. She draws her long braid over one shoulder. "She's not coming."

My automatic response is to turn to Kornelía. As if she was expecting the movement, she meets my curious expression with a serious nod.

"It wasn't her decision," she says. "Her parents thought she needed to focus on schoolwork rather than paranormal studies." Her words are clipped, not quite sarcastic but something close to it. Kornelía's parents aren't overly fond of her attending ghost camp either. I guess she sympathizes with Lu's situation.

I can't say I'm terribly disappointed to realize Lu is not coming back. It's still weird, though. Kornelía and Sabeena are now the only two girls in Shade. I'm sorry they have to be reminded of their missing sector mates every time they go to sleep. But I do envy that they get a room to themselves while the six of us guys are still crammed into a single space.

"It happens for almost every sector," Alex says as she and Robbie walk into the room. "People don't always return. Most sectors end up smaller than they began."

Dylan shifts, leaning against Kornelía's legs.

"We're happy to see the eight of you, though," Robbie says. "And it's nice that we're *cozier* this year."

"It's odd being away from the other sectors," Sabeena says. "I planned to visit Isabis this afternoon but couldn't. Are we going to see the other campers at all?"

"Of course you will," Alex smiles. "The Oracle has hired a crew of drivers this year, and each house is equipped with a phone and the numbers needed to call. There will also be scheduled shuttles for courses."

"Is that what we'll be doing for tonight then, too?" Sabeena asks. "Taking a car to the initiation spot?"

"Well…" Robbie scratches his chin, eyeing Alex in the process. She gives him a wide-eyed stare clearly intended to make him shut up. "They deserve to know," he mumbles, raising his palms in a shrug.

"Know what?" Kornelía asks.

Alex brushes the side-swept bangs that are a new addition to her dark hair this summer. "Things will be a little different this year," she says, her tone careful. "But we're not the ones meant to explain it. You'll find out soon enough."

Robbie purses his lips like he wants to tell us what she's keeping hidden. But then his gaze slides to Kornelía, and his eyes turn suspicious, as if she might be trying to read his mind.

"Stop that," he warns with a pointed finger.

Kornelía rolls her eyes, but she sinks back in her seat and stops staring at him anyway.

"You all relax," Alex says. "Enjoy the company. It's the first time you've been together in a while. We'll talk shortly." She glances at Robbie, and he makes a zippering motion over his mouth.

The leads stay in the room with us, but they don't offer any more cryptic hints. Given that four of us visited the initiation site this afternoon, pretending no one has guessed where we'll be going seems pointless. But Robbie and Alex remain quiet, and their strange behavior—mixed with the altered setting and reduced size of our sector—means the slow tick of minutes is strained.

We struggle to act normal, making small talk or playing cards. But a stilted rift runs among us. For two hours, we attempt to lounge in semi-comfort—a feat I'm pretty sure no one achieves—until a car arrives at our house around ten.

Alex and Robbie give each other impatient glances when the front door swings open. We all pause what we're doing as Mrs. Buxley steps into view.

If you were to ask her what her role at Camp Wanagi is, Mrs. Buxley would claim she is only an instructor. But she must hold a high position in the Oracle. She always seems to appear when ominous things are afoot.

The room grows quiet as Mrs. Buxley walks in. The fire pops, then it too seems to wait—poised to discover what unhappy news she's about to relate.

"Are you going to take us to the initiation?" Reed asks, the only one not cowed into silence by her commanding presence.

"Reed, you dolt," Sefa mutters. "We're not going anywhere."

"What?" Reed glances between us, his face full of confusion. "Why not?"

"Because we need to have a little chat, and this seems like the best time to have it," Mrs. Buxley responds. Her heels tap against the wood floor as she comes to stand by the far sofa. I don't know how she can be wearing such delicate shoes in this kind of terrain.

"Are we going to the initiation afterwards, or are we missing it altogether?" Sabeena asks.

Mrs. Buxley tilts her chin in Sabeena's direction. "The *initiation*, as you call it, is a rite of passage many of our campers enjoy attending," she says. She folds her arms across her chest. "But we feel as though, in this case, it might be more beneficial for us to remain here to talk."

Sefa rubs his hands together while Dylan mutters a curse under his breath.

"Are we being punished for something?" Sabeena asks.

Dylan scratches his head in agitation. "Obviously."

"No one is being punished," our instructor says in a firm voice.

"Mrs. Buxley just wants to go over some things," Alex offers.

"Like how we aren't allowed to go anywhere or do anything?" Sefa asks. His voice is pinched, like he's working hard to suppress a greater show of emotion.

Sabeena studies Sefa, her eyes crinkled with incomprehension. She arrived today, which means she might not know how boxed in her friend's been feeling. "Will it be like this all summer?" she asks, turning back to Mrs. Buxley.

"I flew all the way from Samoa to be here," Sefa grumbles, interrupting before Mrs. Buxley has time to respond. "What the hell was the point if we're going to be under house arrest?"

Our instructor stands still, her face a mask of patience as she waits for us to sort ourselves out before continuing with her speech.

"Shut up, Sefa," I say in a quiet voice.

His head turns in my direction, his eyes set in a glare. "Don't you tell me to shut up," he says. "It's not *my* fault we're in trouble."

The accusation is a surprise, although I suppose it shouldn't be. If Sefa's right and we're being kept under a closer watch, it's not hard to imagine that last year's fiasco in Tonga—the failed exorcism I was part of—is the reason for it.

"No one's in trouble," Alex repeats. Her voice carries the desperate edge of someone eager to keep the peace.

"Of course we are," Dylan says.

"Dylan…" Kornelía begins.

"Will everyone *be quiet*?" Naasir's deep voice smothers the bickering like the sinking of a stone.

The room once again falls silent, and Mrs. Buxley gives Naasir a small nod of thanks before she resumes talking. "I want to assure you that no one is in trouble, and no one is being punished," she says. "We are not holding you under house arrest, either. But we are keeping you from the initiation, that much is true."

"Why?" Sabeena asks.

"Because this sector needs a bit more guidance

than we have so far given," Mrs. Buxley explains. She pauses, considering us before she steps onto the rug in front of the fireplace. "Certain events have occurred that have made us... *cautious* about giving you free rein this summer."

"So we *are* being punished," Sefa says in a dark voice. "For something half of us weren't even involved in."

"Shut it, Sefa," Dylan snaps.

Mrs. Buxley holds up a hand for them both to stop. "*No one* is being punished," she repeats. "You are just going to be monitored more closely. What happened to Mim is only part of the equation. This sector has experienced a number of problematic events, each including a different set of campers."

Sefa sighs, no doubt swallowing a retort that he wasn't involved in any of them. I wonder what that kind of innocence feels like. I'm the guiltiest person here, I suppose. Between digging up graves in the middle of the night and knocking down walls in luxury island homes, I'm fairly certain I was a participant in all of the events Mrs. Buxley is referring to. Me—and Meander.

"So, what does that mean for us?" Sabeena asks.

"Nothing as dire as you seem to think." Mrs. Buxley smiles. "You will still have the opportunity to explore the area and encounter spirits this summer. You will take courses as usual, and you will continue to learn and develop your talents. But, since this is your third year with Camp Wanagi—the time when many of you are undergoing the biggest changes in your abilities— we are going to ensure your encounters are supervised. Just as in your first summer with the Oracle, you will be assigned a lead to oversee your projects this year."

"We're going to help you," Robbie adds from his spot at the back of the room. "To make sure you keep on track. And, you know, stay within the limits of the law."

My lips twitch up, but Mrs. Buxley only offers Robbie a reprimanding glance. "I want to stress that we are not limiting your activities here, only keeping an eye on them," she concludes. "We want you to be successful in your endeavors at Camp Wanagi. And above all else, we want you to be safe. There is no blame to lay. Only a caution to be aware of your surroundings and not to seek adventure without first consulting an official employee of the camp."

"We're being kept on a leash," Dylan scoffs.

Sabeena raises her hand like a schoolgirl. "Even so, why aren't we allowed to attend the initiation?" she asks. She glances at Robbie and Alex before settling her gaze more firmly on Mrs. Buxley. "It doesn't start until midnight. We have plenty of time."

Our instructor shifts her weight from one foot to the other, but she doesn't avoid eye contact with Sabeena. "The spirit the Wraith campers are going to make contact with isn't well suited for this sector," she says with calm assurance.

"Yeah, but don't the other sectors stay back? What harm could it do for us to stand behind everyone else?" Reed asks.

I train my gaze on the fire, refusing to call out Reed's idiocy. He was with us this afternoon when Anna's hair looped around her neck. Three summers into camp, he should understand that some abilities are more dangerous than others. If Mrs. Buxley is holding us back, she's afraid the temperament of this spirit will cause trouble. Guessing whose talent might be problematic isn't hard when only one person here has the ability to make spirits do physical damage.

Still, not everyone else is as oblivious as Reed. The room is tense, and I would say something in Meander's defense except I know he wouldn't want me to. So, I do my best to pretend I'm unaware of everything until Kornelía mercifully directs the conversation elsewhere.

"Can we pick our courses?" she asks. She draws her long legs onto the sofa cushion to sit cross-legged. "If we're staying here tonight, can we at least do that much?"

Mrs. Buxley looks at our leads, shrugging one shoulder. "I don't see why not."

Alex smiles. "I'll go get the sheets," she says, happy to have something useful to do.

Our lead is quick, reappearing with the selection sheets and a bundle of pre-sharpened pencils. She hands them around and, for a few moments, the depressing frustration of learning we're not allowed at the initiation is forgotten as we set about picking our courses.

This summer, I don't waste time thinking about what I will or will not take. At least, I don't intend to. The first selection has been made for us, another mandatory course called Sender Management. I wonder if this class is always the selection for campers now experiencing the full force of their abilities, or if it was chosen especially for us.

One of my other choices is simple. I tick off Hostage Arts, no longer worried about diving too deep. Last year, I ignored the difficult courses because I was afraid of my ability. Spirits still terrify me and, for many months now, I've done everything in my power to keep clear of them. But a classroom at Camp Wanagi is the safest place for me to learn more. The greater my knowledge, the stronger I am when facing unavoidable ghosts and the less likely I'll be to suffer another stupid injury.

My other selections aren't quite as easy, however. I planned to take Resistive Release this year, but it's not listed. Neither is Hostile Spirits. Anger simmers at the base of my throat when I notice the missing course names, but I keep my expression neutral. Pointing them out would be useless. Not every course is offered every summer. Still, I'd be willing to bet that these ones have been removed from the roster for the same reason we're being kept indoors tonight.

Eventually, I select Channeling, thinking a course like that might somehow explain a spirit's ability to guide certain Senders. And then I stare at the sheet, unable to help wondering what courses Meander is going to choose. After how unsubtle our instructor's just been, I doubt he's planning to sign up for any intensive classes. I'm not going to stalk him, but each course we take together increases the likelihood he'll be forced to communicate with me. And since I still have one selection left, I might as well try to find the most non-threatening class he might take.

With a small smile, my pen hovers over Meditative Communication. Meander is not one to meditate. But this is the class that teaches inner strength over outside forces, and I have a sneaking suspicion he'll enroll with the idea he can zone out and pass the summer by faking a few moments of spiritual connection.

At least, I hope that's his plan. I sign myself up for the course and hand in my sheet before anyone sees it long enough to comment.

As soon as he's handed in his selections, Meander retreats from the living room in favor of reading on the screened porch. I watch him leave, then spend the next half hour listening to Sefa complain while Reed blabs to the girls that Robbie took us to the initiation spot earlier today. When I'm sick of Sefa's comments and Sabeena's questions about what little we saw, I skulk to our room to retrieve my violin.

On my way back to the classroom, I pause, lingering in the living room before steeling myself to open the porch door. Standing on the threshold, I watch Meander read for a few seconds before awkwardly clearing my throat.

"You're probably regretting your decision to come right now," I mumble, my head bent and my voice low. "But, uh, I just want to reiterate that I'm glad you're here, Meander."

I don't wait for him to respond, nor do I check to see if he's even bothered to look up from his book. With a quick turn, I step back into the house. Pulling the door shut, I draw my violin case to my chest until I'm inside the classroom and ready to play.

8

ISABIS APPEARS THE NEXT MORNING TO FILL US IN ON THE INITIATION WE missed.

"I thought it was going to be a disaster," she says to Sabeena, Kornelía, and I over cups of coffee and juice at the kitchen table. The Entity camper takes a slow, careful sip of her drink before lowering her tremoring hand. "They asked me to help. In case the ghost acted up. They wanted me there to manipulate it—if it started doing something dangerous. Like a guard."

She smiles, her light pink lipstick matching the pastel shade of her headscarf. She must be proud they wanted her help. Since the Shade sector wasn't even allowed to attend the initiation, their concerns about this spirit's tendencies must have matched my panicked freak out yesterday.

"Did anyone get hurt?" Sabeena asks.

"No," Isabis says. "Two kids saw the ghost. A boy who just talked to it. And a girl who—well, she made it... brighter, somehow. It wasn't dark out, even at midnight. But we all felt like the sky grew brighter."

Sabeena wraps her hands around her mug, a dreamy expression in her tired, round eyes. "Ghosts grow bright when they cross over," she muses. "Maybe the girl's power is to give them energy and bring them closer to the divide."

"If she has an ability like that, the Oracle will love having her around," Kornelía says.

"I don't know if that's what it was," Isabis says. "But it was interesting. Much calmer than last year."

"Yeah, well don't go around telling everybody that." Sabeena taps her cup. "They kept us away because they think we're the trouble sector."

"They don't think we're *trouble*, exactly..." Kornelía begins.

Sabeena gives her a pointed look, and Kornelía sighs before turning her sights on me. She studies my face, perhaps considering my drained appearance. I didn't sleep well last night, and having to get out of bed to wake Dylan from a bad dream at four o'clock didn't help. Not that my restlessness is anything new. I haven't had a good night's sleep since sometime during the winter. But at least I'm not alone. Dylan and I aren't the only ones having nightmares this summer. And even Kornelía and Sabeena look half-asleep sitting next to Isabis. As far as appearances go, I'd guess most of my fellow Shades are faring about the same when it comes to the struggles of sleep.

"It was awful, what Mrs. Buxley said," Kornelía mumbles after a moment. Her gaze is still fixed on mine. "She should never have singled him out like that."

The hairs on my neck prickle at her abrupt change

of topic. I gulp down the rest of my orange juice and push back from table, avoiding her probing stare.

"No, she shouldn't have," I agree.

I don't want to start talking about what happened last night, not with Sabeena and Isabis listening in. So, I cut off the discussion by walking over to the sink to rinse out my glass. I can feel Kornelía's eyes on me as I cross the few steps from the table to the counter. But she doesn't say anything else, which I'm grateful for.

She knows what happened at the end of last summer. She's even emailed Meander a few times to try and make him talk. He's managed to ignore her better than he's ignored me. And as far as I know, she hasn't tried to renew her efforts since his arrival in Greenland. Still, I'm glad she's not blaming him for being kept away from the initiation.

"Hey, Cal, you ready to go?"

I glance away from the sink to see Dylan standing in the kitchen doorway. While Kornelía may believe that Meander is blameless, most of our sector has made it clear they don't share her opinion. Dylan and Sefa bonded over dark mutterings last night, barely managing to contain their talk while we were all in the room preparing for bed.

When I agreed to go on a run with Dylan yesterday, I didn't realize we'd already be at odds again. But I don't have it in me to pick a fight this morning. Besides, it's hard to stay angry with someone as ridiculous as Dylan. Even now, the sight of his florescent green track pants—clashing horrendously with a blue shirt decorated with purple lightning streaks—brings an unexpected laugh to my lips.

"Yeah, let's go." I grab a bottle of water from the

fridge and follow him out of the kitchen, relieved for the excuse to exit the room. On our way to the front door, Dylan hands me the mosquito net I stuffed in my dresser when I unpacked my bags yesterday afternoon.

"We don't *actually* need to wear these," I say in dismay.

"If you don't, you'll pay for it," Dylan replies.

He shoves the net, along with a thin pair of running gloves, into my hand before slipping on his headgear. When he's pulled his net to rest on his shoulders, he looks like a bank robber wearing a poorly fitted stocking.

The events of last night notwithstanding, the idea that this net is a necessity makes me immediately regret my decision to tag along on Dylan's run. Looking like an idiot while also screwing up my hair is not something I'm currently willing to endure. So, I slide on the gloves and stuff the net in my pocket before heading outside.

Dylan sets our course and, for a short time, I run in near-peace. The sky is clear, and the cool air is refreshing after the stuffiness of the crowded house. My eyes sweep the coastline to our left, the deep waters calm in the brightness of the morning. I listen to the gentle lapping of waves and the soft thudding of my sneakers, letting the brisk air fill my lungs.

Despite yesterday afternoon's awkwardness, and my annoyance over what happened last night, I feel better this morning. I'm tired, and a terse cord of anxiousness still strains against my chest. But something unexpected occurred yesterday, and I don't try to quash the note of quiet hope humming under my bones. Meander is here. And although he's keeping his distance, avoiding me in person will be far more difficult than ignoring the emails I've sent throughout the previous year. I won't push too hard and send him into full-on hiding. But I'm going to make sure he doesn't forget I'm only ever one bunk bed away.

I keep up with Dylan's strides over the rocky mounds, our trail veering right until the ocean is no longer at our sides. The terrain is considerably more varied than the straight track of my treadmill at home. I like the challenge. The zigzagging paths cut between rocks, dipping into valleys, then curving over stony mounds and cresting hills before snaking again.

We run for ten minutes in content silence. When we head down a hill and a buzzing noise sounds next to my ear, I swat the air, annoyed to have the peaceful moment disturbed.

Dylan watches the irritated motion with a grin. "Something *bugging* you, Cal?"

"It's just one mosquito. Hardly a swarm worthy of that monstrosity," I mutter, nodding towards the head net.

"Whatever you say," he laughs.

I swat the air a few extra times for good measure, satisfied when the sound fades. At least, until another buzz begins on the other side of my head. And another. And another. It soon becomes painfully obvious that the initial attack was only the beginning of the buggy onslaught. Thirty seconds later, I run into a small swarm of mosquitoes. I make a jerky half-step to the side to avoid them. One of the stupid things lands on my ear, and I clap a hand over it too late to avoid getting bitten.

I hold out for another few minutes, dodging and cursing while Dylan mocks me under his protective covering. When I do give up, grumbling as I slip the net over my face, he slaps me on the back like I've been welcomed to a miserable club.

The buzzing continues, but the bites end once I've donned the net. I'm relieved for the barrier, and I appease myself with a promise I'll shower and comb my hair as soon as we return to the house. I glance around, wondering how far we've ventured from our front door. When I do, I realize that, while I was preoccupied with mosquitoes, I failed to notice we'd gained a different sort of companion.

"Geez, Dylan, do you attract dogs everywhere now?" I ask as the husky fur ball of a puppy bounds on gangly legs, nearly tripping over itself in its joy as it runs at Dylan's side.

Dylan pats the puppy's head. "Sometimes," he admits. "I'm starting to get a reputation at home. Probably a good thing, given the crappy downward spiral of my good looks." He grins, then shakes his head. "Some of the jerks at school thought it'd be fun to start calling me Sludge."

"They didn't do anything to you, did they?" I ask. I had no idea Dylan was being bullied, although the idea is not baffling. With his short stature and interesting fashion sense, Dylan's always been a peculiar sight. Since Mim went into a coma, he's lost a bit of his carefree attitude too.

"Nah," Dylan says. "I told them I'd sick my dogs on them if they got in my way. They didn't believe me— at first." His eyes glint with mischief as he glances at me. "One day, I saw them playing baseball near my house. So, I collected a few of the neighborhood mutts and went for a walk to the field. The sight of seven dogs off-leash awaiting my command did wonders to convince them."

I laugh. "Well, at least you have an army at your disposal."

The dog darts around Dylan's legs and runs between us. Its fur is a dirty white with black strips across its back and hind quarters. Spots freckle its nose, and its eyes are a startling blue, a few shades lighter than the nearby ocean. It tilts its head at me and yips again before bounding forward to lead us on.

"Are you bothered at home?" Dylan asks once the dog has moved ahead of us.

"Not anymore," I sigh. "When I was younger, I got pushed around a bit, but mostly people just leave me alone now. Helps that no one was ever murdered at my school."

Dylan smiles and offers me an appraising, sidelong look. "How long has it been now, anyway?" he asks. "Since you last saw a ghost?"

"January," I admit.

The last spirit I saw was a woman hanging from the rafters of the converted post office one of my violin recitals took place in. She wasn't the first ghost I'd seen whose murder had been disguised as a suicide, but this woman wasn't upset she'd been betrayed— she was furious. She screamed and cursed, and I held my ears and slid along the wall until I could stagger out of the room.

Mom and my sister, Rose, trailed after me, failing to hide their embarrassment despite their best efforts to act like nothing unusual had occurred. Once I made it to the performance area, I was out of the spirit's range. But odd glances from the kids who witnessed my panic followed me onto the stage, and the lingering roil of my gut made me desperate to get out of the building and back to the solitary comfort of my bedroom. Fury like that of the ghost's swelled, but I played through it, rough on my strings and more melodramatic than my pieces called for. The determination in my features must have counted for something to the judges. I took first prize and, after the performance was over, I left through the building's back exit.

I haven't seen a spirit since.

"Sometimes I think I should be relieved," I confess to Dylan as we head down a steep, grassy slope. "But then I remember that it won't last. It can't. And when I *do* see a spirit again…"

"You're afraid your skin will turn gray," Dylan says with a sage nod.

I smile, eyeing his off-putting appearance. "Is that what you think this is? Something related to your talent?" I ask.

He shrugs. "It has to be. The doctors can't find anything wrong. Besides, I don't feel sick. In fact, I feel… better? More attuned with my surroundings or something. And I swear my hearing's gotten stronger."

I slow to a stop, waiting for Dylan to glance back at me before I nod in the direction of our furry companion.

"Like a *dog*?" I question.

Dylan halts with a groan. "They're going to start calling me wolf-boy, aren't they?"

I unscrew the lid of my water bottle and take a sip, remembering too late that there's a net blocking the way to my mouth. Water spills down my front, and I curse, glaring at Dylan when he snorts.

"Better than being called Sludge," I say, reaching a hand under the net to wipe water from my chin. "You don't want *that* in your senior yearbook."

"True," Dylan agrees. He whistles, and the puppy circles back to his side. Dylan gives the dog a scratch as it jumps at his leg. "Maybe I should start wearing a collar. Think I could pull it off?"

"No," I laugh. "But when has that ever stopped you?"

Dylan grins. He kneels down to pet the dog while I swat at the mosquitoes long enough to wring out the net and guzzle a few gulps of water.

DESPITE MRS. BUXLEY'S CLAIM THAT WE'RE NOT UNDER ARREST, FOR THE first few days of camp, our small house feels like a prison. We're stuck inside, only given the chance to escape when a car comes to take the people who have Tuesday courses to their respective classrooms. Tuesdays are a free day for me this year, which means the shuttle service offers no release. Sefa, Sabeena, and Meander leave while the rest of us stay shut in.

At least we've got Dylan's puppy to keep us entertained. The dog stayed with Dylan until we finished our run Monday morning. The next day, it was back to join him on a solo trek. When Dylan returned to the house, the puppy hung around, whining at the front door until Kornelía took pity and let it inside. It stayed until the dinner hour, bounding outside when a startled Sefa opened the front door on his return from class.

Still, a puppy doesn't dull the boredom of staying

indoors. Nor does the fact that, when it's finally time for my first course of the summer to begin on Wednesday, I only get to travel as far as the classroom in our house. One more way to keep us trapped within these walls. At this rate, I won't see any ghosts this summer, anyway. I won't be out of the house long enough.

Sender Management starts at two o'clock Wednesday afternoon. In-house or not, when we're called into the class, I'm happy to at least get out of the living room. Even Dylan doesn't seem to mind leaving the stray dog curled up by the fireplace in favor of a lesson about ghosts.

Mrs. Buxley is teaching this course and, while I'm not surprised, I do wonder if she is *supposed* to be the instructor. It's been two years since we were all in a classroom with her. But the moment she starts talking, it's like we're back in our introductory Basics of Paranormality course.

"The aim of Sender Management is to help you explore the new facets of your talents." She leans back against her desk, her eyes roaming the room. "Most of you have already turned sixteen. And those who haven't yet will soon."

Three members of the remaining Shade sector have yet to reach their sixteenth birthdays. Reed will be sixteen at the beginning of August, and Sefa at the beginning of September. Kornelía won't have her birthday until November. But the other five of us have already reached the not-so-sweet age.

"Discovering new aspects of your abilities can be frightening," Mrs. Buxley says, her expression warm despite her solemn tone. "Particularly when major developments happen in a relatively short span of time.

Being a Sender is difficult. It's important for you to remember that your leads and instructors understand what you're going through. We've all gone through it ourselves. With that said, however, I know that facing these unique changes can be a solitary fight."

"Mrs. Buxley," Sabeena begins, her pen tapping nervously against her notebook, "are these changes permanent? Not the way we see spirits, but... the other changes. The *physical* things."

She stares at the pen, watching its uneasy bounce while Mrs. Buxley considers her from afar. A few seconds tick by before our instructor steps up to Sabeena's desk and places a hand over the pen to stop its movement.

"Yes," she says, no qualifier floating behind her words.

Sabeena doesn't look any different to me, and I'm curious what physical changes she's talking about. Of course, Sabeena's not shy. That she's nervous making a vague illusion to her change means it's probably something I don't need to know.

"I was afraid of that," she half-whispers, her pen dropping to the table.

"Come and see me after this session is over," Mrs. Buxley says. She moves her hand to Sabeena's shoulder. "We'll talk."

Sabeena looks up and nods, her eyes shining. Mrs. Buxley squeezes her shoulder, then walks on, circling the room as she continues to speak.

"These changes may also be confusing," she says. "Your ability does not always develop the way you expect. But unfortunately, the only way for you to truly understand your development is to confront spirits and gain practice managing your talents."

"So, you're sending us out to find ghosts?" Sefa asks. His voice is hopeful, like maybe his summer hasn't been ruined after all.

"Certainly." Mrs. Buxley smiles as she returns to the front of the room. "The main purpose of this course is to teach you coping mechanisms and tactics you can use to keep from being overwhelmed in a spirit's presence. These tactics will, like your abilities, be unique. So, the best way for us to help you is to have you interact with a spiritual entity."

She pauses as if she's waiting for someone to interrupt her. No one does. I suspect everyone wants to know the details—or the catch.

"Because we want to ensure your success," she continues when the room remains quiet, "we will be overseeing your projects. You can pair off as you see fit, and each pair will be working with a lead to choose and make contact with a spirit."

Sefa leans back in his chair, his hands laced behind his head. "We don't need to be babysat," he mutters, his voice low even though everyone in the room can hear him.

Mrs. Buxley fixes him with her no-nonsense stare. "You'll be doing all of the work," she says. "No one is going to clean up your messes. Think of the leads as a bonus. If you insist on being moody about it, think of them as a road block instead. They're not going to hold your hand, but they will warn you if they sense danger ahead."

"This all seems a little excessive," Dylan muses. "Mim did her exorcism planning in secret. And our first year Cal was being, like, possessed or something.

What the hell is having a lead going to do if he's possessed again? He'll be in the freaking ocean before any road block can stop him."

"Thanks for that, Dylan," I mutter. I rub my hands over my face, banishing memories of the time I worried a ghost would, indeed, push me over some precarious ledge.

"Let's not dwell on what's happened," Kornelía says with a sharp look at Dylan. "I'd like to hear what else Mrs. Buxley has to share."

"Thank you, Kornelía," our instructor says. She crosses her ankles and sits on the edge of her desk. "As I said, you will pair off and work in groups of two. You'll have the entire summer, so each group can choose to work with two spirits, if you wish. But we are not going to push you." Her eyes are almost sad when she surveys us again, like it's painful for her to admit this. "If you'd rather, your group can stick to one spirit. Teamwork is important, and if you want to work together on a single project, that is okay."

I'm sorry she's so bothered by telling us we can play it safe, but none of us look too upset by the news. The campers who still want to venture forth and take charge are able to do so. But not all of Shade wants to spend their summer with ghosts. Even if it goes against the Oracle's mission—not to mention budget—I'm glad they're giving us the choice.

Our instructor lets us partner up, and I instinctively glance across the room to where Meander sits next to Reed. I didn't plan on cornering Meander today. I haven't, in fact, spoken to him since Sunday night. But I can't deny how pleased I am by the idea of working with him all summer. This project is the best chance

I've got to get him to talk with me. Plus, Mrs. Buxley has given him a pass on finding a ghost himself. I can take charge, and we can ensure he—and I—stay safe. No one else will give him a guarantee like that.

Meander doesn't look like he intends to do any choosing. His eyes wander aimlessly over the room until he catches me watching him. His shoulders tense, and he sits upright in his chair as our gazes lock. For a second, I think he's about to nod in approval of my unspoken plan. When he shifts to face Reed instead, my anticipation dims. When I hear his mumbled suggestion the two of them partner up, any lingering hope is completely snuffed out.

My mood clouds with something like petty jealousy as Reed shrugs in agreement. Facing front, I slump in my chair, fighting the sting of tears. I'm not shocked Meander doesn't want to be forced into close contact with me. But I'm unhappy he was so quick to ensure we wouldn't work together. After everything that's occurred since last summer, I suppose this small slight shouldn't hurt. Still, I grip the edge of my table until my fingers turn white.

Sefa twists in his chair, and I try to keep the pain out of my face as he directs his gaze at me.

"Looks like we're stuck with each other," he grumbles, which I guess means we're the last two Shades without partners. He's clearly not thrilled with the arrangement. Though I imagine he's less bothered by working with *me* than with anyone who was involved in the incidents that have made him feel cheated this summer.

"I guess we are," I agree in a tight voice.

Sefa turns back around with a sigh as Mrs. Buxley

starts writing down our groups. At least we don't have to start working together right away. Once she's made her list, our instructor continues explaining what we'll be doing during our weekly class time. Then we talk about management techniques—like schedule keeping and having an emergency backup—until about halfway through our four hours, when Dylan's puppy starts scratching at the house's front door.

With a *tsk* of annoyance, Mrs. Buxley gives into Dylan's bouncing agitation and allows us a break so he can let the dog out. She opens the door and steps into the hall, scolding Dylan for keeping a stray in the house while he bounds away to release the pup. My other sector mates get up as well, glad for the chance to stretch and grab something from the kitchen.

I stay sulking in my seat, watching the others pass until only Meander and I remain. He gets up to leave too, and I wait for him to disappear so I can brood by myself. He crosses the room. When his steps falter at the edge of my desk, I raise my head to find him watching me. His eyes are imploring, a surprise given his continued avoidance over the last few days. But the unexpected appeal doesn't override my disappointment.

"Reed? Really?" I ask, my voice more desperate than I'd like.

Meander takes a careful step forward. "He never sees spirits, Cal," he says, his voice stuck somewhere between emotionless logic and quiet pleading. "If I let him take the lead, we'll fail our assignment and have an uneventful summer. That's what Buxley wants anyway. For me not to get involved. I bet they wouldn't let us pair off even if we wanted to."

"Even if *you* wanted to," I correct.

His jaw tightens as he begins his retreat. "You knew this would happen." The words snap with a flare of anger, but I don't let them jolt me out of my stony glower. "I didn't come here to do coursework and hunt for ghosts, Cal. I'm here for information. That's *all*."

The coarse declaration rakes against my skin. But when I register what he's actually said, the hard line of my mouth melts and my features soften with incomprehension.

"What information?" I ask. I knew Meander was lying when he said his mother forced him to attend Wanagi this summer. But this isn't the secret I thought he was keeping.

Meander startles, unprepared for the question. Whatever his secret is, he didn't mean to disclose it. Long seconds drag by as he considers me, contemplating if he's going to divulge the truth—or maybe offer up another lie.

"Nothing," he mumbles at last. He shakes his head and looks at the doorway. "I've got to go."

"Meander, wait—" I start.

He doesn't falter a second time. As Sabeena and Naasir walk back into the room, Meander pushes between them and slips out the door.

WHEN SENDER MANAGEMENT IS OVER, SEFA TRAILS ME TO THE LIVING ROOM so we can discuss our project. He wants to take the lead for the first part of the summer. He's on edge when he suggests it, his wide shoulders relaxing only once I'm quick to agree. Sefa was unsuccessful with his spirit release in Tonga. Given how serious he is about developing what he considers to be his "gift," the failure has probably weighed on him for months. Since he blames me for at least part of his lackluster start in Greenland, alleviating his worries about the future is the least I can do.

I assure my sector mate he can plan whatever the hell he wants for this summer. Then, while I'm still moping over my conversation with Meander, Sefa leaves me alone and gets to work. By the time I'm attending back-to-back courses on Thursday, he's already roped Robbie into a meeting so the two of them can discuss potential subjects for release. I don't mind being absent. Sefa is content to take total charge. And since he's not the partner I wanted this for this assignment anyway, I'm not eager to put in full participatory effort.

He makes up for my disinterest, staying up late Thursday and Friday to pore over case files Robbie's produced from Oracle-related sources. By Saturday, the two of them have narrowed the field to three reports of dead elders who haven't quite settled into their graves. The start is promising, and I'm impressed by the swift progress Sefa's dedication makes. But after the initial flurry of research, a slow, uneventful week sails by before a spirit is finally picked.

"Y'all better pack," Robbie says as Sefa and I step into the kitchen on our second Friday at camp.

I sit at the table, folding my arms on its top. "Pack? For what?"

"For your first attempt at meeting a ghost," Robbie says with a smile. "We've found a case for you two. But it's forty-five minutes away, so we've got some travelling to do."

Sefa rips a piece from the loaf of marbled bread resting on the table. He slathers it with jam as he considers what Robbie said.

"Forty-five minutes isn't far. Why do we need to pack?" he asks.

Robbie's smile slides into a grin. "Forty-fives minutes by *plane*. Greenland's towns are not all connected by roads. You can't get far by driving around here. We'll be doing an overnight trip."

"You're coming with us?" I ask.

I'm not as nervous as I expected to hear we'll be looking for a spirit soon. The past week has been dreary and boring, and the idea of doing *something* intrigues me. Last year, I had plenty to keep me busy between ghost sightings. But now Meander's nearly non-existent, spending most of his time out of our house and ignoring me when he's forced to be here. Dylan's been focused on the puppy, and Kornelía splits her time between him and Sabeena. The result is sort of like being back at home. I spend vast majority of my days alone, without the creature comforts of my house to keep me placated.

But besides all that, Sefa is leading this project. Once we complete it—if we manage to do so—we'll talk about whether I'm willing to lead a second ghost-hunt before the summer's end. For now, I'm content to be the watchful bystander.

"Sure, I'm coming along," Robbie says with a nod. "Can't let you two have all the fun, can I?"

"More like can't leave us alone to get ourselves killed," Sefa grumbles.

Robbie gives me a knowing glance, like we're two adults smiling above the head of a petulant child.

I lean back in my chair with a small smirk. "We're only going overnight, though? Don't you think it'll take more time than that?"

"Oh, it likely will," Robbie says. "This is just the introductory meeting. We're leaving tonight, and we'll be back tomorrow around lunch. Gives you enough time to see the ghost and ask some initial questions. When you're back, you can start the research."

"What if…" I begin, before Robbie cuts me off with a laugh.

"We're quite sure the body's not buried anywhere in the house," he says, picking up my thought as clearly as Kornelía might. "We've been assured his bones were properly put to rest."

"So, it's a man?" Sefa asks, perking up when he realizes there are details to discover.

"Yep." Robbie nods. "His name was Albert Timmons."

I quirk a brow. "That doesn't sound like a Greenlandic name."

"It's not," Robbie agrees. "Albert was an American. The town you're going to was an American air base during the second World War."

"He was a military man," Sefa says, repeating the information as if he's jotting notes in his brain.

"That depends on when—and why—Albert lived there," I remind him.

"You said it's a military town," Sefa says to Robbie. "That means he was involved in the war, right?"

Robbie shakes his head. "I don't know for sure," he admits. "They only told me his name. I had the same reaction as Cal, so they mentioned the air base. I'd assume that means the two are connected, but I can't say for certain. There's more information waiting for you when we arrive, so you'll know soon. Y'all better get packing, anyway. We leave for the airport in an hour."

While Sefa finishes his bread and jam, I make quick work of packing. I stuff a change of clothes, my toiletries case, and my phone charger into my backpack. I'm curious to know why we have to leave on such short notice. But I can't say I'm bothered by having to hurry. Being in this house is claustrophobic. Particularly when night falls and I have to keep the volume on my phone loud enough to drown out the sound of rifling book pages.

I finish packing my overnight necessities. Then, with a hesitant glance around the room to make sure no one is secretly peering over my shoulder, I pull out my duffel bag. The outfit I left folded within two weeks ago is still there, the clothes a neatly pressed reminder of the delirium I must have been suffering when I decided to bring them along. For the briefest of moments, I consider pulling out the ensemble and stuffing it in my backpack with everything else. But the flutter of thought makes my neck prickle with embarrassment. I'd look like an idiot wearing this outfit on a spirit-hunting mission. I'm not sure why I ever thought to pack it in the first place.

With a sigh, I close the bag and kick it under my bunk, the clothes still inside.

The house is empty while we pack, and only Reed has returned from his course by the time we're ready to leave. He waves us off as we climb into the hired car, and soon Sefa, Robbie, and I are on our way to the Greenlandic town of Kangerlussuaq.

The flight is short and, when we land, a local guide waits to take us to the hotel where we'll be staying the night. I assume she's another hired driver. But when we arrive at the hotel, she hands us files about the spirit we'll be visiting in the morning.

"Why don't we go tonight?" Sefa asks. He's annoyed we've rushed to carry out these last minute plans for no apparent reason. I'm less troubled by the trip, though it would have been nice to at least let the other Shades know we were leaving.

"The house is occupied," the woman tells us. "We only managed to get a few free hours for you to explore. The owners aren't happy having us in their home. They're giving us a small frame of time because they truly believe the house is haunted."

"Couldn't we have caught a flight tomorrow, then?" I ask.

"You'll be visiting the house early," she clarifies. "The owners work in the morning. So, we're allowed in from four until six. Travelling today was the only way to arrive in time."

Sefa sighs. "Guess that means we're turning in for an early night, too."

We check into our room, and Sefa flips through TV stations while Robbie goes for a shower. I'm happy to see that my phone has a network connection here, so I can check for messages from home. Rose has sent me an email asking about camp, and there's a note from Kornelía dated an hour ago wishing me luck on tomorrow's venture. I reply to both emails, then I hunch over my phone so there's no chance Sefa can remark on my music choices as I browse through symphonies and concertos.

When Robbie steps out of the bathroom dressed for bed, his hair is pulled into a high bun. The alternating colors twist together in a thick, black-green strip across the top of his head.

Sefa and I stare at him open-mouthed.

"What?" he asks, his brows arched high as he looks between us.

"This is the first time I've *ever* seen you without your mohawk up," I say.

Robbie laughs, tugging at the bun and flopping onto one of the three small beds. "I'd keep the mohawk all the time," he says with a grin. "But it's a bitch to sleep with."

I smile, shutting down my phone as Robbie switches off his bedside lamp. I'm not tired, and—early morning start or not—I suspect I'm going to have trouble getting to sleep tonight. But I make an effort to prepare for rest, taking a turn in the bathroom to brush my teeth as I ponder what I'm going to face when the morning comes.

Throughout the night, I toss and turn, starting awake around two thirty when Sefa yells something in his sleep. At three, an alarm rings on Robbie's phone, and I'm glad I can stop trying to pretend I'm relaxed enough to rest. The sun is out all twenty-four hours at this time of the year so, when Sefa begins doing finger push-ups and Robbie tinkers with some kind of antique timepiece he's fished out of his bag, I grab my phone and go for a walk outside until it's time to face the ghost.

THE HAUNTED HOUSE IS NOT UNLIKE THE PLACE WE'RE STAYING THIS
summer. The building is small and square, the siding
green-gray with white trim around the wide windows.
I wonder if the interior will have a similar layout
as the Shade house in Ilulissat. I'd like to ascertain
the similarity for myself, but Sefa halts us outside,
wanting to get a sense of the place from its exterior
before venturing in.

The sky is overcast, and the breeze is cold. I huddle
into my jacket, but the windbreaker is not enough
to keep the chill at bay, even with my Camp Wanagi
sweater underneath. I stamp my feet as I wait for Sefa
to make his rounds, annoyed that Robbie gleefully left
us here while he ambled away in search of coffee. I
wish I had tea right now. The promise of a hot mug
when this expedition is over is hardly enough to help
me endure the frigid weather.

"Are you ready to go in yet?" I ask after at least

fifteen minutes of watching my sector mate wander around the building and its surrounding land.

Sefa swings a massive oak walking stick like a giant baton as he rounds the front of the house for the fourth time. "Cool it, will you?" he snaps. "I'm doing my process."

"Does your process usually take this long?" I mutter. "No wonder you're the golden boy of Shade. You know you have to get *near* a spirit to communicate with it, right?"

"You want a smack with this?" he asks, waving the stick in my direction. He insisted on bringing it with him from Ilulissat. I haven't measured its length, but I'm pretty sure it's as tall as me.

I roll my eyes in response to Sefa's threat, and he continues around the house. Sefa and I have never worked together before, but I didn't expect we'd be such hostile partners. He's been out of sorts all summer, annoyed we're being monitored because of things he hasn't been a part of. I get why he's mad. But I also resent that he thinks he's been burdened with a trouble-maker.

Still, I didn't plan on being an ass. The gray weather and lack of sleep has made me grumpy. So has standing outside when we could be getting this encounter over and done with.

When the first patterings of cold rain drizzle over my hair, I give up on waiting.

"I'll meet you inside!" I call as I rush up to the house.

Sefa doesn't respond, either because he's out of hearing range or he's pretending I haven't spoken. Regardless, I ascend the inclined ramp leading to the front door and push inside, glad the house is already unlocked.

With a shiver, I step into the entryway and stamp my shoes on the welcome mat to kick off any bits of soggy dirt. The air is as cold in here as it was outside, but I unzip my jacket anyway, hoping I'll warm up once I'm further in.

When I'm convinced my sneakers won't leave prints on some stranger's hardwoods, I continue into the carpeted living room. The fireplace is small compared to ours, and I'm disappointed it's not lit. The chill hasn't faded, and I zip my jacket again, hunching my shoulders against the lingering coolness.

Rubbing my nose, I approach the fireplace as a sour smell wafts from the carpet fibers beneath my feet. The scent is musty and old, like an alcohol stain from a glass spilt seventy years ago. My brows furrow at the thought, peculiar and precise as it is, and I stare at the carpet, trying to detect any sign of a stain.

A flash in my peripheral vision makes me raise my eyes to the glass-encased fireplace. When I catch the blink of a white spot behind my shoulder, I swivel in a panic. My head clouds with the movement, and my heart thuds heavy in my chest as the sour smell grows stronger. The room is empty, but something pools between my ears—a quiet sound I haven't heard in many months.

Static.

"Damn it." I turn back towards the entryway, the static growing louder as my stomach begins to churn. The distant sound of the front door swinging open and shut pushes through the fuzz, and I cringe when the static morphs around it, whining and burbling like someone's fiddling with a radio dial inside my head.

Groaning, I bring a hand to my temple as the more distinct scent of hard liquor makes my vision swim. I shuffle forward, taking small steps until the solid support of the hallway's wood floors rests beneath my sneakers.

And then the music starts.

The spinning dial in my head stops and, with the force of a gunshot, my ears are assaulted by the huge, clear sound of a big band playing a jazzy tune. The volume is horrendous, the whole house overcome with the noise of clarinets and trumpets blasting notes inside my brain.

I cry out and fall to my knees, my hands squeezing tight to my ears. I don't understand what the hell is happening, but I can only assume this is a trick, a nasty joke played by Sefa—or else a spirit with the capacity to mess with the house's sound system. My stomach aches, but the noise is far, *far* worse. I'm not sure I can breathe. If I take too large of a breath, my focus might slip and my eardrums might burst.

When a bass begins playing, the plucking notes sting like they're snapping hard against my veins. Then the clarinet takes over again, the shrillness of its improvised tune setting me groaning through gritted teeth.

I don't hear Sefa approach. When he shakes my shoulder, I start and open my eyes, unaware I ever closed them. He mumbles something I can't make out, and I shake my head.

"What?" I yell, and he starts back, looking pissed at my question and mumbling something again. "I can't hear you! The music's too loud!"

He stares at me, his expression perplexed. He utters words I don't hear at all. When I shake my head again, he brings his face close to mine.

"*There's no music,*" he mouths.

Annoyance gives way to curiosity as he appraises my confounded expression. Either he's deaf or I'm insane. I can't for one second believe no one else can hear this hellish sound.

Sefa looks like he might try speaking again. But then his head snaps up, and his attention shifts to something behind me. Understanding and discomfort bloom in his brown eyes. He stands, taking a single step forward before stumbling back. The walking stick— its wood-length carved with flowery designs— digs into the floor as he leans his weight against it.

Drums beat, and a swing time rhythm shakes my brain with thrumming pain. I never thought I'd ache for the static I heard briefly before the music began. It feels like the band is struggling to contain a concert hall's worth of noise within the tight constraints of my head.

My head.

Sefa droops over the walking stick, his skin assuming a weary pallor and fading from soft brown to a spotted, sandy shade much like the windswept and sun-bleached skin of an elderly person. He says something I can't understand, his eyes still fixed behind me. I count the beats of the song raging through my head, working up enough will to half-turn, half-fall onto my back. I twist my head to the far side of the room and finally see the wispy mass of the ghost watching us.

The spirit of Albert Timmons is not well-formed. Every part of him is misshapen and, in a few spots, the blue-white smoke is missing, leaving gaping holes through which I can see the wall behind him. Another unexpected murder victim. This time with a musical addition I could never have fathomed.

The man peers at us, and I think Sefa must speak to him because the vague shape of what was once his head tilts to the side. After a pause, a hole in the mist yawns open, and he speaks.

"*Go away,*" he says, the words mixing into the music like counter beats to the heavy drum.

"We're… we're here to help!" I yell.

The shrieking melody of the clarinet returns, and I wince as the man shifts his transparent face towards me. A waft of what I think might be gin sweeps under my nose. My stomach bucks with the smell, but I don't dare lower my hands from my ears. The noise is inside of my head, apparently. But that doesn't change the fact I feel like gray matter will seep out if I give up my desperate grip.

"*Go away,*" he repeats. The words sound like part of the music—lyrics rising over the melody, so much clearer than I'm used to spirits sounding.

The ghost looks back at Sefa, who is using the cane to hobble forward as if he doesn't have the strength to keep himself upright without aid. His stance is fragile, an astonishingly odd sight given his mass of bulky muscles. He must be transferring power, offering the spirit some of his strength. The closer he gets to the spirit, the worse Sefa looks—while the holes in the ghost's energy continue to cloud and fill.

Sefa says something to Albert, and the ghost shakes his head. He looks far more solid than he did before Sefa approached him, and it dawns on me that I couldn't even see the spirit before Sefa came up to the house.

"*I just want to forget,*" the ghost says in response to a

question Sefa asked.

The song's melody has shifted. The noise is almost beyond making musical sense, and I'm not sure if a new tune has begun or if this is the same song stretching in a new, terrible direction. The brass section blazes, the sound swelling and crashing like obnoxious waves. I gasp, the enormity of the score sending a spike of pain rocketing down my body.

I roll onto my side, shivering as I wonder how hard it would be for me to crawl out of the room. I can't take this. Sefa can hunch over his walking stick like some badly-cast drama production trying to pass off an in-shape youth as a withered elder. But my eyes are leaking from the agonizing music, and my chest is tight with the effort to breathe.

Screw the ghost. This is *not* worth it. I need to get out before my brain short-circuits under the pressure.

"*No,*" the old man says.

Sefa must still be talking. The two of them are welcome to converse as much as they want. I'm getting the hell out of here.

I push onto my stomach and brace myself to drop my arms. The pain is no different without the security of my hands against my ears, but I feel more vulnerable. I groan, sniffing through the cold and my tears of pain. My palms press into the carpet, and I start to army crawl away from the scene.

"*I just want to forget,*" the old man says again.

Halting to breathe, I twist away from the stinking rug and get a clear enough view to read Sefa's lips.

"Forget what?" he asks the spirit. He looks exhausted. I'm not sure why he hasn't given up trying to stand. He's stronger than I am. But I'm already flat on the ground, and I'm not giving the ghost any of my strength. I can't believe he's kept his footing this long.

The alcohol ferments in a blossom of stench, and I gag as I crawl forward again, trying to match my movements to the speedy tempo of the band. I reach the hardwood and pull myself completely out of the room. The distance is enough to make the music crackle, like an old record popping as it turns. I keep moving, the static sharp but nevertheless a relief. The band whines, fading before it surges in volume as the old man's voice cuts through the cacophony.

"Marmalade."

I cringe, the very idea of food roiling my gut. Pushing forward another foot, I'm relieved when I lift my head to the quiet—but noticeable—sound of the front door swinging open down the hall.

Robbie enters the house and takes in my stance with a barely contained grin. He steps forward, nodding as he looks beyond me to Sefa.

"Thought I'd check on you," he says. He moves out of view, disappearing into the living room before returning to my side and helping pull me up. His smile is no longer hidden as he gets me to my feet and ushers me towards the door. "Thought it might be time for a break."

"I'll stay a little longer," Sefa says from behind us. I'm glad I can hear him through the static that's swallowed the sound of the band. My ears are sore, like they've been given a pummeling and will swell in an hour or so. But by the time Robbie helps me across the threshold, the pain begins to ebb with the rainy breeze.

"Have an unplanned visit, did you?" Robbie asks once we're in the rented car.

"I always seem to," I sigh. I rub my temples and lean against the headrest. "You didn't tell me this guy was murdered."

"Yeah, that's the funny part," Robbie says, considering me. He tugs at the bun he's still sporting this morning and shrugs. "I didn't think this guy was."

12

ANOTHER PERSON KILLED WITH NO ONE EVEN KNOWING IT.

My head quiets with the soothing drizzle of rain on the car roof. But when Robbie goes back into the house ten minutes after helping me out, I'm still ringing with the music of the big band and how it could be related to the murder of Albert Timmons. I've never heard music around a spirit before. The song must be important, if he retained the memory of those notes even after his death.

Sefa staggers out of the house with Robbie, and I shut off my brain while we drive to the inn to have breakfast. Robbie doesn't prod us for information and, with strangers nearby, we don't talk much until we're back in the car. There, Sefa asks if we can return for another round with the spirit. I don't argue. But when the car brakes before the house for the second time, I stay in the backseat.

"Suit yourself," Sefa says with a shrug. He's quick to

slam the door shut, and I think he's secretly pleased I don't want to join him. He wasn't expecting company on this sighting. He's keen to continue leading the project, which is fine by me.

A meal and an understanding of what's to come bolsters Sefa's ability to withstand the ghost. Robbie and I wait for thirty minutes before he hobbles outside, too weak to continue. I'm impressed by his strength. The few pounds of muscle I've managed to develop over the past year have done nothing to keep me from practically falling on my face in the spirit's presence. Of course, I've spent a long time with ghosts before, so perhaps it's only the music making me so pathetic. If I'd heard that noise on my first plane ride to Camp Wanagi, I don't think I ever would have made it out of Toronto.

We checked out of the hotel before visiting Albert's home so, when Sefa gives up, we head back to the airport. I sleep on the return trip to Ilulissat, a short nap that's broken by a choppy landing. My head throbs by the time we arrive at the Shade house near noon. But despite wanting to drop onto my bed and sleep away the remainder of the day, I force myself to sit with Sefa in the living room.

"He told me he had a wife," he says, recounting the conversation I wasn't in the house to hear. He's eager to get a jump start on piecing together the information we've gathered. "That's what he seemed fixed on. I'm going to start my search there."

Sefa picks carefully through each page in the manila file folder we were given in Kangerlussuaq. I don't care about any of the documents except the one already in my grip—Albert's death record from 1991.

"It says here he died from complications after going into cardiac arrest," I mumble as I scan the certificate. "No autopsy was performed, and his remains were shipped back to America. He was here for the war, but he didn't die until the nineties. So, his murder couldn't have been battle-related."

Sefa glances up from his notes. "He wasn't murdered," he says, snatching the record from between my fingers. "It says right here he died of a heart attack."

"Yeah, you'd be surprised how often these things are wrong," I say, grabbing the certificate back.

"Well, this time it's not," Sefa argues. "I saw the man myself. We talked—while you were outside. I know that's how he died. His heart gave out."

"His heart may have given out, but it wasn't just nature taking its course," I sigh. "He was murdered. I don't know how, but it was something that made it *look* like a heart attack."

I didn't notice any death marks on the spirit, but I wasn't looking for them either. If I had been more prepared, maybe I would have had my wits about me enough to take stock of my surroundings. I didn't steel myself for the possibility of seeing a murder victim this morning. Then again, I'm not sure anything could have braced me for facing that awful music.

"Listen, we've never worked together before, so I don't know what it's like for you," Sefa begins, his words curt. "But I have a connection to the ghosts I see. I know things, like how this man died. He wasn't murdered, Cal. He died naturally. Almost peacefully. It's not his death that's keeping him around."

"I know things too," I snap. "And maybe the

spirits you see all die in different ways, but the ones I encounter share one commonality. They were killed. Whether it looks like a murder or is hidden under a clever cover up, the truth of their death is the same. I see the ghosts of murder victims. And I definitely saw that man. *Ergo*, he was murdered."

"Okay, fine," Sefa concedes, although I get the distinct impression he's only saying it to shut me up. "If that's what you want to focus on, go ahead. In the meantime, I'll research his wife." He bends over his notes, his mouth set in a scowl.

Maybe this kind of disconnect is normal for campers partnering for the first time. But it's weird. On every other occasion where I've seen the same ghost as another would-be Sender, our experiences correlated and complemented one another's. This is the first time I've ever argued with one of my camp mates when we've both seen the same spirit.

"Whatever," I mutter. I get up, annoyed enough I want to forget all about researching and instead spend the rest of the afternoon with my violin.

I grab my violin from under my bunk before walking through the living room on my way to the small classroom not currently in use. When I pass the couches, Sefa makes an indistinguishable noise I'm sure isn't friendly. My teeth grind together, and I stride to the classroom, throwing the door open with an irritated huff.

I take three steps into the room before realizing I'm not alone. Meander sits at one of the back tables with the old book I've seen him reading over the past couple weeks, a notebook full of neat writing laid out beside it.

"Oh, uh… sorry. Didn't think anyone was here," I mumble. I hold up my violin, then drop it back to my side. "I was going to play, but… I'll find somewhere else."

Meander glances at his book, and I start to turn. But then he raises his eyes. "You're back from visiting that spirit," he says in a quiet voice.

I quirk a brow. "Yeah, how did—"

"Kornelía told me." He shrugs.

"Oh. Right."

I haven't spoken to Meander since he partnered with Reed a week and a half ago. I haven't even bothered trying to talk with him in Meditative Communication, the course I correctly guessed he'd take in an effort to avoid all ghosts this summer. Kornelía had good intentions telling him where I was. But it still hurts to know he's conversing with other Shades while continuing to avoid me.

"You saw him, then?" Meander asks. The question is timid, like he's not sure he wants to start this discussion. His eyes drift to my violin case, and he shrugs a second time. "I heard some of your conversation."

I nod, stepping farther into the classroom and placing the case on a table. "I wasn't supposed to see him, but I did," I say.

"How was it?" he asks in the same cautious way.

"Bad," I admit, my voice shaking with a nervous laugh. "I, uh, heard music. That was a bit of a shock."

"Music?" Meander closes his book and leans back in his chair, his eyes no longer avoiding mine.

"In my head," I explain. "Like the static I hear. Only… in focus. And loud. Like, *incredibly* loud. I thought my eardrums were going to burst. I can safely say breaking an arm was nothing compared to that."

His eyes flit to the arm I fractured last summer during the attempted exorcism that set his reclusiveness in motion. "You've always said the static was like a radio," he mumbles, more to himself than to me.

"Yes," I say, amazed he's so quick to catch the connection. "And this was like the radio had finally hit a station."

I pause, thinking about what that means. I used to assume all Senders heard static when they saw spirits. But at some point between my first and second summer, I discovered the way we hear spirits is different. Meander couldn't explain his experience well. He once told me it was a full, rushing sort of noise, like something he'd heard before but a thousand times more intense. Dylan can't speak to spirits like we do but, last summer, he likened being near a canine ghost to standing in a wind tunnel. I never did ask Mim what it's like for her. I don't want to dwell on wondering if I'll ever get the chance to pose the question in the future.

Meander's expression is reflective, like he's working to find a logical explanation for what I've told him. I watch the contemplation playing in his features, happy he's too preoccupied to notice. He swipes at a loose curl, his teeth running over his bottom lip as his eyes adopt a momentary glint of surprise. But then his face clouds, and he takes a deep breath, his thoughts scattering as he blinks back to the present.

"I'm sorry it was bad," he says, lowering his gaze to the closed book. He starts to collect his things. "I'll go. You play."

"You don't..." I begin, but then I stop, knowing it's

pointless to ask him to stay.

He rises and crosses the room. As he nears me, I glance at the book he's been carrying around since he arrived at camp. The volume is huge, but I can't read what the cover says—because the words are not written in English.

"Learning new languages now?" I ask, nodding at the book.

Meander's cheeks bloom pink. He continues past me, but not before I catch the glint in his eye—the brief return of the imploring look he gave me during our first Sender Management course.

"Something to keep me busy," he mutters. He skulks through the door and pushes it closed behind him.

With a resigned breath, I drop into the nearest chair. Meander is no longer simply distant. He's hiding something. And although he's good at keeping silent, I'm positive I still understand him well enough to know his hesitating glances mean he wants to let me in. My neck prickles. I'm annoyed by his behavior and frustrated with myself for failing so completely to break through this latest coat of armor. I wish I wasn't so oblivious. I wish *he* wasn't so stupidly stubborn.

Pain—completely different from the shocking music—ignites in my chest. But I tamp down the hurt and quash my nagging thoughts as I open the violin case. Right now, I can't focus on Meander's motives for being at camp. My current priority is getting myself under control so I can start uncovering the truth about how Albert Timmons was murdered.

13

FOR THE NEXT FEW DAYS, I RESEARCH THE LIFE AND DEATH OF ALBERT Timmons.

Our records state that he was born in 1920 and died in 1991, which means he was in his early seventies when the heart attack took his life. I start by trying to determine the true culprit of his death. Everyone—Sefa included—is certain cardiac arrest is what did it. I don't care much about coroner reports or death certificates, but I do trust Sefa's judgment—even if he is being a jerk about not trusting mine.

On Tuesday, I decide the best course of action will be looking up ways a heart attack can be faked or induced by malevolent means. Our house doesn't have an internet connection, so I take my laptop and catch a ride into the main part of Ilulissat. There, for the first time in two and a half weeks of camp, I step into Wanagi's library.

The apartment that's been converted is bright and

airy, with windows covering two walls and light wood flooring reflecting the sun shining through the panes. Unlike the previous summers I've spent with the Oracle, this year there is no coming and going of campers as people wander from room to room or fale to fale. Everything is separated by short car rides or long treks on foot. The only campers in the library have come with a purpose.

I sit at a table and use my laptop to search for murder cover-ups involving heart attacks. I'm not sure what I'm after but, if I can pinpoint how Albert was killed, it might give me a better idea who did it. A skilled, drug-induced reaction would suggest a professional—a doctor, perhaps, or a person with money to spend on precision hitmen. If the manner was crude, it could mean Albert was involved in bad dealings with a group of ruffians. I make a mental note to check the files later to confirm where, exactly, he died. For all I know, he did have a genuine heart attack—after someone pushed him down or threatened his life.

An hour into my research, Reed arrives at the library. Plenty of spaces are still available in the open room, but he takes a slim book from one of the shelves and sits next to me, flipping open the pages and getting out his phone to take notes.

"Working on your project?" he asks. He glances at the database of recorded murders I morbidly bookmarked years ago.

"Yep." I ignore Reed's prying eyes as I scroll through accounts of cardiac arrest due to the shock of being stabbed or shot.

"Sefa thinks you're crazy," he says, turning back to his book.

I blink away from my computer screen, annoyance cutting through my focus. "He said that?" I ask, shocked less by the statement than the fact that Sefa's been saying it out loud.

"Oh yeah," Reed says, unfazed by my indignant glower. "Says you've been out of your mind since you went to the house. Something about you rolling around on the floor, screaming about music?"

"I wasn't *rolling...*" I start. "I *rolled*, like, once. And there *was* music. I just didn't know he couldn't hear it."

"Well, he thinks you don't know what you're talking about with this ghost," Reed shrugs. "Says you believe the guy was murdered when he wasn't."

I ball my hands into fists, working to remember that Reed is only conveying the information, not spouting it as the truth.

"I see murder victims," I reiterate in short, staccato beats. "I've never worked with Sefa before. Or you, for that matter. So, I get that you guys don't automatically take my word as fact. But this is how I see spirits. It'd be nice if you stopped assuming I'm an idiot for a minute, okay?"

Reed stares at me, his freckled face void of reaction. "Sorry," he mumbles, not sounding sorry at all. "Just what he said."

"It doesn't matter." I sigh, turning back to my screen. "He'll believe me when I've found proof. Until then, he can think whatever he wants."

"Hey, at least you've picked a ghost already," Reed says. "We're still looking. Well, I am, anyway. Meander spends most of his time researching that old Latin crap."

I'm sore about Reed working with Meander, but

I have no intention of stooping to pressing him for information about what Meander's been doing over the past couple weeks. Even so, Reed's latest comment sends my head swiveling in his direction.

"Latin?" That must be the language the worn book is written in. But why would Meander be researching Latin?

"I think so. Some old language, anyway," Reed says. "He said I could take charge of our project, though. Which is pretty cool. No one ever lets me do anything. They think just because I haven't seen a ghost since I was a kid, it means I'm useless. Kind of pisses me off, to tell the truth. If anyone else had let me be in charge of a project before, maybe I would have found a ghost. But no one ever thinks about that."

"No, I guess they don't," I agree.

"I know Meander doesn't care about the project, but it's still cool of him to let me choose the ghost," he adds. "I'm working with Alex, and can you believe she's already found three nearby drowning victims who have been seen after their deaths? There's one in particular I want to find. They call her the Siren. She makes a wailing noise like no other ghost, and she's lured at least two ships to crash on the rocks where she died. She's strong. I want her to be mine."

"You think you'll be able to see her?" I ask. "You haven't had much luck before."

Reed ruffles his rusty hair, the frizz as long as it was our first summer at camp.

"This year is different, though," he says with a smile. "I'll be sixteen soon. And I think I can almost feel it? The changes. I know they're not superpowers or anything. But *something* is going on, and I'm sure it means I'll be able to see a ghost soon."

The theory is suspect, but his enthusiasm is hard to discount.

"I'm glad you're getting a chance, Reed," I tell him. "You seem to be having the best summer of all of us."

"Weird, isn't it?" He nods. "Everyone is miserable this year except for me and Naasir."

He turns to a chapter in what must be some kind of folklore compendium. An illustrated mermaid-like picture graces the left page, and I swallow a scoff when I notice the chapter is titled "The Siren." If Reed thinks this is the spirit he's going to see, he's in for a rather grand disappointment. No wonder Meander chose him for a partner. Reed Vodden is clueless when it comes to ghosts.

"Naasir's having an okay go of things, too?" I ask, resisting a crueler response. Naasir's so stoic I hadn't noticed any swings in his mood one way or the other.

"He doesn't need a mosquito net, for one thing," Reed laughs. "That's enough of a reason to be happy here."

Greenland is a beautiful place, but I haven't spent nearly as much time outside as I should. Part of it is my gloomy attitude. But another, shallower reason is a hatred of the head nets and what they do to my hair.

"True enough," I say as I return to my research.

"I wish you guys would sleep better, though," Reed grumbles. He picks up his book and leans back in his seat to read. "Someone should have brought sleeping pills."

I roll my eyes and focus on my work, refusing to allow Reed to get any further under my skin. Over the last five months, I've been subject to periodic nightmares—

visions I suppose fit more into the category of terrors. On those nights, I'm lost to dark dreamscapes wherein the ghosts from my past, the ones I have not been able to help, suffocate me with their begging wails and clawing fingers of frozen smoke.

I was worried I would make a fool of myself when I got here, crying out in my sleep and pissing off my sector mates in the process. But I was quick to discover that this is one trait I share with most of my fellow Shades. Sefa, Dylan, and Meander have also had nightmares this summer. And at least once I've heard a shriek from the girls' room down the hall. While I'd prefer us all to get a good night's sleep, there is a crooked sort of comfort in knowing this isn't something I'm suffering alone.

Only Reed and Naasir seem to be immune. Naasir is quiet on the subject, but Reed has never been good at holding his tongue. Today is not the first complaint he's made, and not even threats of a beating from Sefa have managed to make him shut up.

Reed would be a far less annoying sector mate if he would stop whining all the time. Still, I do pity him and Naasir. They didn't bargain for a summer of being woken nightly by someone else's dreams, and it's not their fault they don't have to deal with the frustrating effects of being a Sender even while trying to sleep. I long for a night of a peaceful rest. I feel bad for the two occupants of our room who can still manage to have one for themselves.

CORRECTION: I FEEL BAD FOR THE *ONE* OCCUPANT STILL TRYING TO GET some uninterrupted rest.

Naasir and Sabeena are working on two projects at once this year, maximizing their efforts so they'll each have ample time to complete their tasks. Naasir's been scouting people who are sick, old, or both—looking for someone who is likely to die and might still have unfinished business when they go. Dylan refers to it as death-stalking. Naasir prefers to view it as a final act of mercy.

Whatever the case, Naasir is waiting on two people. One is in the town of Nuuk and being monitored by a local with Oracle ties. The other is close by and being watched by Naasir. He's waiting for the woman to reach her death bed, the short frame of time in which she's fading fast but not yet gone. Sefa asked how he'll know when that point's come. Naasir only shook his head and said it wouldn't be a problem.

What he meant was, it wouldn't be a problem for *him*.

Almost a week after my conversation with Reed in the library, I slip into the first notes of a nightmare. A world of black surrounds me, and soft static crackles in my head. But then the static turns to buzzing, and I jerk, swatting the air around me. Something pricks my neck and, with a startled gasp, I sit upright in my bed. For a moment, I blink dazedly into the darkness of the room, listening to the sounds flying past my ears. Then the tickling sting on my neck brings the shady spots dancing before my eyes into focus.

"*Mosquitoes,*" I hiss.

I wave my arms, horrified to realize that my bunk is full of mosquitoes. The insects swoop at my face, and I scramble out from under my blanket until I'm standing between beds. I put an arm against my mouth, gagging with disgust as I see that the entire room is pulsing with the swarm.

"What the hell is going on?" I mumble against my arm, my neck already itching as another bug lands on my skin.

"Wha—what is that noise?" Dylan groans, rolling onto his back and opening his eyes. He blinks a few times before making a strangled sound and pulling his sheets over his head. "What the—where did the freaking mosquitoes come from?"

The others begin to wake, everyone addled until they connect the loud buzzing with the insects making the noise. Then they curse and bury themselves under their covers while I continue standing in the middle of the room like a blood-filled target. The only one who doesn't wig out is, of course, Naasir. He sits up in bed, calm as he watches the insects milling before him.

"How did they get in?" Sefa asks from beneath his pillow.

"They came to find me," Naasir says in his deep, quiet voice.

"Why the hell are they in here, though?" I ask, swatting uselessly at the air.

"Cal, get back under your covers, you idiot," Meander says from his bunk.

I glance at my bed, and can't see how I'll ever make it back in there. The space above my pillow is teeming with insects, their numbers so thick I could grab handfuls if I wanted to. I take a step towards the bed, reaching for my comforter. As soon as I do, the mosquitoes circle my arm like a shirt sleeve, and I snatch it back to my side in retreat.

"I can't get under there," I groan.

"You should have stayed still," Naasir says as he rises from his bed. "They wouldn't have bothered you."

"Great information to know," I mutter. I flick a mosquito off my cheek, and Naasir holds up a menacing hand.

"Don't harm them!" he says, his palm outstretched.

I stare at him, incredulous. "You make them stop sucking my blood, and I promise to stop swatting them dead."

"Bloody hell, Cal," Meander mumbles. He reaches an arm out from under his mound of blankets. "Get up here, will you?"

If I was a practical person, I would consider my options and perhaps see if something as simple as leaving the bedroom might give me space to breathe. But I don't know if the swarm extends beyond our doorway, and I don't really want to risk finding out. For half a second, I hesitate, wondering if taking Meander up on his offer is a good idea. But desperation to be free of the bugs—and my weakness making sound judgment calls when it comes to this particular boy— means I swing around to grab his hand.

I catapult up the ladder, crawling onto the top bunk while Meander lifts his blankets. Diving beside him, I'm momentarily pleased by the mosquitoes' appearance as his arm settles over my back. Keeping me close to his side, he tucks the blankets around us both. His breath is hot against my ear, and the cocoon of covers is stifling. But I breathe deep, glad I don't have to worry about accidentally inhaling a bug.

"Seriously, Naasir, what is going on?" Sefa asks from across the room.

I can't see from under these covers, but I can hear Naasir's footsteps even through the buzzing. He must be wearing shoes now. The heavy tread crosses the room, and the door creaks open.

"They're here for me. I have to go," he says, like everything that's happening is totally normal.

"Wait, is this your thing? That old lady that's dying?" Reed asks.

"Yes," Naasir says. "The mosquitoes have come to warn me I need to go to her."

"Wait a freaking minute," Dylan calls from beneath us. "Warn you? Naasir, man, are you *speaking* to the bugs now?"

"You shouldn't talk, dog boy," Sefa chuckles.

"That's different," Dylan protests. "I don't have packs of dogs—"

"Flocking to your side whenever you're close?" I

offer.

Meander lets out a quiet breath of laughter, and I take the moment to risk snuggling closer to him. Lying on my stomach, I shift until his chest is pressed against my side. He tightens the blankets around us, his hand curling around my waist and holding me against him. For one fraction of a second, his head dips low, his lips brushing the tip of my ear.

"Yeah, okay, well... I don't *talk* to them," Dylan mutters.

"I don't either," Naasir says. "It's not like that. We understand each other. Insects have mental capacities we couldn't dream of. They understand what I need, and they're letting me know."

"Does it work in reverse?" Reed asks. "Like, can you tell them to *get out*?"

"They will go with me," Naasir says, his voice fading as he steps through the door. "I must leave now. I don't have much time."

He walks out of the room and, for several minutes, the rest of us don't say anything. The buzzing continues but slowly starts to quiet as the swarm moves in droves out the door to trail behind Naasir. I focus on the sound of the insects for about two seconds after Naasir leaves. Then I direct my attention to being tucked under covers with Meander.

I'm sure he doesn't notice he's doing it, but his thumb is stroking my side as we lie together. I close my eyes, reveling in the heat of our makeshift hideaway. This close, I can even smell his shampoo, and it's dizzying to be near enough to experience a simple sensation that—a year ago—I completely took for granted.

I drift into the tranquility, ignoring that we're still

technically not on speaking terms. I'm covered with bug bites and, in a short time, this night is going to leave a very uncomfortable set of reminders all over my skin. Until then, I'll allow myself the joy of pretending this is not an atypical moment.

"The bugs are gone," Sefa says after a while.

My eyes snap open, and my face rushes with heat. Without realizing it, I started to doze off. I'm so comfortable, my own bunk seems like a block of cement in comparison. I'm tempted to ignore the call, to let myself fall asleep in Meander's bed. But prolonging the moment will draw serious questions from everyone around me. So, I push away the covers and Meander's arm draws back as we both sit up to survey the now insect-free bedroom.

"Okay, please tell me you all thought that was bizarre," Dylan says.

"Um, I'd say so," Reed mumbles. He stretches his doughy arms over his head as he yawns.

"What's going to happen when he arrives at that person's house, though?" Sefa asks. "If I had a dying relative, I wouldn't let some strange teenager into my house—even if he *wasn't* trailing mosquitoes."

"Who knows," Dylan says. He swings out of bed and heads for the door. "Naasir doesn't seem concerned. Maybe the bugs will help him pick the lock or something. They got in here, after all. Anyway, I'm going to check on the girls. See if they were attacked, too."

Dylan leaves. With a reluctant shift, I pull away from Meander so I can head back to my own bed. He doesn't say anything and, after I've climbed down, he pulls his covers over his head. I cross the room and shake out my comforter to make sure no stragglers are still waiting to steal more blood. When I'm sure the bed is clear, I drop onto my mattress and let the exhaustion from the commotion pull me back into slumber before I give into the already growing urge to scratch at my bites.

15

By morning, I'm covered in spots. Scratching my neck before I've even opened my eyes, I scrunch my nose in revulsion when I feel the landscape of swollen lumps on my skin. My fingers flex, and I can't resist itching a few of the bigger bites as I pull myself up to survey the quiet bedroom.

I'm the only one left in the room, and the solitude almost makes me wonder if last night's swarm was part of a twisted dream. If I weren't so itchy, I'd probably assume the whole episode was a fractured fantasy. As it is, I stretch my legs and my foot kicks something near the end of the bed. When I lean forward, I see a small container of medicated salve resting on my comforter. It confirms my sanity, at least. I grab the plastic jar and read the attached note.

You're going to be itchy. This will help.

Smiling, I peel off the message jotted in Meander's neat handwriting before I unscrew the cap and start taking inventory of the dots covering my skin.

When I finally emerge from the bedroom, dressed and lathered in salve, I don't have to look hard to find where the others have gone. The rest of the sector is in the living room, listening as Naasir talks about his adventures.

"She was a waitress," he says as I squeeze onto the sofa next to Kornelía. She pats my knee and gives me a sympathetic smile as she surveys my blotchy skin.

"And that's why she was going to become a ghost?" Reed asks. "Sounds like a waste of unfinished business."

"No, you fool," Naasir says, his tone flaring with a rare note of impatience. He eyes Reed, who turns red and quiets down. "She was a waitress, but she really wanted to be a dancer. When she was a child, she would practice alone in her room. When she was older, she decided to leave Greenland to see if she could make it in Europe."

"Was she successful?" Sabeena asks from her spot next to him on the far sofa. She sits hunched into herself, her fingers twisting in the ends of her long hair. In her fluffy, lavender bathrobe, she looks like a girl of ten.

"She never tried," Naasir says. He stares at his feet while he relates the woman's tale. "She had a beau. He didn't want her to leave, but she told him she was going. She thought his heart was broken. She got as far as Iceland and couldn't make herself leave him behind. Within a week she was back, only to discover he had started seeing someone new. Coming back broke *her* heart, and she couldn't bring herself to make the leap and depart again.

"She told her beau that she tried and failed, hoping he would return to her out of pity. But he stayed with his new girl, and they married and had children together. Haldora—the old woman—eventually moved on and had a family of her own. But it always bothered her that her first lover thought she was a failure. She had already made peace with not becoming a dancer. But she never made peace with the way he viewed her."

"So, what did you do?" Kornelía asks.

"Her daughter called the man and told him. He heard Haldora's confession and apologized for what he did to her all those years ago."

"And that's it?" Reed asks.

Naasir nods. "She died half an hour after the phone call was complete. Her business was finished, so she was able to let go."

"That's incredible, Naasir," Sabeena says with a proud smile. "I'm sorry I missed it, but I'm so glad you achieved your goal."

"So early in the summer, too," Sefa nods. He looks troubled. In a week of researching, neither of us has found any useful information regarding the unfinished business of Albert Timmons. We have another six and a half weeks left before we leave Greenland in August. Still, Sefa is antsy. He won't say as much, but I'm positive he didn't expect to have trouble sorting out this spirit.

"What happened to all the mosquitoes?" Dylan asks from where he sits on the floor, the stray puppy resting in his lap.

"They dispersed once I was outside," Naasir explains. "They only came to warn me, so I wouldn't be too late."

"Interesting," Dylan mumbles. His eyes glaze over as he strokes the dog's soft fur. I watch him for a moment, wondering if he's dazed from our late-night interruption, or if there is deeper thought going on in his brain. Dylan's hard to figure out that way.

"I'm going to clean up and go to bed," Naasir says once he's finished the glass of water he's been nursing. He stands, eyeing me on his way past the sofa. "I'm sorry you were bitten. You moved and swatted. They thought they were under attack."

I sulk into the sofa cushion. *"They* were under attack? That's rich."

Naasir contemplates a few of the spots, his expression somewhere between pity and annoyance—like he feels bad for my discomfort but fully blames me for its presence. "Hope you feel better soon," he says with a shrug as he continues towards bedroom. "I've heard those bites can be quite itchy."

Naasir disappears into the hallway, leaving the rest of us hushed in awed silence. I wonder what it must be like to have a built-in safeguard against bug bites and bee stings. Naasir's experience with the Oracle is so different from mine. As my spiritual encounters become increasingly unbearable, Naasir's seem to take on a far more peaceful—and impressive—quality.

"Anyway," Sabeena asks once the sound of the bedroom door clicking shut breaks our reverie, "what is everyone else up to this morning?"

"I'm going to get a car over to the library," Sefa says with determination. "Do some more research."

I suppose his declaration should spur me into action as well, but I'm not interested in studying old murder cases this morning. Meander's salve has dulled the itch of my skin, but a couple of the biggest bites still throb. It's requiring most of my willpower to keep from scratching until they bleed—there's no way I can direct my focus to ghostly studies instead.

"I'll come with you," Reed says, taking my place as dedicated Sender-in-training.

"Korni, do you want to come have breakfast with Isabis and me?" Sabeena asks.

Kornelía considers the offer before giving her head a shake. "No, I've got some work to do here," she says. "Tell Isabis I say hi."

Sabeena nods, and our sector starts to shift, everyone getting up and preparing for their day. Meander's sitting on the floor by the fire, a thin paperback open on his lap and an empty mug of tea next to his leg. He's still wearing his pajamas. I study the black cotton of his turtleneck, my memory of the soft fabric recent enough I can still feel it against my arm.

He glances up from his book and, when he sees that people are leaving, he grabs his mug and stands as well. I try to catch his attention, wanting to at least thank him with my eyes. But he ignores me, passing without pause.

My chest constricts, and I breathe deep to keep my frustration under control. Beside me, Kornelía pats my knee again, and I try to reel in my emotions, reminding myself there's a minder-reader to my left.

"Dylan, are you going for a run?" she asks. She gathers her long hair into a bun while Dylan stirs from his own thoughts.

"Huh?" He blinks up at her. After a beat, he nods. "Yeah... A run... Yeah, that sounds good. Come on, boy."

He scratches the dog's ear, and it hops out of his lap before bounding for the door. Dylan climbs to his feet and heads in the same direction, already dressed in his running gear.

Kornelía waits for the pair to leave, then she turns to me. "Want to go for a walk?" she asks.

"Are you kidding?" I laugh, pointing to my spotted face.

She smiles, her head tilting to one side. "Breakfast, then? There's a café in town we can go to. We'll catch a ride with Sabeena."

Kornelía stands, pulling me up alongside her before I have a chance to question why she told Sabeena she was busy if she was just going to hang out with me this morning instead. Pushing me towards the front hall, she ventures off to inform Sabeena of the change in her plans.

It only takes a moment before the three of us are ready to leave the house. But waiting for a car and dropping Sabeena off in-town means it's nearly an hour before Kornelía and I are on our own. Sitting in a busy café, we order eggs, yogurt, and bread with a selection of jams. Kornelía sips on a latte. Once our food has arrived, she studies me until I'm so uncomfortable I start to physically squirm.

"Stop it," I say. I push a spoon through my yogurt without taking a bite.

"Sorry." She continues to stare, her hands cupped around the wide, white mug. "You're just so... sad."

"The perfect thing to say to cheer someone up," I grumble before looking at her with an apologetic shrug. "Sorry. I know you mean well."

"It's been a tough few weeks for you," she says.

I raise my yogurt-covered spoon and point it at her. "Okay, level with me, Kornelía. Can you read minds *all* the time now?"

"No," she promises with a grin. "It doesn't work like that. I get... not words, exactly, but ideas? I mean, I'll look at people and have a good *sense* of what's going on in their heads. Not always. Sometimes things appear randomly, little sparks of thought that jump out. But usually, it's got more to do with someone thinking a lot about a certain place, event..." she gives me a knowing look. "Or person."

I groan, dropping my spoon and running a hand over my face. "Am I that pathetic?" I ask, my whining voice enough of an answer.

Kornelía smiles. "Well, if it makes you feel any better—he is, too."

My eyes fix on hers. Her tawny pupils are magnified behind the myodiscs. I don't want to ask the question. But Kornelía seems to sense that as well.

"He thinks about you all the time," she says with a gentle sigh. "He watches you when you can't see. He sits on the floor outside the classroom when you play the violin."

I lean back in my chair, surprised. After years of listening to other musicians and hearing the complaints of my family, I have good reason to believe my violin can be heard in many parts of our small house. If Meander wants to listen, he could do so without staying close.

"I... didn't know that," I mumble. I pick up my tea and blow on it before chancing a cautious sip as I wonder at the oddity of this newest revelation. I'm not sure how I feel about Meander sitting outside the room while I play. He knows perfectly well I'd let him sit inside. I'm happy he wants to hear, but it nevertheless hurts that he refuses to be near me while I'm aware of it.

"Despite what you might think, I don't know what's going on," Kornelía says after taking a sip of her latte. "Nothing more than what you told me. He blames himself for what happened to Mim, and he thinks you're safer not being around him. But if you're worried about him not caring, don't be. I'm not sure that helps, but I thought you should know."

"Thanks," I say. Knowing he cares doesn't make our situation any different, but it does make me feel... *something*. Less foolish, maybe? Less lonely?

I drink some tea, and push aside my yogurt in favor of the bread and jam. Then I glance at Kornelía with a forced smile. "What about you?" I ask, changing the subject. "How has your summer been?"

She ducks her head, meek for a brief second before giving me a goofy grin. "It's been good," she says. "Much better than I thought it would be. Between Mim not being here, and these ridiculous things—" she points at her glasses with a frown "—I didn't think I'd enjoy myself much. But Dylan's..."

"Good company?" I finish for her.

She nods, hiding another smile behind her cup.

I'm glad that, for a moment, I have the chance to do the prodding. "You never told me about you two."

"There wasn't anything to tell," she admits. "We talked last summer, but nothing happened. We wanted to wait until after the night in the cave, so Mim wouldn't be distracted. And afterwards, it seemed pointless for us to even discuss it. We meant to stay friends. But when we arrived here… things changed."

I fold my arms on the tabletop, hoping I'm not pushing my bounds. "Do you feel guilty?" I ask, my voice quiet and—I hope—kind.

Kornelía purses her lips before taking another sip of her drink. Then she gathers a forkful of eggs. "For a long time, I didn't understand what went wrong at the exorcism," she says at last. "I was so stuck on what Mim *did*, I didn't focus on what she hadn't done. She kept information from us, thinking she had everything under control. She knew full well what that spirit was capable of. She told us it wouldn't matter—but she knew it would."

She pauses, her fork hovering halfway to her mouth.

"*That's* why she didn't want Dylan there," she explains. "Because she understood the spirit would attack couples. And the reason she never mentioned it was because she knew Dylan's loyalties didn't lie solely with her. If she thought the only danger was for the two of them, she would have told us—she would have at least confided in me. But she didn't tell me a thing. Which means she knew Dylan had feelings for me, and—I suspect—that I had feelings for him too. She didn't want anything to jeopardize the exorcism, so she kept the truth hidden to keep him safe and me unburdened."

Kornelía takes a bite of her eggs, chewing slowly and letting the information sink in. Much of what she's told me fits with my own theories about what went wrong in Tonga. I'm certain Mim knew Anjelo Savou's ghost had a vendetta against couples. But I'm impressed how confident Kornelía is in her assertion that Mim kept the information to herself to protect friends who were less than faithful.

"I thought what happened in the cave couldn't be helped," Kornelía continues after a moment. "But Mim messed up. She should have told us. Even if she only mentioned it to me, I could have informed her of the relationship she *didn't* see. And if she told you in order to keep me out of the loop—well, you wouldn't have come. She didn't think. And I miss her, Cal. I want nothing more than for her to be okay, and I'm so, *so* sorry for what happened. But it's not your fault. It's not mine. And it certainly isn't Meander's. This is on Mim."

"I never thought of it that way," I say, staring at the red smear of jam on my bread.

"We don't want to blame the person who got hurt." Kornelía smiles. "And the truth is, I do feel guilty about being with Dylan. Not because we're together now, but because we should have been together last year before the exorcism in the cave. However," she adds as straightens her back, "I'm not going to let those regrets ruin my summer."

I nod, and try for one more prying question before I let her be. "So, you're happy? With Dylan?" I ask.

"Yes," she says, her expression mild but content. "I mean, I'm not in love with him. He's a good friend, and he's fun to be with. We're enjoying each other's company, which is nice. I'm fine with it being nothing deeper than that." She takes another bite of egg and brushes a loose strand of hair behind her ear. "But I am happy."

"I'm glad you're enjoying yourself," I say. "And I'm sorry my obsessions keep bothering your mind." She smiles, and I raise a hand to keep her from responding. "I promise I'll try thinking only nice thoughts when

I'm around you from now on. Okay?"

"Sure," she grins.

"Just one thing," I say. "You know what you said about none of us being to blame for what Mim failed to say? Well, if you get a chance, I'd really appreciate you sharing that tidbit with Meander, too."

Kornelía's eyes widen, and she brings a hand to her chest in indignation.

"You don't think I've already tried?" she says with convincing alarm. "What kind of friend do you take me for, Cal?"

"A very good… and somewhat peculiar one," I say.

Her serious expression cracks into another grin, and she reaches across the table to snatch the uneaten bread from my hand.

16

"I'VE BEEN THINKING ABOUT WHAT NAASIR SAID," DYLAN WHISPERS WHILE we sit in Channeling on Thursday afternoon.

I was intrigued to find Dylan taking this course, until I realized he'd chosen his classes more or less at random. I'm glad for his company, at least. The rest of the course is made up entirely of Entity campers.

"About what?" I ask. I slump low in my seat, my eyes trained on the slideshow playing at the front of the room.

"About communicating with his bugs," Dylan says. He shifts lower in his chair as well while the slideshow advances to an image of a Sender mid-channel. "Maybe that's what I'm missing. I've never figured out how to communicate with the ghosts I see. But, you know, maybe I could. If I tried hard enough."

"You want to try talking to dogs now?" I ask with a smirk.

"*No,*" Dylan says. "Not holding a conversation.

But like Naasir said—communicating. Letting them tell me things. Letting them show me what they need from me."

"So… talking to them," I repeat.

In my peripheral vision, I catch Dylan rolling his eyes. "I'm going to work with Naasir, see if he has any tips," he says, ignoring my remark. "The puppy. I don't think he's just a friendly stray. He's trying to get my attention."

"Ah, attention, what a lovely concept," Ms. Tahan, our instructor, says with a loud clap of her hands.

I start at the unexpected sound—as does half the class—and Ms. Tahan gives us a probing smile.

"Sorry, Miss," Dylan mutters, but his apology isn't enough.

"Please, do tell us what so completely stole your *attention* away from this lesson?" she asks. She crosses her arms over her chest, awaiting our response. Ms. Tahan is a short, petite woman, and her blue patterned hijab is a perfect complement to the metallic blue suit all the Wanagi instructors wear. Her expression is not a severe one, but her big, expectant eyes still make me uneasy.

"Dylan was, uh, thinking about channeling," I stammer, trying to come up with a plausible excuse for our chatter. "He wants to talk, uh, *communicate* with canine spirits. And he thought channeling might be the way to do that."

Dylan's looks at me like I've sold him out over some petty crime, but Ms. Tahan's expression softens into one of appreciation.

"Yes, that is true," she says.

She motions for Gianna—the Revenant lead acting

as teaching assistant for our channeling course this summer—to shut off the slide show. We wait for the images to stop flicking past. When the room has lost the projector's hum, our instructor continues.

"Often, Senders think of channeling as a way to get clearer speech from a weak ghost," she begins. "Using the strength of our living bodies as a vessel for the spirit—whether through speech or writing— allows us to get more coherent and complete answers to our questions. Channeling is not used extensively, however, as it only works one way. We can hear from the spirit, but we cannot convey information back to them in the same manner. And many Senders don't need the intermediary step. They *can* communicate with the spirits they see, without the aid of channeling. Gianna, you've witnessed successful *and* failed channeling sessions, yes?"

"I have," Gianna agrees. "It's an amazing sight— when it works. But more times than not, it doesn't. Some Senders don't have the kind of connection necessary for channeling."

"That's true," Ms. Tahan says with a nod. "Not everyone can be a vessel. However, channeling does have its purpose. Not only for weak entities in need of a signal boost, but also for those Senders—like Mr. Benowitz here—who do not have the ability to communicate with the spirits they see."

Dylan sits up straighter in his chair, intrigued by what she said. "You mean I could channel dogs?" he asks. Under the table, his knee starts bouncing with quiet excitement.

"To be honest, I haven't a clue," Ms. Tahan admits. "I've never had occasion to witness or study a case of non-human channeling. However, it seems quite within the realm of possibility. There are a lot of factors that go into it. You need to be capable of acting as a vessel, and the canine in question must be able to connect with you in order to speak." She considers him for a moment, then gives a twinkling laugh. "A successful channeling may only result in you barking answers. But… it could work."

"It could work," Dylan repeats, his voice thoughtful.

Ms. Tahan raises a finger to her lip and taps her mouth. "Come and see me at the end of the class," she tells him. "I know someone you can talk to. Not a canine expert, but a channeler. He might have some insights for you."

"Thanks," Dylan says, his gratitude more genuine than anything I've ever heard him say to an instructor.

Once the session is over, Dylan stays behind to talk with Ms. Tahan while I dash to my next class. But as soon as I return to our house that night, he seeks me out.

"There's a guy in Argentina," he says as he paces the living room, his steps quick and springy, like someone eager for a run. "He knows all about this channeling stuff. Ms. Tahan said she'd set up an interview between us. But I need your help."

"My help?" I ask, distracted by his frantic movements. "Why?"

"The guy doesn't speak English well." Dylan shrugs. He plops down beside me and ruffles his unruly hair. "I need a translator. And Ms. Tahan said I should ask one of the Entity leads to translate for me. Daniel, she said. He's the one you know, right? Your old mentor?"

"Yeah, he is," I agree, "but I still don't get why you

need my help. Afraid to ask him yourself?"

Dylan huffs. "Ms. Tahan said he'd be busy, so she couldn't guarantee he'd be available to help. But if *you* asked, I'm sure he'd be willing to offer his services."

"That sounds oddly menacing," I say. But when Dylan gives me an impatient glance, I raise my hands in surrender. "Okay, I'll help. You're really excited about this, aren't you?"

He pops up and starts rounding the room again. "If I talk to Naasir, and talk to this guy in Argentina, maybe something will click. We're supposed to pick a project for the summer, anyway. So, I might as well try this out."

"You haven't picked something already?" I ask. "What about Kornelía?"

"Nope," Dylan says. He scratches the back of his neck, his expression mischievous. "We thought it'd be *fun* to work together." He gives me a knowing glance that quickly fades into melancholy. "But we didn't think about the fact neither of us has anything useful to do here."

He turns away, but not before I notice the sad glint that's appeared in his eyes. Kornelía may have separated the events of last summer from her current situation, but I don't think Dylan has. When he's with Kornelía, he acts like she's always been his girlfriend. But when they're not together, he refrains from talking about their relationship and looks guilty when it's alluded to.

Part of me wants to offer to discuss it, but I shove the inclination away. I'd never be comfortable talking to Dylan about my relationship problems—even if he hadn't settled into a dull dislike of Meander this summer—so I can't expect him to open up to me.

Instead, I turn my thoughts to his project—and his partner. Ms. Tahan told us this afternoon that channeling can be done by people who can't otherwise communicate with spirits. Which means that maybe Dylan's not the only one who could benefit from this new information.

"Hey, Dylan, has Kornelía ever taken Ms. Tahan's course?" I ask.

He turns back to me, his brows drawn. "No idea," he says, while I wrack my brain to recall Kornelía's past Wanagi schedules. "Why, you think she might know something?"

"No. I think she could use the information, though," I say. "Channeling might be worth exploring for her, too."

Dylan pauses, staring at me for a few seconds before he bounds out of the room. I wonder what the hell he's doing until a couple of minutes tick by and he returns with Kornelía in tow. Her glasses are off, and her eyes are tired. She's wearing pajamas, and her messy bun is a good match for Dylan's wild style. She must be having—*trying* to have—an early night.

"Sit down," Dylan says, pushing her onto the sofa.

She yawns, giving me a sleepy wave as she draws her knees up to her chest. "What are we doing?" she asks, unperturbed by the sudden interruption to her rest.

"Cal has a good idea," Dylan says. He sits next to her and ruffles his hair again. "And we've finally got a plan for our project."

17

KORNELÍA'S NOT CONVINCED SHE OR DYLAN WILL BE ABLE TO CHANNEL anything but, after some flirtatious goading—a spectacle I find difficult to watch—she agrees to try channeling as the basis for their summer project.

Dylan explains his plan, which at this point is nothing more than a couple of interview sessions with Senders more knowledgeable than him. After he relates what little he knows, Kornelía stumbles back to her room. When she's gone, Dylan sets me on the task of hunting down Daniel. I remind him it's nearly 9 p.m., but he quickly points out the ever-present sun and the fact Camp Wanagi officially runs until the stroke of midnight.

Despite my protests, he calls for a car and, within fifteen minutes, I'm kicked out of the house by someone too eager for his own good.

I haven't a clue where to start looking for Daniel. With the campers so spread out this year, I haven't really seen anyone outside of Shade except during course times. Honestly, I forgot Daniel was even in the country. Our summer has been fairly boring so far. Nevertheless, I've been preoccupied with enough annoying and troubling thoughts, I haven't given my former mentor any consideration.

Taking a car into town, I stop at each of the main houses, trying to locate the familiar face. At least Ilulissat is small, with a population that only reaches about 5,000 people. And I can't deny the scenery is beautiful. Rocky peninsulas slope down to bay waters speckled with ice while, in the near-distance, the massive icefjord rises like a white cliff that makes me shiver even in the warmth of the car's backseat. The landscape is brown, green, and icy blue, with vibrant squares of color from the houses dotted throughout.

I watch the surreal country pass by my window as we make our way from stop to stop, until we reach a yellow-sided house resting at the base of a peaked hill.

Daniel is not in the house when I step through its front door, but someone else I recognize is.

"Hi Isabis," I say, standing in the entryway like an awkward stranger.

I've been in this building a few times since the beginning of summer. In fact, I was here only an hour ago for my Hostage Arts course. But walking straight through the door and up to the classroom on the second storey is different than entering when no one but the Entity campers should be inside.

Isabis doesn't seem bothered by my presence, although the girl beside her is annoyed I've interrupted the cooking competition they're watching.

"Hi, Cal." Isabis smiles. "Want some vetkoek? It's

got apricot jam."

"It's so good," the other girl says. Her glower disappears as she holds up a golden puff of bread dusted with sugar and oozing warm jam.

I take too long staring at the creation. My back-to-back courses—combined with Dylan's attack as soon as I returned to our house—means I haven't had dinner. Isabis must see the hunger in my eyes. She wraps a puff in a napkin and holds it out to me.

"Take it. I made too much," she says.

She's obviously lying. She's got an entire sector housing with her. I'm sure at least a few of them would be delighted to help her finish these off. Still, I'm not going to refuse now that she's wrapped it up.

"Thanks." I step into the room and take the dessert. The dough's warmth has already spread through the napkin, and I want to tear the paper off so I can eat the whole puff and then maybe push my luck for a second helping. But I don't know Isabis that well, and I'm not even sure what the other girl's name is. Besides, I'm here on a mission. If I return home without locating Daniel, Dylan will have me up at four in the morning so the two of us can resume the search.

Isabis's gaze is curious, but it's the other girl who speaks first—saving me the trouble of excusing myself for barging into their home.

"Are you looking for someone, or..." She pushes her shoulder-length hair behind her ears. The purple ends of the otherwise dark strands remind me of Mim.

"Yeah, uh, is Daniel here? I need to ask him something," I say.

The question earns me a peculiar look from the girl with the purple hair. Her skin is darker, her frame fuller, and her height taller than Mim's. But her forward nature and the territorial gleam in her eyes makes me wonder if this is Entity's version of the girl Shade is missing this year.

"He's not in," Isabis says with a shake of her head. She stands, grabs her crutches, and makes her way to a pad of paper and pen resting on a sideboard table at the back of the room. Her hand shakes as she writes, but the numbers are drawn in a deliberate, careful hand. "I'll give you the house number. He'll be here tomorrow."

She hands me the paper, and I take the number—along with my dessert—with a nod of thanks.

I call the next morning at eleven.

"He wants to channel a dog?" Daniel laughs when I explain the situation.

"Well, a dead dog. At least, I think that's what he means," I say.

Dylan stands at the kitchen counter beside me, glaring at my less-than-convincing spiel.

I shrug in apology and twist away from his stare. "Anyway, he needs to speak with this Sender from Argentina. Would you be able to sit in on the conversation, help translate? It would mean a lot. And, if you don't, I'm pretty sure Dylan's going to make me learn Spanish in your place."

"Sure, I'll help," my old mentor says with another laugh. "Let me talk to him, and we can work out the details."

Dylan grabs the outstretched phone and babbles like a kid talking to his hero. Five minutes after their conversation begins, he ends the call and dials the number for the shuttle service so he can go meet with Ms. Tahan.

The remaining arrangements come together swiftly. When Dylan returns to the house around five, he happily informs us his interview is set for tonight. I'm pleased by his newfound dedication, even if Kornelía's convinced it'll be short-lived.

"As soon as he realizes how much work goes into something like channeling, he'll want to call it quits," she says with a fond sigh as we watch him hunt for a notebook so he can do research at the library.

She follows Dylan into the living room while I venture as far as the doorway before coming to an uneasy halt. After four tedious hours spent learning the myths surrounding telepathy during Meditative Communication this afternoon, watching Meander load into a separate car so he wouldn't have to share the ride back to our house was irritating. Seeing him in the living room now is vexatious—particularly when I notice the cup of tea that's acting as his only form of dinnertime sustenance.

Meander's never been a huge eater, but lately he's been skipping a lot of meals. My temper flares knowing he ignored the stew waiting on our stovetop when we returned from our lessons. I want to berate him into eating some actual food. But I doubt he'd even listen to my rant.

Kornelía surveys the room and sidles back next to me. "Want to come to the library with us?" she asks in a soft voice.

"Yeah, I'll come," I say, appreciating her inclusion. "Just give me a sec."

I return to the kitchen, grabbing a loaf of bread and some sliced ham from the fridge. I compile a sandwich, cheese and mustard the fanciest toppings our meager supply of food allows. I grab my backpack from the bedroom. Then I take the sandwich and drop it silently beside Meander on my way out the door.

Once we reach the library, Kornelía's quiet skepticism gives way to support as she aids Dylan's efforts to discover if there have ever been recorded cases of non-human channeling. I trail behind them for a few minutes. But they don't need my assistance. Besides, Dylan's keen attitude is wearing off. As my friends continue working on their project, I decide to once more focus on the death of Albert Timmons.

My efforts don't prove productive. Still, the library offers a good distraction from the monotony of the house. Two hours in, Kornelía joins me seated in the stacks, flipping through an account of Greenland's role in World War II.

"How's your project coming along?" she asks. She slides down next to me and pushes her glasses onto her head.

"Terrible," I mumble. I turn to the book's index without hope I'll see any subject headings worth investigating. "I haven't found anything. Nothing about his death or ties with shady figures. I'm trying to determine if he did anything extra-horrific during the war, but I don't think that's really where we should be focusing."

"Has Sefa found anything?" she asks.

I give up and drop the book onto my lap. Kornelía picks it up, though she doesn't open it.

"No, his research has been as useless as mine," I say. "He thought Albert's business had something to do with his wife. But she died five years ago and, as far as Sefa can tell, they had a simple, happy marriage."

Sefa convinced the Oracle to let him return to Kangerlussuaq last week to talk to some locals. He didn't ask me to come with him, but I can't complain since I wouldn't have gone anyway. He may be sure I'm wrong about Albert's death being suspicious, but I'm positive he's heading down a false trail trying to follow up with the dead man's family.

Albert told us to go away. He wouldn't talk about his reason for staying around, and what little he did say amounted to a declaration that he wanted to forget. I lean against the bookshelves, replaying his sparse conversation and remembering the other thing he said—the last thing I heard before his voice disappeared.

Marmalade.

"Why do spirits like to give us such obscure clues?" I ask.

Kornelía smiles. "They don't always... In our first year, one of my instructors told us about a spirit she encountered—his unfinished business was that he liked talking so much, he felt a single lifetime wasn't enough to get his fill."

"Okay, maybe a one word response isn't the *worst* thing," I amend with a laugh.

"I take it that's what this spirit gave you?" she asks.

"Yep." I raise my hand to hover over my head, checking to ensure the strands of hair I swept to one side are still in place. "He did talk. A bit. I think Sefa got more from him than I did. Which isn't a surprise, since he spent longer in the house. But neither of us got any useful information. Except maybe *marmalade*. Which doesn't seem useful, either. Only I know from experience not to write off anything a spirit utters as fodder."

"Hey guys, I found something!" Dylan's head appears around the corner of the stack. Hair hangs over one of his eyes, while the other is wide with excitement. The gray pallor of his skin is still alarming, even four weeks into camp. But his eye, yellowed as it is, is bright with a determined gleam that makes him look immensely alive.

"You found someone who's channeled a dog?" Kornelía asks, her voice high with hope I know she doesn't feel.

"No," Dylan says. "But I found a woman who claims she once channeled a parakeet."

I try hard to hold in my laughter, but it still escapes as a hard breath through my nose. "You're kidding," I say while Kornelía nudges my side.

"No, I'm serious!" Dylan exclaims. He looks offended for half a second, but his excitement returns as he faces Kornelía. "This is close. Different species, but still not human. That's something, right?"

"Of course it is." Kornelía beams. She scrambles up from her spot, giving me a stern look before following Dylan to his table.

18

DYLAN SPENDS THE REST OF FRIDAY NIGHT AND THE FIRST SEVERAL HOURS of Saturday morning— reviewing his interview notes. After a brief bout of sleep, he disappears for a long run with the puppy. When he gets back, he corners Naasir for a lengthy chat about the similarities between insects and dogs.

"Is he losing it?" Sefa asks over the kitchen table at lunch.

"He's just… invested," I offer.

Sefa stares at me, unconvinced. "He definitely seems like he's losing it," he declares. He serves himself another bowl of soup from the giant stock pot a staff member delivered to the house an hour ago. I rip a chunk from the bread loaf in the middle of the table and scrape it along my bowl to gather remnant bits of tomato.

"Give him a break," Reed says from beside me. "He wants to know what it's like. You guys don't understand. You've both released ghosts before."

"I haven't," Sefa says.

Reed's mouth hangs open, his slack-jawed expression a good match for my surprise.

"You've never released a spirit?" I ask.

Sefa scoffs, sitting with a heavy thud. "No," he says, tearing off a quarter of the bread loaf. "Not one I could see, at any rate. Sabeena took charge of our group project in France. And last year, the project I led was unsuccessful. I've never witnessed a ghost cross."

I swallow my last bite of bread and push away the empty bowl. "Wow. I figured you'd dealt with some spirits on your own. You know, outside of camp."

Sefa shakes his head. "Despite what you all seem to think, I don't delight in seeing ghosts," he says with a mild sneer. "It's an important job, and I'm grateful to have it. But when I'm not with the Oracle, I don't seek them out. Maybe when we've finished our training, I will. For now, however, I'd like to keep my encounters contained."

No wonder Sefa wants to be successful with Albert. I've been a part of three spirit releases—and one failed exorcism—without really trying. I never saw the spirit of Anjelo Savou in Tonga. But I saw all the others, and now I've seen Albert too. I've encroached on what was supposed to be Sefa's mission of glory. And by insisting he's wrong about the old man's death, maybe he thinks I'm flaunting my experience in his face.

"Well, then you should understand how Dylan feels," Reed says. "He wants to know what it's like to be a proper Sender. We all do."

Reed might be right, but that doesn't stop us from debating our friend's sanity. As Saturday rolls into

Sunday, Dylan continues flitting between activities, running too much and sleeping too little as he prepares for something he won't explain.

"You'll know soon," he says when we prod him for answers. He ruffles his hair as he downs an energy drink, his tattered, neon green sleeveless tee reeking of sweat, dirt, and bug spray. "We'll be ready soon."

He disappears from the house again that evening, leaving even Kornelía fretting about where he's gone. At midnight, he bursts into our room and shakes me from sleep.

"Come on, Cal," he says.

I push him off with a groan and sit up, disoriented after only half an hour of slumber.

"Come on where?" I ask with a yawn.

He doesn't answer. Instead, he tosses my running shoes onto the sheets and motions for me to follow him.

I fumble into my sneakers then, with a second thought, kick them off long enough to switch from pajamas to jeans. When I get to the living room, Dylan's wrangled Kornelía and Naasir, insisting they come along as well.

"I'm going, too," Sefa says with a laugh. "I want to know what the hell you've been up to."

"Whatever," Dylan says, bouncing on his heels. "You can all come, if you want. But we need to get moving, so hurry it up."

Sefa gets his shoes while Kornelía and I put on our coats. With only a moment of hesitation, Reed and Sabeena decide to join the crew as well. Dylan's not happy it takes us a full ten minutes to get sorted. But once we're outside, he leads the way into the rocky hills.

"Where are we going, Dylan?" Kornelía says, her

voice full of worry. He walks at a quick speed, but her strides are long enough to keep pace.

"To see some dogs," Dylan says. He points upwards and glances at us with a smile. "They'll be nice and active tonight."

I follow the line of his finger. The sky doesn't reflect the late hour, the midnight sun keeping our surroundings bright with daylight. Still, even with the light, it's easy to make out the round, full moon hanging above us.

We walk up the rocky slopes and down into gentle valleys. No trees block our view, which at least makes getting lost in the wilds of Greenland a hard feat to accomplish.

"I don't like this," Naasir says after a few minutes. "We shouldn't be looking for dogs during the full moon."

"Calm down, Candyman," Dylan replies. "We won't be finding any werewolves tonight."

I smirk, peering around the group, surveying my fellow Shades. But it's not long before my thoughts turn to the sector member still back at the house. If he *is* at the house. Meander wasn't sleeping when Dylan woke me, and I didn't catch sight of him in the kitchen or living room as we prepared to leave. The car service from house to house ends at midnight, and sector leads always check to ensure everyone's back before official lights out. But Alex and Robbie were missing when Dylan took us on this adventure, too—I wonder if they were elsewhere in the house, or if they were trying to track Meander down.

I wish he was here. Even if he only skulked in the back, not saying a word to anyone, he should be part of this. My fingers clutch the phone in my pocket, itching to text him. But even if I believed he'd respond, there's no signal out here to send a message.

We head down an uneven path, and our house disappears from view. I give my phone a final squeeze before pulling my hand from my pocket so I have both arms ready should I fall on my way down the slope.

"Okay, Dylan, what are we doing out here?" Kornelía tries again.

The way she speaks sends a chill of recognition through me. This is, in most ways, a completely different experience than last summer's trip to a Tongan cave. But Kornelía's question has highlighted the key similarity—Dylan has brought us along on his ridiculous mission without any of us knowing what the hell we're in store for.

"I figured it out," Dylan says. He pauses to look around before heading to the right. We follow a rough path of mossy green that winds around the base of a rock—one that peaks in the formation of a perfect, miniature mountain. "For weeks, I've let that puppy follow me on my runs. But I never knew how to *listen* to him. Until now."

"What's he on about?" Reed asks, trailing at the back of the group.

Sabeena hushes him. "Let him talk, and you'll find out," she scolds.

Reed opens his mouth to say something else, and Sabeena claps a hand over his lips to shut him up. At least with Naasir nearby, a bit of repellant spray is enough protection to make the ghastly head nets unnecessary. I still have a few souvenirs from the swarm in our room six days ago. I don't need any additional reminders marking my skin.

"I found the dog, and I let him lead me," Dylan says. He looks back at us, his grin wide. "It took a while, but I figured out how to do it."

"Do what?" Reed asks as soon as Sabeena drops her hand.

"*Listen*," Dylan replies. He stops and points to the wide hill that stretches about thirty feet high. At the top, the puppy sits as if awaiting his arrival.

"Dylan," Kornelía whispers, the worry gone from her voice. "I'm so proud of you."

He looks at her and, for a moment, they share matching expressions, their eyes and smiles wide with excitement.

"I haven't done anything yet," he says when he glances at the rest of us. "That's what we're here for now. I'm going to see if I can make this work."

The puppy watches our ascent as Dylan leads us on. The way up the hill is steep. Without any path to guide us, the hike feels like it's halfway rock climbing. I slip twice on loose stones, and—our leader excluded—everyone else struggles too.

When we reach the top, Dylan pets the dog, crouching next to it as he stares at the valley below us. A small inlet of water pools at the bottom of the hill's far side, and Dylan nuzzles his face in the dog's neck before the two start towards it.

"How much further are we going?" Kornelía asks as we begin the careful trek down.

Dylan doesn't respond, but the way his manner shifts with every step is answer enough. His breath becomes labored, first sounding like he's winded from the hike, then deepening into heavy, rhythmic huffs through his nose. When Kornelía asks if he needs a break, he looks at her with eyes ringed in pure black, the dark circles full like bruises.

His eyes are yellow, a disturbing shade on a human but—I realize with a grotesque sort of amusement—normal for a canine. We may not see any werewolves tonight, but this feels eerily close. Dylan's not turning into a dog. But his manner and appearance have altered, and he now seems vaguely inhuman. The epiphany is simultaneously unsettling and reassuring. I'm not sure why being close to spirits would have this kind of effect on him. But at least this confirms Dylan isn't wasting away from some undetectable disease.

"We're almost there," he says, his eyes shining with a vibrancy the rest of his body does not share.

He loses his footing and slides the last several feet down the hill. With a quiet growl, he brushes dirt from his palms before pushing himself into a half-run, half-stagger to the water's edge.

We follow, helping each other so we don't end up falling as well. When we're on more or less flat ground, we jog to the water, hanging back as Dylan sits cross-legged next to the puppy at the pool's edge. From behind, it's like a photographer's dream—a hiker and his dog enjoying the radiance of the midnight sun in the lonely foothills of the Greenland wilds.

After he settles, Dylan turns his head slowly from side to side, his hand gliding through the air. I half-expect him to start talking—or barking—but he doesn't say anything. He sits with the living dog and what I assume is at least two dead ones. He seems to switch his attention between them, his movements careful and calm, probably to keep the pain in his head as low as possible.

Kornelía remains standing but, after ten or so minutes, the rest of us sit. Watching Dylan's slow movements in this quiet landscape is actually quite peaceful. I draw my legs up and rest my chin on my knees. Before long, my eyes start to drift closed, though the chill of the air keeps me from being comfortable enough to fall asleep.

When the dog yips, my eyes fly open in time to see Dylan pet its head. He struggles to his feet, his gaze casting about until his eyes find us.

"Bones," he says, his voice cracking with the strain of speech. "The litter was killed a couple months ago. Some of the bones were eaten, but others are scattered in this valley. We need to gather them."

"*We?*" Sefa asks as his thick arms cross over his chest. "You want us to go hunting for dog bones?"

"You came, you help," Naasir says.

Sabeena stands, looping her hands around Sefa's arm to haul him up. "Naasir's right," she says as Sefa reluctantly gets to his feet. "Come on. It's only one dog, and you don't have to get close. Besides, the sooner we find the bones, the sooner we can go back inside where it's warm."

"Do you think they're spread far?" I ask, stretching my arms over my head to stave off my drowsiness. "We might not get them all tonight."

"How many dogs are we talking about?" Kornelía adds. She walks to Dylan, wrapping her arms around his shoulders and giving him a moment to slump against her side.

"There were six puppies," Dylan murmurs. "Only one survived. The mother and three of the pups are gone. But two of them are still here. We're looking for *their* bones."

"Anyone good at canine anatomy?" Sabeena asks. "How many bones do they have?"

"Three hundred and nineteen, on average," Dylan says. "Per dog."

"You're joking." Reed balks.

Dylan steps away from Kornelía, his eyes shifting to the water. "A lot of them ended up there," he says, pointing to the shoreline. "We don't need those. Like I said, some were eaten. But a few are still around. If we look, we'll find them. Let's start over there."

He signals for us to head west. With only a few uncertain glances passed behind his back, we set off on Dylan's midnight scavenger hunt.

I'm not sure how we're supposed to find random bones amongst the hills and mossy grass, but Dylan seems to have the situation under control. He directs us to various places, unrelated spots that nevertheless yield results. I can't fathom what the purpose of this venture is, since the dogs won't have complete skeletons regardless of how thoroughly we search. But then again, I have no idea why these spirits have stuck around. Dylan's the only one with even half an inkling of what is going on, and he seems to believe this is the task that needs to be done.

Reed finds the first bone, which Dylan claims is part of a tail. The piece is small and, with a sad pang, I realize I was expecting to see a full-sized skeleton instead of tiny fragments from a newborn puppy. But Dylan is pleased, and his happiness rubs off on the rest of us as we continue our search. For the next hour, we wander the not-night, picking through the grass and moving small stones until we locate the bones.

Sefa tries kicking a bit of a leg towards the water, but Dylan yells at him, insisting we treat the bones with reverence and carry them ourselves. I'm not keen to pick up the first bone I see bare-handed but, when I spot what I think is half of a ribcage, I don't want to chance Dylan's wrath. Pulling my jacket over my hands, I balance the bones on my covered palms, holding them out before me like I'm carrying something perched on a tray.

"Think you're going to get rabies?" Dylan asks with a laugh. He walks beside me, a nearly whole skull grasped lightly in one hand.

"No," I grumble, my nose scrunching with uncertainty. "But how should I know what kinds of diseases *could* exist in a half-rotted bone?"

"You'll be fine," he assures me.

"I'm taking extra precautions anyway," I say.

We lower the bones into a heap by the water. After an hour, we've collected a sizeable pile.

Dylan appraises the bones with a nod. "I think that's good enough."

"Please tell me we don't have to, like, arrange them into dog-shapes," Reed says.

"No," Dylan says, eyeing him with annoyance. "We'll put them in the water. Less likely they'll be dug up there."

He spares a moment to pat the live puppy trailing our movements. Then we take careful measures to lift, carry, and lower the bones into the water. The whole scene feels like a children's game that's far more important to the participants than to any outsider watching from afar. I'm sure we look ridiculous, all of us placing the bones in the shallow pool, as silent as if we're giving a loved one a nautical send-off.

But our actions have an effect. A shift in the air— like the wind changing direction or a shadow falling across the low sun—makes a shiver rifle through the group. We huddle into our jackets, Reed the only one unaffected by the cool breeze. Even Kornelía, who has never minded the crispness of a spirit close at hand, hunches her shoulders as Dylan clutches his temples with a gasp.

"What's wrong?" She reaches for his arm, but he shakes her off.

Staring at the puppy, Dylan tilts his head to one side and his eyes shift to the empty space beside the dog. He grabs his stomach, doubling-over with a groan of pain.

The puppy yowls and bounds off. Dylan rakes in breath, panting as he watches the dog run away. Then he nods, sparing us a quick smile before he starts after it.

"Dylan, where are you going?" Kornelía calls.

He once more fails to answer, leaving us behind as he follows the mostly-dead pack.

"What are we supposed to do now?" Sefa asks.

I survey the group. "Anyone know how to get back to camp?"

One by one, my sector mates shake their heads.

"Well, then, we'd better go after him," Naasir says.

"Oh, great," Reed mutters. He cups his hands around his mouth and calls into the distance, "Dylan, wait up!"

Dylan doesn't stop, and we can't afford to waste any more time. With a final grumble of self-pity, we start to sprint, trying to catch up with the dogs and their boy.

My sneakers pound across the rough terrain, and my calf muscles strain to keep me from sinking in the moss or slipping off the rocks. I'm glad I've kept up my fitness routine for the last year but, even so, my lungs burn as I speed across the hills and work to keep Dylan in sight.

Kornelía runs ahead of me, her lithe frame gliding across the landscape like a blowing leaf while Naasir runs heavy and solid a beat behind her. The other three are farther back, though their thudding footsteps stay close.

"Dylan, wait!" Kornelía yells.

Ahead of us, Dylan finally halts at the top of a nearby hill. He bends over, his hands on his knees like he's trying to catch his breath or keep from vomiting—from this distance, it's hard to tell which. He calls out, but his voice is muffled, and I can't decipher what he says. He waves for us to hurry, then he disappears beyond the peak of the hill.

We push ourselves, ascending as quickly as we can manage.

"How is he so fast?" Sabeena moans when we're halfway up the hill. "I can't even walk when I'm around a ghost. How can he run like that?"

"Stop wasting breath questioning it," Sefa scolds. He propels her forward with a push.

When I crest the hill, I see another valley below us. I don't know what direction changes we've made, but somehow we've approached the coast again. Our house is nowhere in sight, which makes me uneasy. But a different house sits back from the rocky shore, a fence cordoning off a large portion of its land.

At least a dozen dogs run out of a barn, all of them

bolting to the fence with wagging tails. Dylan stops at the base of the hill, fifty feet away from the property. I make my way to him as the puppy bounds to the fence and wriggles its way underneath.

The dogs greet their missing pack member, and Dylan laughs. "He's not a stray," he says, surprised. "He has a family now. He needed to let his litter mates know."

Dylan slumps to the ground, sitting hard as he grips his head. A whipping wind has blown from the shore. I shiver, the air frigid and biting against the exposed bits of my skin.

When Dylan glances up again, squinting like he's staring at a bright light, I smile. But then the rush of wind kicks up so hard, I'm knocked off balance. Stumbling forward, I fall to my knees, glad we've stopped in a grassy patch. Another gust of wind wipes over us, and I push against it—nevertheless failing to keep upright. I flatten onto my stomach, drowsiness sweeping over me. My eyes flutter closed, a familiar sensation of light rushing in, and I steel myself against the draining sweep as I prepare to lose consciousness.

When the drain lifts and the lightness passes, I blink a few times and look around. The others are on the ground, too, and further away, the dogs have become subdued. I turn to Dylan, who nods.

"They're gone," he says with a relieved sigh.

I've never been around dogs crossing over before, at least not that I've been aware of. But my guess is the small size of the puppies—combined with the mass of living bodies nearby—means the energy was shared between enough sources we didn't pass out. I'm tired, but I was tired before this venture began. Mostly, I'm happy we didn't end up blacking out here in the cold.

"You did it." Kornelía smiles. She crawls over to Dylan and kisses the top of his head.

"I did, didn't I?" he says. He looks up at her, the yellow of his eyes duller now, the gray hue of his skin a little less intense. "What do you know... I'm a Sender, after all!"

Across the way, the puppy has struggled to its feet. It raises its head and lets a long, low howl escape. The other dogs join in, and an eerie wail echoes towards the full moon.

Dylan laughs, collapsing onto his side before rolling onto his back. He runs his fingers through his wavy hair, tilts his chin up to the sky, and lets out a reedy howl of his own.

WE WALK BACK TO THE HOUSE OVER THE COURSE OF AN HOUR, A BRUTAL
trek full of cool weather and no energy to spare. By
the time I drag my tired feet into the bedroom, I don't
even bother taking off my coat. I flop onto the bed,
glancing up only long enough to see Meander is still
absent before weariness drags me into troubled sleep.

My worry and total exhaustion make me a prime
target for haunting dreams and, at some point during
what remains of the night, black visions of howling
spirits grip me. The nightmare rages for longer than
the others I've suffered so far this summer. Normally,
we're quick to shake each other awake. Tonight, my
roommates must be too tired to notice my distress.

When I do bolt upright—gasping as the dream finally
cuts to an end—I'm face-to-face with Meander. He sits
on the edge of my bed and, even in the darkness, it's
easy to make out the strain in his eyes. I'm not sure
what the time is, but I'd wager it's nearly four or five

in the morning. When he asks me if I'm okay, his voice the low murmur I remember from the few middle of the night chats we used to share over video, my eyes drift to the thick sweater he's still wearing from yesterday. Either he just returned from his own late adventure, or he camped in the classroom and heard my cries from down the hall.

I want to question him, or at least tell him to get some sleep. But after a quiet moment in which I rest my head on his shoulder and mumble apologies for bothering him, I can no longer keep my eyes open. He peels away and, with a heavy sigh, I lie back down.

When I wake again late in the morning, Meander is once more absent. But our other roommates are awake. Sefa and Reed are questioning Dylan about what happened with the dogs.

"Man, but how did you know about the bones?" Sefa presses from the bunk above me.

"I can't explain it," Dylan says, lying with his hands folded behind his head. He glances over as I flex my feet and pull myself up with a stiff groan. "It wasn't like I could hear their thoughts or anything. But when I sat with the spirits, I sort of... knew. I got this weird idea in my head that I had to find the bones."

His explanation shares similarities with Kornelía's description of her ability to read minds. The coincidence is interesting, though I don't make mention of it as I slip out of bed. While the others talk, I throw off the coat I'm still wearing from last night before walking to the door's mirror. Pushing my fingers through my hair, I make an attempt at neatness, studying my reflection until I'm satisfied the strands are not a total mess. Then I shuffle out of the room.

The tile is cool on my bare feet as I step into the kitchen. Stifling a yawn, I fill the kettle and grab two mugs, dropping a tea bag into each. While I wait for the water to boil, I check the living room for signs of life. Alex lounges on one of the sofas, the space's only occupant. I give her a wave before returning to the quiet of the kitchen.

When the tea is steeped and flavored with milk and sugar, I leave one cup on the counter and take the other to the classroom. Leaning against the door frame, I close my eyes against the dull throb in my temples and knock on the closed door.

"Yeah?" an uninterested voice says from inside.

I sigh, push open the door, and step into the room. Meander glances up at me, and I give him a small salute with the mug.

"Brought you this," I say, placing the cup on the nearest table. "For waking me earlier."

His pale, gaunt cheeks show a hint of pink as he eyes the mug. "Thanks," he mumbles. He's seated far back, books and notebooks laid neatly across his desk.

I'm used to him reading at all hours of the day, but I've never seen him with so many study materials before. I'd ask what he's doing, if I thought he'd tell me the truth. Not knowing sucks. But I'd rather be clueless than have him spout another lie.

I force my eyes away from the table and turn to leave. Halfway to the door, I pause, unable to resist a final glance at him.

"Hey, have you been sleeping much?" I ask. Mysterious all-night study sessions are one thing. But Meander's still wearing the same sweater as earlier, and I'm starting to seriously worry about the habits he's formed since arriving in Greenland.

He runs his teeth his over his bottom lip, his eyes fixed downwards. "Enough," he says, each syllable unconvincing. So much for not being lied to again.

"Well..." I pause, struggling to keep my voice steady. "Just, uh, try to get some rest soon."

He doesn't respond and, with nothing else to add, I leave the room and shut the door behind me. I wish it wasn't Monday. No one has course time today, which means no one will force Meander out of hiding. Maybe if he hasn't left by this afternoon, I'll pretend I'm eager to play my violin. I hate having to contemplate such ridiculous schemes. But as frustrating as he is, I don't want Meander to suffer a breakdown because he hasn't slept in a week.

I walk back through the kitchen and grab the tea I made for myself before returning to the living room. Sabeena, Kornelía, and Dylan have joined Alex on the sofas, so I sit on the floor by the fireplace. The stone is as cool against my back as the tiles were on my feet. Sabeena flips through a magazine while Kornelía talks to Alex about something she learned in one of her courses. Dylan lounges on the sofa, his eyes closed and a content smile on his face.

When Robbie enters the room a few minutes later, he shares a look with Alex before she nods.

"Okay, so are you going to tell us where you all went last night?" she asks, cutting off Kornelía mid-sentence.

Sabeena peers over the top of her magazine, her eyes wide. "You knew we were gone?"

"We'd be pretty awful leads if we didn't notice that *none* of our campers were in their rooms in the middle of the night." Robbie grins.

Kornelía's head tilts to the side, and she gives me a questioning look. I nod in the direction of the classroom, and she frowns.

"I released two spirits," Dylan says, his hand sliding against Kornelía's thigh. Her attention shifts, and she pats his knee with a smile.

"He did," she confirms. "Two puppies. It was incredible."

"Good work," Robbie says as he steps behind one sofa. "But did it ever occur to you that you guys can tell us when you're setting out?"

"Why, so you can force us to stay inside?" Sefa asks as he walks into the room.

"We wouldn't do that," Alex protests.

Sefa looks annoyed. "It's hard to believe you."

"I didn't know it would happen," Dylan interjects. "I wasn't planning for a release."

Robbie sighs, twisting his neck from side to side until the joints crack. For a brief moment, he looks tough, the flat line of his unsmiling mouth menacing. But then he shrugs and nods.

"We get that," he says, leaning forward so his elbows rest on the back of the sofa. "Don't forget, we were Shades before you started camp."

"And did you tell your leads whenever you ventured out?" I ask.

Alex looks like she wants to tell us they did, but Robbie doesn't give her the chance.

"Absolutely not," he says with a short snort of laughter.

"No," Alex agrees, her voice a touch more serious, "but that doesn't mean we want you to ignore us.

We're here to help. And to keep you safe."

"We're not kids," Sefa insists.

Robbie lays his arms flat on the back of the sofa. "No, but you are sixteen," he says. "And that's a helluva time for Senders. Plus, little as we talk about it, one of our own has already been pretty damn hurt because she didn't tell us what was going on."

Dylan's hand falls from Kornelía's leg. Her frown returns, and her tawny eyes fix on her jeans.

I sip my tea, my eyes sliding to the closed classroom door. Telling our leads everything that happens to us feels like stepping back and becoming newbies all over again. But Robbie has a point. If they'd known of Mim's exorcism, she wouldn't have gone through with it. Two years ago, if I'd had enough sense to let Robbie or Alex know about the spirit that had me under its guiding influence, I could have avoided getting hit in the head with a rock while in France.

If those injuries hadn't happened, Meander wouldn't be hiding, desperate to keep out of everyone's way.

But being a Sender is complicated. And I can't help wondering if telling our leads everything we do would have changed our paths in less favorable ways. Two summers ago, Meander ventured off during a class trip. If he hadn't gone—if I hadn't followed—if anyone had informed our leads what we were doing, Meander and I never would have walked through a cemetery or seen the spirit in his aunt's apartment. If I hadn't realized there was more to him than his brooding silence suggested, our friendship would never have grown. And if it hadn't, there's a decent chance Meander wouldn't have returned to camp after his first year.

If we'd been good students, we could have avoided getting hurt. But maybe hurt is an inescapable part of the equation.

Without pain, perhaps our stories are incomplete.

MEANDER DOESN'T HEED MY ADVICE TO GET MORE SLEEP. WHEN THE CAR arrives to take him to Meditative Communication on Friday, he's too tired to resist me tagging along. The short ride is enough to make him doze and, when we stop, he's so dazed he exits the vehicle before realizing we've arrived at the wrong place.

"Where the hell are we?" He stares at the harbor, his features clouding with annoyed incomprehension.

"The driver must have gotten the location wrong." I shrug.

We should be at the Wraith house for Meditative Communication, but instead we've come to the shore. A large ferry boat and several smaller fishing vessels bob alongside a long loading dock while a few small houses sit farther back from the water. I'm frustrated I paid so little attention to our direction. The constant back and forth in cars this summer means I'm used to zoning out, listening to music and letting the scenery blur past my window until we stop.

Meander talks to the driver. The middle-aged man insists we're at the correct address. He points to the ferry boat then shifts the car into drive.

"A bloody boat trip?" Meander mutters, eyeing the ship with trepidation. I'm not sure if he's having flashbacks to last summer's final boat ride, or if he's only nervous at the prospect of doing something out of the ordinary. Either way, I can tell he regrets the small sliver of sleep he got in the backseat.

"Maybe we're going to try yoga at sea," I suggest in a casual voice. "Which, come to think of it, might be horrendous. I can't imagine my attempts at a Crow Pose would be very nice to watch. Hell, a handstand would probably send me overboard."

Meander tries to keep his face serious, but a smile twitches at his lips. "The fact you know what a Crow Pose is makes me wonder if you're taking this course too seriously," he says with a soft, teasing breath of laughter.

Ignoring the hopeful patter of my heart that he *made a joke*, I shake my head in exaggerated dismay.

"Hey, I've told you my parents do yoga. *Together*," I say in a horrified voice. "Mom's okay at it, but Dad is awful. Rose and I are taking bets on which appendage he'll strain first."

"Oh yeah," Meander says with a genuine smirk. "You said they were trying to get you to join them. You sure they didn't succeed?"

"*Please.*" I smile. "If I could do yoga, I'd be all for it. But we both know I'm not coordinated enough for that."

"True," he agrees. "But you're wrong about one

thing. I think I'd have a wonderful time watching you attempt a Crow Pose."

I don't think he meant the remark to be suggestive but, the second he says it, his cheeks brighten in time with the heat that flushes my skin. His eyes rest on mine for several long beats then, with an embarrassed turn, he hunches forward and heads to the water.

The white and red ferry is massive. Even from a distance, it's easy to see that people are already on board. I trail behind Meander as we approach our instructor, who waits on the crowded dock with the other campers who have arrived. Ms. Lind offers no explanation for why we're here. When we reach her, she hands us tickets and tells us to wait, shooing us off to stand with the others so she can keep a lookout for the students yet to come.

Meander's expression is dark when he takes the proffered ticket, his step hesitant as he follows her instructions and stands to one side. I can't believe he doesn't ditch class altogether. I recognize the cagey glint in his eye—I've experienced it myself every time I've gone somewhere new over the last several months.

When the rest of the class arrives—the total count being seven campers—Ms. Lind ushers us to the ferry. But even once we're on board, she withholds lengthy discussion until the boat has drifted out to sea.

"Thus far in the course," she says when the ferry has left the dock and reached its full speed, "we've learned how to focus our energies and open our minds to spiritual communication." Her deep voice is quiet amongst the rush of wind, water, and mechanical noises of the boat. I inch closer to hear her better. "Which is all fine and well for non-Senders," she continues, her eyes shining with amusement I'm not sure the rest of us share. "But for those who see ghosts on a regular basis, spirit-focused meditation may seem a bit, well... pointless."

I blink, surprised she so accurately captured my sentiments about the first five weeks of this course. The class has admittedly been a calming experience, often straddling the line between relaxation and boredom. Some of the techniques Ms. Lind has shared will come in handy if I'm stressed out and unable to play my violin. But so far, we've yet to learn anything directly related to ghosts. Our lessons are focused on the *possibility* of spirit communication—we haven't been taught any specifics for when communication is already a sure thing.

"Today, we're going to explore a new perspective," Ms. Lind continues. "And for our purposes, this is the best—well, the *only*—mode of transportation." She beams at the open water before returning her focus to us. "I'm sure you are all eager to know what we'll be doing. But since the ferry is loud and we are far from being alone, we'll wait until we disembark before diving into the details of today's lesson."

The ferry trip is about an hour long and, as far as course time is concerned, it's a nice way to let the minutes pass. Ms. Lind escorts the campers who don't have their sea legs into the boat's interior to minimize the unsteady sway. The remaining five of us spread out along the upper deck.

I stand next to Meander, who doesn't talk but doesn't try to escape my company either. He folds his arms atop the railing, his eyes fixed over the water.

His jeans and navy wool turtleneck, combined with the way his curls blow in the wind, make him look older than sixteen. My stomach tightens with the realization, a taunt that perhaps I've missed more than a few months with him.

With an inward sigh, I pry my eyes from the high collar of his sweater and gaze instead at the giant chunks of ice floating by the boat. From the land, the ice looks like small flakes of snow drifting in the sea. Now that we're on the water, the ferry boat is tiny next to some of the massive glacier hunks, the crystalline blue of the frozen rocks glinting like blocks of uncut jewels.

Rose bemoaned the camp destination this year far more than I did. When she found out I wouldn't once again be on a tropical island, she pitied me. I never thought Greenland would be a bad choice though. My sister wishes summer could last year-round, but I've always enjoyed milder temperatures. Besides, I didn't want the weather reminding me of last year's location. My memories of Tonga are abundant enough.

When the ferry docks at a small settlement off the coast, Ms. Lind gathers us together to head inland. There, a local woman guides into a town spread out in a similar fashion to Ilulissat. Colored houses dot the uneven landscape, the properties separated by sloping rock and rough roads. Our instructor didn't hint at this excursion, so it's lucky no one was foolish enough to wear sandals thinking they'd be spending their afternoon indoors. Only one Entity brought his mosquito net, however. The rest of us swat at bugs on our way, thankful the swarms are not as severe today as they've been on other occasions this summer.

We approach one of the bigger houses. Its siding is

painted a deep, farm barn red. The guide beckons us through the front door, and we file in one by one until we're all huddled within the cramped foyer. Ms. Lind shuts the front door, and the guide uses a brass key to unlock an inner room behind where we stand.

She opens the door to what I assume was once a sitting room. Now, a large, circular table is situated in the middle of a wide oak floor. Nine chairs stand around the table's edge, and three unlit candles decorate its middle. The room is void of any other furnishings.

"What's going on?" someone asks as our small group ambles inside.

I step into the room second-to-last, leaving only Meander in the foyer. He halts in the doorframe, his eyes clouding with doubt as he takes in the table.

"Today, we're going to do a live demonstration of meditative communication," Ms. Lind says with an excited smile, oblivious to her student's unease. "We're joined here by Sardlik, a local resident and expert at performing séances."

"We're doing a séance?" one of the girls asks, her voice as enthusiastic as our instructor's.

Ms. Lind nods. "If you'll all take a seat around the table, we will show you how the power of your mind can be utilized to talk to the deceased."

Meander doesn't move. His feet stay planted in the doorway while he offers Ms. Lind a firm shake of his head.

"I-I can't," he stammers. He glances at me, and I falter, unsure how to respond. A year ago, I would have grabbed his arm and pulled him into the room with me. But I know what happened in April, and I'm still living with the consequences of what occurred the last time I convinced him to participate in someone else's spiritual endeavors.

A hand rests on my shoulder, and I look over to see Ms. Lind standing beside me. Her gaze is focused on Meander, and she wears an expression of surprise—like she's only just realized that he's one of the Shade kids she's been warned about.

"You don't need to worry, Mr. Rhoades," she says. "The spirit we will be attempting to contact today is not an angry one."

"That you know of," he says, his stare hard.

He's ready to bolt, on the verge of turning tail and leaving the house altogether. But our instructor doesn't accept his brooding look or his anxious stance. Her own stare turns stern, and she lets go of my shoulder in favor of stepping over to him.

"Both Sardlik and myself have communicated with this spirit," she insists. "This woman does not hold any anger. I promise you that."

She sweeps an arm, directing him to the table. The other campers are watching, and Meander's cheeks burn under their stares. He doesn't believe her, and I can see the uncertainty in his hazel eyes as he considers everything—and everyone—in the room. He's weighing his options, and I'm not sure what choice he's going to make until he steps across the threshold with a resigned, shaking breath.

Ms. Lind moves to the far side of the room while Meander and I sit next to each other at the crowded table. His knee bounces against my leg, and I resist the urge to stifle the movement with my hand. I don't like seeing him so nervous. Yet even in this uncomfortable place, I can't deny a weird sense of relief keeping my mood light. So many of our sector mates are, in some way, happy to see spirits. I'd almost forgotten what it was like to be with someone who shares my own fears about what each ghostly encounter will bring.

Sardlik pulls a curtain over the room's only window. I can't see her through the blackness but, without stumbling or even making a sound, she resumes her place at the table and strikes a long match so that light flickers before her face.

"Senders often wonder how a séance could be useful," Ms. Lind says as Sardlik lights the three candles. "Because many fail to realize that the situations of the dead are diverse. The divide between life and death is often compared to that of a veil, and many people believe that ghosts are dead beings hovering on the wrong side of the fabric. Which is true, much of the time. Yet a more accurate description of the divide would be not a veil—but a corridor."

"Death is a corridor?" the only Entity boy says. "Very poetic."

One of the girls chuckles, but Ms. Lind is not impressed.

"The world of the living is one room," she continues after giving them a sharp look. "The realm of the dead is another. And those two planes are connected by a corridor. We all travel the corridor when we die. The dead world's door only opens one way. Once you are through, you cannot come back. Life, however, has a swinging door. Often, the dead we see don't know how to enter the corridor and are stuck in the room of life. But a select few start their journey without completing it. They stay *in* the corridor, occasionally swinging back into the living world."

A girl I think is named Océane raises her hand. "My grand-maman believes in what she calls visiting spirits," she says. "Is this what she's talking about?"

"Could be," Ms. Lind replies with a nod. "Some spirits do travel back and forth, though not because they are visiting. It is because they are lost, unaware they are dead and confused by how to move on. Or, in the case of today's spirit, their unfinished business keeps them in the corridor, as if the doorway to death's room is locked—and the resolution of their business the only key."

She eyes Sardlik, and the other woman nods. "Spirits that are lost between our world and the next—those stuck in the corridor between rooms— can be called forth through séances," Sardlik says in a voice heavy with the Greenlandic accent. "By focusing our energies, we can reach through the door and draw them back into our world."

Sardlik takes charge of explaining how the séance will work. Some of the pieces—like her explanation of how the candles' flames and drip patterns can tell us the spirit's attitude—seem like wasted moments of showmanship. I don't think this woman is connected to the Oracle. She's obviously conducted séances before, but I suspect this is her first time doing so with a whole group of Senders-in-training.

While part of her spiel seems pointless, however, other aspects have a semblance of sense. We're told to be quiet and not to speak over one another in order to give the spirit the best chance of communicating with us. We're also told to hold hands, making a circle to join our energies. I'm not totally sure energy can be shared between living bodies through the simple act of touching skin. But the idea that we're stronger together is sound.

I imagine Meander will hesitate to join hands with me but, when we're instructed to take hold, his grasp is quick and firm. He's uneasy, and we're in a group setting. So, with the room dark and everyone else's attention focused on what Sardlik is saying, I stroke his hand with my thumb, hoping the warmth of my touch will offer at least a hint of comfort.

"Today, we call upon the spirit of Jytte Feldt," Sardlik says in a low, musical voice.

"Focus your energies," Ms. Lind tells us once Sardlik has finished speaking. "Close your eyes, and think about the corridor. Help us open the door."

I don't close my eyes so much as roll them before fixing my sight to the table in compromise. A half-glance to my left shows me that Meander has his eyes open too. He stares at the space above the lit candles, his back straight and his expression tense.

The two of us aren't doing our part to help the spirit appear, but the attention of the others is enough to have the desired effect. A chill sweeps over the room, and the candles begin to flicker. Meander squeezes my hand, and I hold it tight. One of the candles blows out, and two of the campers gasp. A low groan issues from Ms. Lind's throat, and Sardlik opens her eyes, staring around the room with a delighted smile.

"She's here," she says as if she knows for sure and is not only going off the expressions of the people in the room who must be able to see her.

Meander glances around the table. Three of the campers still have their eyes closed, but the two who gasped have given up the pretence of keeping their energy focused. They, along with Ms. Lind, watch the middle of the table.

"Good afternoon, Jytte," our instructor says in a husky voice.

I don't see the spirit, and Meander must not either. With a deep breath, the grip on my hand loosens, and he relaxes so much he doesn't even pull away when I lace my fingers with his.

21

"WE'D LIKE TO ASK YOU A FEW QUESTIONS," MS. LIND ANNOUNCES.

One of the Entity campers makes a muffled sound of pain, and the two remaining candles flicker. Ms. Lind looks around the group, asking if anyone would like to pose a question first. One of the kids who can see the spirit is quick to offer.

"Do you… know you're dead?" she asks.

The question is awkward but, when the girl looks to Ms. Lind, our instructor nods. Silence follows, in which the spirit may or may not answer. I have no idea what communication is happening, and I'm content to keep it that way.

The other kids have stirred from their concentrated stupors and are now glancing around the table. After a moment of quiet has passed, one of them clears her throat.

"Ms. Lind?" she starts, the question uncertain. "I don't understand. I can't see anything. Isn't the point of a séance that we *all* connect with the ghost?"

Ms. Lind shakes her head. "Only certain Senders are capable of interacting with a spirit during a séance," she explains. "Just as with any other spiritual encounter."

"So, what's the point of having all of us here?" the other boy in the course asks. He drops his hands, and everyone else follows suit.

I let go of Sardlik's palm, and Meander releases the girl to his left. When he tugs against my hand, I think he's preparing to let go of me too. But he keeps a firm grip as he brings our hands under the table, and I bite the inside of my cheek, my heart thudding fast as our still-laced fingers settle on his thigh.

"The point is that no one saw this spirit when we entered the room," Ms. Lind says. "She was not visible to any of us until we joined our hands and focused our energy to call to her. She's drawing strength from us now, and she'll continue to use what energy she can until our connection is loosed and she returns to the other side of the door.

"Can I ask a question next?" the other girl who stares at the middle of the table says. Ms. Lind nods, and the girl smiles at the empty air. "Are you waiting for someone?" she asks. A wince of pain crosses her face, and she shakes her head. "No, not waiting. Do you miss someone?"

Meander's hand clenches mine. For a moment, I stupidly think the motion is a reaction to girl's reference to missing someone. But then he whimpers, and my chest tightens as I turn to him. He takes a labored breath, his eyes finding mine in the darkness. I grab hold of his arm with my free hand as panic spreads across his face.

"Do you—" I begin before another candle blows out and Meander's gaze slides to the space above the table. He moans, coughs, then swallows hard.

"What's going on?" Sardlik says, like she has no idea why everyone keeps groaning and flinching in pain.

Meander tries to stand, dropping my hand as he gets to his feet. He grabs at the neck of his sweater, stumbling back with a wheeze of breath.

I round on our instructor. "You said she wasn't angry!" I seethe, upturning my seat as I stand. The wooden chair clatters to the ground as I hurry to Meander's side.

"She's not," Ms. Lind says, her voice strained.

"Like hell she isn't," I mutter. I grab Meander's forearm but, when he winces under my touch, I remember the old wound that must now be flaring with pain. Cursing myself, I slide my grip to his elbow as he gasps, the breath weak and shallow.

"She's not angry," one of the girls says from behind me. "She's only sad. She misses someone, and… She's sad about it."

Meander staggers back until he hits the wall, his hands rising to his face. He slides to the ground and presses his palms over his eyes. The sleeve of his sweater pulls back a little with the movement, and I'm stunned. Even in the low light of a single candle, I see the grey-black bruise spreading along the underside of his right arm. My eyes flick to his neck, and my stomach churns as I notice a darker, purpled bruise peeking from above his high collar.

"We need to get you out of here," I whisper, my voice breaking with worry.

I grip his arm tight and try to pull him up. But he's not paying attention to what's around him. Eyes still covered, his head jerks slightly from side to side. When his hands suddenly drop and his eyes fly open, the whites are bloodshot. The scar on the left side of his jaw has deepened in color too, the white-pink line now looking fresher, like the blood's rushing up under the skin.

"We need to stop this," Ms. Lind says. She no longer sounds confused by what's happening. Now, she stands, her manner commanding. "Sardlik, end the séance."

"Y-Yes, of course," Sardlik mutters. "Go back to the other side, Jytte. I will extinguish the final candle. Someone needs to turn on the light."

"I'll do it," Ms. Lind says. She crosses the room and finds the switch.

The room brightens, but Meander doesn't slump with relief. He gasps like he's having trouble breathing, his eyes wide and fixed on the space above the table.

"It didn't work," Sardlik says, her voice puzzled. This one is definitely not a Sender. She doesn't understand that Meander's offering enough power to make up for the loss of focus from everyone else.

He mutters something I can't hear, and I lean in close.

"What?"

He grabs at his neck, a harsh cough spluttering from his throat. I hold his side, and nod when Ms. Lind comes to help me pull him up.

"Mary Thorne," Meander gasps.

The name makes no sense to me and, when I glance at Ms. Lind, her face is blank. But then Meander retches, and I forget about the random declaration.

"Let's get him out of here!" I half-yell.

Ms. Lind doesn't stop to scold me. She helps me lift and drag him from the room, through the foyer and out into the bright, gray day. Outside, Meander catches his footing, stumbling and collapsing on a patch of grass. His whole body trembles as he draws his knees up, folding himself into a ball.

I don't realize I'm also shaking until I bring a hand up to my neck as I glare at Ms. Lind. She doesn't meet my gaze. Instead, she studies Meander, her expression curious.

"Mary Thorne," she says at length. "Who is that?"

"Who the hell cares?" I start, ready to accuse her of being a horrible instructor who doesn't give a damn about her students' safety. But Meander raises his head to reply.

"It's a character. In a book," he says with a sniff. "The spirit... She misses someone. Mary Thorne— she was..." He stares at nothing, his expression hard as he works through his thoughts. "She was born illegitimately and was raised by a relative. Maybe the spirit never knew her mother? Or her baby."

"Her baby?" Ms. Lind repeats. "I'll have to tell Sardlik. She didn't mention—"

Meander cuts her off. "Could be no one knew she ever had a child," he suggests in a voice rough and scratched. "That'd certainly give her a regret to cling to."

"How the hell did you make that connection?" I ask, bewildered by everything that's happened in the past five minutes.

Meander eyes me for a second before he folds into himself again without responding.

"Thank you," Ms. Lind says to him. She sighs, glancing over the sea. "There's a ferry leaving in fifteen minutes. You can return early if you wish. Callum, go with him. Make sure he gets safely back to camp."

22

MEANDER DOESN'T SAY ANYTHING AS MS. LIND ESCORTS US TO THE FERRY, nor does he talk during the hour long boat ride back to camp. He sits on a bench, shaking for a good twenty minutes before calming enough to be still. I'm burning with questions. But the ferry is busy, and, even once we're in Ilulissat, we're stuck in a car with a stranger in close proximity for the duration of the trip.

When we reach our house, however, the place is quiet. I'm not sure if others are nearby, but no one is in the living room or the kitchen when we arrive. Meander goes straight to the bedroom, and I follow him, standing in the doorway as he moves with mechanical purpose to his dresser drawer. He fumbles, pushing items around until he finds the container of salve he let me borrow for my mosquito bites.

Sitting on my bunk, he unscrews the lid with clumsy fingers. I step into the room and close the door behind me, crossing the space and taking hold of the container.

He grips it tight, trying to keep it from me, but I tug it away with a stern look.

"Let me help," I say, my words sharp.

A long pause stretches between us before Meander finally nods. His fingers reach to the bottom of his sweater to peel it off. Then he stills, his expression uncertain as he moves instead to pull down the sweater's high neck. After all this time, he still doesn't know I'm aware of the scars on his chest. The reminder of our distance is painful. But when he pushes back the navy fabric to reveal the wide, pink lines circling his neck, my remorse dissolves into a different kind of ache.

My fingers threaten to shake as I scoop salve and press it gently to Meander's skin. With forced steadiness, I rub the thick lotion into his newest scars.

This is the first time I've seen Meander's neck wounds up close. But it's not the first time I've seen them. Three weeks into April, I broke from my usual repertoire of writing about the mundane events of my week to wish Meander a happy birthday—and to check he was okay after turning the big sixteen. It was one of the few messages he responded to over the ten months we were at home, a simple message to assure me he was fine. But about a week later, he called to ask if we could talk over video, the way we used to chat every day.

I knew something was wrong when I saw his number on my phone. But I was unprepared when his image appeared on my computer screen. His eyes were red, and his neck was covered in bruises and burns—the skin all shades of purple, green, and black.

For three hours, the silence between us was forgotten. Meander didn't pretend I no longer existed, and I didn't try to convince him he still needed me in his life. For a while, I said nothing, listening quietly as he detailed what happened. He told me how he'd come across a spirit, one who was strong enough to accost him with a bit of nearby rope—garroting him until he managed to scramble far enough out of its reach to keep from being choked unconscious.

Meander made it through the first portion of his tale with flat resolve. But his jaded expression cracked with a quiet sob when he related what occurred afterwards.

When a stranger found Meander staggering on the street, they called an ambulance and had him taken to the hospital. Given his track record of incidents and injuries, no one listened to his half-hearted attempt to make up a plausible excuse. His mother didn't help matters either. She told the doctors he was troublesome and better off restrained. What Meander said didn't matter. In the end, he was forced to stay in the hospital undergoing psych evaluations until the doctor finally sent him on his way—with a referral for a therapist he could never afford, even if he did believe it would be of any help.

I listened while he spoke, cried, and ranted about what everyone believed. Then I did my damnedest to comfort him with all the agreements and arguments I could make in his favor. He smiled at my rant on his behalf, and laughed when I told him I'd happily fly to England to tell off everyone in person. Slowly, his fury diminished. When only exhaustion remained, his guard came down and we spent an hour and a half talking about nothing of importance—until he could barely keep his eyes open, and I knew I needed to let him get some rest.

Meander's been careful not to let anyone see the scars on his neck this summer. He's kept himself covered day and night since we arrived, and this is the first moment I've even glimpsed the startling wounds that—at the very least—look so much better now than they did a few months ago. But today feels a little like that night in April. It's as if the solitude that's gripped us both all summer means nothing in this moment of closeness.

I work the lotion in small circles, relieved when the tension in Meander's shoulders loosens. My fingers glide across the damaged skin, soothing what I hope is only phantom pain left over from today's episode. For a few minutes, the room is quiet as I focus on my task. When Meander leans back, the movement automatic as he relaxes into my touch, I sigh.

"Why do I have the feeling I'm missing a few crucial bits of information?" I murmur.

"Hmm?" Meander stirs like I've brought him out of faraway thoughts—or from a tranquil place with no thoughts at all. He shifts, his muscles stiffening once more when he realizes what I've said. "What do you mean?" he asks, like he doesn't already know.

"Where do I start?" I say with a laugh that's part amusement, part scoff. "When that spirit appeared, she was choking you, wasn't she?"

"No," he says. "Not exactly. It was the wound. It—I don't know. It felt like the rope was back... like it was happening all over again."

"That started last year, didn't it?" I ask. My memory floats to the night we spent in the cave when Mim's exorcism caused Meander to grip his arm in pain.

He nods. "Yeah, but only at the end of the summer.

Now, it happens each time."

"Is it every wound?" I'm unable to keep the questions from pouring forth. This is the first time he's given me any kind of response. I'm not going to spare him my prodding now. "And does it hurt anywhere else? Are there new wounds when it happens? Or, like, if you cut yourself in a totally non-ghost related shaving mishap, does that hurt too?"

He tilts his head to the side so he can see me as he smirks. "I'm not sure," he admits, his smile fading. "I've only seen two spirits since..." He motions to his neck, and I resume massaging it. "The woman today, and one at the beginning of June. Even before April, I only saw a couple. I think it's just the old wounds that hurt, and it seems like the fresher ones hurt more. Or maybe that's wrong. Could just be the ones I've gotten since my ability's developed a bit. Might be it depends on the spirit. But no, non-ghost related shaving mishaps aren't triggered."

"Did you know the scars get dark?" I ask.

His brow furrows. "Get dark?" He lifts the sleeve of his right arm and studies the now-faded scar from the glass shard that stabbed him a year and a half ago. "I thought they just hurt. I didn't know they looked any different."

I nod. "It was dim, and you've got most of them covered," I say, my hands sliding deeper underneath his sweater to rub his shoulder. "But it looked like they were changing. Even your jaw."

"I had no idea," he mumbles. His voice is full of quiet mortification.

"You *did* know about the spirit, though," I segue. "When I saw a ghost a few weeks ago, I could barely move, let alone think coherently. You had trouble breathing, but you still managed to pinpoint what the spirit needed. How did you do that?"

"I'm not sure," he says again. He lets out a heavy breath and shifts so he can lean into my touch while still keeping me in view. "The process is hard to remember afterwards. It's like… pages. Like my brain is a giant index flipping through thousands of pages until something sticks out."

"The character?" I ask, thinking of the random name that fell so confidently from his spluttering lips.

"Not the character so much as the story," he clarifies. "Something I've read before. I knew it applied to her, in some way."

"Wow." I catch his eyes, and my own muscles tighten as he holds my gaze. "So, are you some kind of genius?" I ask. "All this time, and you never even told me?"

He laughs, the sound a soft and joyful music to my ears.

"No," he says, his eyes still on mine. "I don't think it's my intellect at work. It's something… deeper. More primal."

His words taper off, and we fall once more into silence. Heat flushes my neck as he continues to stare at me but, unlike earlier at the ferry dock, this time Meander doesn't hunch away from my gaze. For a few seconds, the world freezes. Then the sun shining through the bedroom window glints off the jade in Meander's irises as his body shifts closer to mine.

One of my hands is still on his shoulder, and I allow my fingers to creep up his neck. As my thumb strokes the skin beneath his ear, I revel in the soft hitch of his breath. Meander's hand slides onto my knee, his touch hot even through the thick fabric of my jeans.

"Cal?" The word is gentle, a whisper that is half-question, half-plea.

My free hand itches to grab his waist and pull him to me. But I don't want to risk any sudden movements, so I settle for inching my face nearer to his. Meander swallows, his head crossing a fraction of the distance between us. I press my fingers more firmly into his neck, a soft pressure I hope will spur his speed. For an instant, it works, and his lips draw steadily closer to mine.

When a wince of pain sweeps across his face, his expression falling as he blinks out of his daze, the hurt is echoed in my chest. He stares at where his hand still rests on my knee. With another sharp breath, he pulls it back to his side as he stands.

"I'm sorry," he mutters. "I should go. I've still got work to do."

I study the empty space on my mattress, my emotions twisting into slithering snakes of frustration, anger, and despair. Processing everything is impossible in such a short span of time. So I cling to the last thing he's said, and push myself up amidst a flurry of heated speech.

"First of all, you are *not* doing any more damned work," I start, the words harsh and loud. "After what you've been through today, you're going to bed—and if I catch you out of bed for anything other than food, I'll find whatever you're working on and tear it to shreds."

Meander glances back at me, his expression caught between surprise and amusement. But when he sees my furious glare, his features fall into an apologetic frown.

"Fine, I—" he begins, but I don't let him mutter his way through another solemn farewell.

"And second of all, did you ever stop to think that if you weren't being so idiotically stubborn, this afternoon's debacle could have been avoided?"

"I… What?" Meander stares at me, confounded by an outburst I didn't intend to make.

"Ms. Lind told us that spirit wasn't angry," I say, the words shooting from my mouth like daggers. "The ghost missed someone. You said it could have even been her baby. Why would she be mad about that? The other camper said she was sad, and that makes sense. *And* you didn't see her until someone asked the question that uncovered her sadness."

"S-so?" He looks lost. Under other circumstances his perplexed expression would make me break into a pathetic grin. But right now I'm too riled up to think about smiling.

"So clearly, you didn't draw the anger out of that spirit. You drew out her sadness," I say. The idea only occurred to me on the ferry ride back here. But saying it out loud makes it feel like this is a certainty I've always known.

"And if that's true?" Meander asks, attempting anger but failing to achieve more than annoyed incomprehension. "I'm still trying to figure out all this shit, Cal. I don't know what the hell is going on."

"Yes, but I might have!" I throw my arms in the air, barely managing to hold back the stomp of a full temper tantrum. "Don't you see that? I've already figured it out. I know it's a shock for me to be quick on the draw, but it's happened. Because Naasir is working alongside mosquitos, Dylan's reading the minds of dogs, and Kornelía is seeing dead people almost like they're still alive. Our abilities are not getting stronger, Meander… They're *changing*. And if I'd known the details of the other spirits you've encountered, maybe I could have helped you figure out that you're not just seeing angry ghosts anymore. Maybe we could have understood that before you were attacked in the middle of a damned séance!"

He studies me, his eyes widening before his brow furrows, like he's wondering if I'm right or if I'm just spouting nonsense. I expect his muddled thoughts to pool into a shouting retort. But after a tense moment, he only gives me a hard stare.

"Have you solved your project's case?" he asks.

My head spins, the words cycling through my mind twice before I'm assured of them. My momentary triumph sinks back into the bog of cluelessness, and my anger fizzles as I give him my own questioning look.

"N-not that it matters, but… no," I stammer, unable to keep my voice strong. The reality is I haven't found anything to help with Albert's unfinished business. But a lack of information about my own case doesn't dampen the fact I've put together a small piece of his.

Meander's face softens, his eyes apologetic as he takes a single step towards me. "Have you researched the music?"

"What music?" I ask, before I understand what he's referring to. "The music I heard in that house?" He nods, and I shake my head. "No. That's not… That's unrelated."

He looks guilty again, the same expression he wore

when we talked after I first saw the spirit of Albert Timmons.

"I should have told you earlier. I'm sorry," he says before turning away.

I watch him cross the remainder of the room, my whirlwind of thoughts now mixing with remnant chords from the big band's song. Meander reaches the door and turns the handle. When the door creaks open, I make sense of my confusion long enough to blurt out one final question.

"Should have told me what?"

He doesn't look back at me, but his shoulders slump, and his neck bends with fatigue.

"Start with the music," he says.

His shoulders straighten, but his head stays low as he walks out of the room.

THE MUSIC.

In all the time I've spent researching the death of Albert Timmons, not once have I considered that the music I heard might have something to do with his reason for being a ghost.

Meander disappears into the bathroom, taking a short shower before he returns to bed. Sneaking into our room half an hour after it goes quiet, I expect to find him reading and am pleased to discover he's fallen asleep. For a moment, I stand like a creep at the foot of the bunk, watching the soft rise and fall of his blankets. The rhythm is soothing, though the secrecy of how I'm viewing it makes me sink into self-pity over what almost happened before our fight.

Fight. The word itself should make me more morose, but instead it brings a small smile to my lips. What we just did could hardly be construed as a fight. And it resulted in a new direction for my project. Maybe I should be bitter that Meander didn't point me to the music sooner. But my obliviousness is not his fault, and the fact that we shared a moment this afternoon is enough to keep me going for now.

With a gentle sigh, I leave Meander to sleep. Once I've closed the bedroom door behind me, I walk to the kitchen to call for a car.

The library is busy when I arrive. Sabeena is working at one of the tables, and several Wraiths are clustered together at the computer stations. I take my laptop and veer to the back of the room, finding a small corner next to the empty librarian's desk. Slumping down, I connect to the internet and start reading up on the history of swing music.

I spend a lot of my time listening to—and playing—music. But as well-versed as I am in classical compositions, other musical genres are foreign territory. I don't know anything about big band sounds, except that sometimes they're featured in movies and people seem to like them for grand functions like weddings. Which means I haven't a clue where I should be hunting for a possible connection between the spirit and the song I heard in his house.

History seems like a decent place to begin. So I start by researching how—and where—swing music came into existence. My search leads me back to the early twentieth century in the States, which corresponds to when and where Albert Timmons was born. But a better connection, the one that makes me nod in excitement, is the link between big bands and wartime tunes.

I smile when a nagging thought makes me look up popular wartime era swing songs. Plugging my headphones into the computer, I cycle through music videos. A couple of songs make my ears prickle with familiarity, but only from soundtracks they've been included in. Most of the tunes are strange, and while the music's not to my taste, I do my best to listen through them—trying to pull out the melody that raged war on my earbuds a few weeks ago.

When the autoplay cycles to the eleventh video, my heart thuds as the first notes begin. An ache starts in the middle of my head like a bolt twisting into my brain. I reach up to my earbuds, ready to pull them away. But then I remember that I'm not in the spirit's presence. This time, I have full volume control of the sound now streaming quietly through my head.

The song is the one I heard in the house, and I stop reading about swing instrumentation to focus on the tune. The beat is there, the rattling cymbal followed by the brass introduction that leads into the quick-fingered clarinet feature.

"This is it!"

I raise my eyes as I declare my success out loud, only to be greeted by a row of books. I was so wrapped up in my studies, I called out to someone who isn't even in the building, and I'm thankful that at least no one is near to witness my embarrassment. Pretending nothing is amiss, I close my mouth and dig in my backpack, ignoring the humiliating heat of my neck as I search for a notebook and pen.

Despite my intentions to be a dedicated student this summer, my course notes are scarce. As it is, I only have to flip to the second page in my Meditative Communication notebook in order to find blank space for jotting down the song's title.

I click away from the article on instrumentation

and turn back to the music videos. Then I stare at the screen, reading the song's title and feeling like I've unlocked a new level of gameplay—all while thinking I need to go back to year one of Camp Wanagi so I can learn to stop being such an ignorant fool.

Clarinet Marmalade.

"Damn it," I mutter, my voice stuck between a groan and a laugh.

I listen to the song three times. The melody is irritating as it rattles through my head. Each quick beat reminds me of being in Albert's house, the smell of alcohol and the stabbing pain of his unexpected presence senses I can almost feel even now. But I force the music to continue, listening hard as if the clues might be in the chaotic dance of the clarinet or the jazzy notes blazing fast through the trumpet horns.

After the song plays for the third time, I close the page and shut my laptop. For a moment, I sit with my earbuds still in place, my outstretched foot bouncing in time with the rhythm no longer flowing. Then I stow my materials and head for the library tables.

Sabeena jumps when I speak.

"Hey." I step back as her head flies up. She takes a startled breath and glowers at me in annoyance.

"You scared me," she says, dropping her pencil on what appears to be a journal full of small, cramped Devanāgarī script.

"Sorry," I offer. "I was just wondering if you know where Sefa might be."

Sabeena looks like she's going to say she can't help. But then something sparks in her eye, and she nods. "He and Reed were going scouting," she says.

I quirk a brow. "Scouting for what?"

"A ghost, I think," she says with a shrug. "Meander put Reed in charge of their project, but Reed doesn't have a clue what he's doing."

"I thought he'd picked a spirit. *The Siren* or something."

Sabeena's giggle is soft and childish. "Yes, something ridiculous like that," she agrees. "He wanted to go check out the area. They should be back by dinnertime, though. If you can wait, I'll be finished in the next half hour. We can return to the house together."

"Sure, thanks," I say with a nod.

Using the library's landline, I call ahead for a pickup before leaving the building to walk down the nearby streets. Ilulissat is small and lacking in variety compared to somewhere like home. But only a few minutes of wandering leads me to a small café similar to the one where Kornelía and I ate last week.

I head inside, happy to discover a few freshly baked cakes and cookies on display. Two people are in line ahead of me, allowing me time to survey the goods before I order. A slice of chocolate cake first catches my eye. But when my turn arrives and I shuffle to the counter, I notice a swirl of pastry drizzled with orange marmalade. I order the pastry, my foot tapping, my ears ringing, and my smile bigger than it's been since sometime last summer.

When we get back to the house, I slip into our bedroom. Meander is still asleep, so I place the small pastry box in the top corner of his bed, the note I wrote on the car ride over a little crooked but nevertheless legible.

You're too stubborn for your own good. But you were right about the music.

I take a deep breath, wishing I didn't have to sneak him things in secret. Then I head back to the living room to wait for Sefa's return.

SEFA SITS ON ONE OF THE LIVING ROOM SOFAS, HIS ELBOWS ON HIS KNEES and his hands clasped together in thought.

"Marmalade. That's what he said? All this time I thought he'd been talking about mermaids."

"*The* Mermaid? Like... The Siren?" Reed asks from beside him. "Maybe they're related."

Sefa rolls his eyes. "I said I *thought* he said something about mermaids," he reiterates, giving Reed an irritated glance. "I heard him wrong."

"How did your scouting mission go?" I ask Reed. He doesn't seem interested in leaving Sefa and me to talk on our own. He's wound tight with pointless excitement, like a kid hopped up on hot dogs and cotton candy after a day at the carnival.

"Great!" he exclaims. Sefa gives him a sidelong stare, and Reed shrugs. "Well, good. I found the area, and I think I felt something."

"Yeah, the wind from the sea," Sefa laughs.

"No, it was her," Reed says, unperturbed by his friend's lack of conviction. "And I know I could see her better if I had a boat."

"You are never going to get permission to take a boat out in those waters," Sefa scoffs. "Now, will you shut up? We're trying to discuss something important here."

Reed grumbles about his topic being important as he gets up and heads to the kitchen. When he's out of sight, Sefa sinks back into his contemplative pose.

"Okay, so marmalade. It's a song... The song you heard when you were in the house," he says, recapping the information I relayed when he and Reed returned from their outing. "And now you think that's got something to do with his unfinished business?"

"It has to," I say. "Why else would that particular song play? He gave the clue to me, not to you. You said yourself you couldn't even understand him when he said it. He knew I was hearing the song. It's connected. I just don't know how."

"You don't still think he was killed, do you?" Sefa asks, his voice wary. "I'm not looking into this if you're just using it as some weird excuse to research more murder cases."

I bristle, biting back a curse as he once again blows off the fact that my ability is as valid and accurate as his. Trying to unravel the cause of Albert's death has led to nothing. Right now, focusing on his connection to the music seems the better path.

"Let's just worry about the song," I say. "Big bands were an American thing, and they were popular during the war. That's what I keep coming back to."

"I don't think Albert's death has anything to do with his time in the military," Sefa says, a statement that rings true for me as well. "Besides, he was here during the war."

"Yeah, you're right," I sigh. "Maybe there was a travelling band? Kangerlussuaq was a military base, after all."

Sefa considers the possibility. "Do you think they'd send a whole band all the way up here?"

I lean back against the sofa, my foot still tapping the rhythm my head can no longer keep a hold of. "Probably not," I admit.

"Maybe it has something to do with his wife," Sefa offers. "She could have brought a favorite record with her or something."

"With her?" I ask, sitting up straight again. "She wasn't from here?"

"No, she was American, too," Sefa says.

I stare at the low flicker of the fire as I ruminate on this newest piece of information. I don't think the song was something played on a phonograph. The sound was too lively in my head. Like the recording I listened to on my computer, the song I heard in Albert's home came from the burned memory of a live performance.

"When did they marry?" I ask.

Sefa looks confused by the question. "Nineteen fifty-two," he says, his voice curious.

"*Where* were they married?" I ask next, and this time he catches the direction of my thoughts.

"I don't know," he says, already rising from his seat. "But I have a copy of their marriage certificate. Hold on, I'll get it."

He starts for the bedroom, and I halt him just before he throws open the door.

"Be quiet, Meander's sleeping," I call.

Sefa looks like he's about to ask why someone is asleep half an hour before we're supposed to eat dinner. But then he must remember that nothing at this camp runs on a tight, cohesive schedule. He nods, entering the room with quiet footsteps and reappearing less than a minute later holding the folder of information.

He sifts through the papers, pulling out random sheets of notes, family statements, and photocopied documents. Aside from Albert's marriage certificate, the other pages seem irrelevant to our current search. But I stay silent as Sefa hunts. When he's about halfway through the stack, he plucks out the paper we need.

"It looks like they were married in New York," Sefa says. "That's where he was born, too. I'm not sure about his wife, but there's a decent chance she was from the same area."

"They were married late, given the time," I say, studying the certificate. "He was in his thirties, and long since back from the war." I raise my eyes to meet Sefa's. "But he did come *back* from the war. He didn't stay in Greenland the whole time. He must have returned to the States at some point, and then moved here later."

"You're right," Sefa agrees. "Does that help us at all?"

"I think it makes things more complicated," I say with a laugh.

Sefa laces his fingers and puts them behind his head. "Okay, so what do we think? Albert was born in New York, and was stationed in Greenland during the war."

"Then he returned to New York and married his wife in fifty-two," I add. "The music is American. And I'm sure he heard it live. Since it's unlikely a big band was playing here during the war, I think Albert's unfinished business is related to something that happened back at home."

"We're screwed, aren't we?" Sefa groans. "How are we supposed to figure out what his business is if it's got nothing to do with this place?"

"We're not done searching yet," I remind him. "But we are working with a wide range. We need to find out when he left New York, when he returned, and when he moved to Greenland for good. And we need to figure out where and when he may have heard that damned song."

We eat dinner with Reed and Sabeena before calling another car to bring us back to the library. The constant trips and the fact our own house lacks an internet connection makes being efficient an aggravating impossibility this summer. I never thought I'd miss the ramshackle French château where we stayed our first year of camp. But having everyone—and every resource—in one building has definite benefits.

My motivation is high when we bunker down in the library, prepared to spend several hours untangling the threads of Albert's story. But the spark of determination snuffs out like the candles during this afternoon's séance when I realize that "Clarinet Marmalade" has been a popular jazz tune for pretty much a century—played by musicians in countless venues around the world.

I sit back and stare at my computer screen in dismay. "Couldn't be some obscure symphony by a recluse composer who only played one live show his entire life."

"Yeah, cause that's everyone's idea of a fun night on the town," Sefa scoffs.

"I'd think it was fun," I mumble.

"Of course you would," he says with a shake of his head.

Paying no heed to Sefa's ignorance on what it means to have a refined taste in music, I focus on the more important matters at stake. The fact that this particular song could have been played at any point from Albert's birth to his death is overwhelming. I wish he had heard the song here in Greenland—it would make things a lot easier if I could pinpoint a single performance with only a few searches. But I have a feeling New York is going to be our target state, which means our range has hardly narrowed at all.

"Here's something interesting," Sefa says after an hour.

I glance at his computer screen, which is logged into a genealogy site. I don't recognize the name of the woman whose profile is up. Sefa points to a chart showing a marriage date of nineteen thirty-eight.

"This is Albert's wife," he says. "It looks like he was her second husband. She married young… eighteen. And her first husband—" He clicks the link of the first husband's name, then nods with a solemn face. "He died during the war. That explains why her second marriage was at a later age. I wonder…"

He stares at the screen, then turns his eyes to me.

"What?" I ask, unsettled by his intense expression. An idea is forming in his head, but I haven't a clue what it could be.

"Maybe Albert had a first wife, too?" he suggests, before frowning. "No. I would have found that out already."

"What if it wasn't a wife, but a fiancée or a girlfriend

or something," I offer. I'm not sure this has any bearing on our case, but if Sefa's got an inkling, I'm not going to shove it aside—not when our current search seems so hopeless. "That kind of relationship wouldn't be marked in official records."

"That's true," Sefa says. He pushes his computer aside and grabs the folder of papers again. After flipping through the pages he pulled at random earlier this evening, he takes one out and smiles. "His sister. She talked to me about his marriage. She might know of a relationship he had before that."

"Can you chat with her again?" I ask.

He nods. "I think so. I'll ask Robbie if I can call her tomorrow."

"Do you think this has anything to do with the song?"

"No idea," he says. He rereads the testament Albert's sister gave him regarding her brother's life. "But it's a start. At least a temporary one. And who knows? Maybe by tomorrow we'll have all the answers we need."

WE DON'T HAVE ANSWERS BY SATURDAY. IN FACT, SEFA'S NOT ABLE
to speak with Albert's sister again until Thursday
evening while I'm in Hostage Arts.

Robbie said I could skip the course if I wanted to
take part in the interview. But Sefa's better equipped
to talk to the woman than I am. Besides, Hostage Arts
is my favorite course this year. While my other three
selections were made in the moment, or by someone
else's command, this is the course I was determined to
enroll in. Hostage Arts is one of the few Wanagi classes
that feels directly related to my abilities as a Sender.
Last year, I was too afraid to take it. Now, I understand
that the more information I have regarding my talent,
the better prepared I'll be for facing spirits in the future.

After last summer, my paranoia about being guided
by a spirit's will diminished. All told, I've been guided
twice in my life—but I've seen far more than two
ghosts. I get now that not every spirit is going to draw

me under its influence. But that doesn't mean I want to forget what happened a couple summers ago. As easy as Meander finds it to blame himself each time something goes wrong, I claim fault in the problems we've had had at Camp Wanagi too. He thinks he caused me a concussion when we were fourteen because he gave a ghost enough strength to hurl a rock. But he absorbed the ghost's energy—an amazing feat that could have proven deadly—all because he was trying to help me out of my trance-induced trouble.

And last year, well… If I had stayed back with Dylan, Mim's exorcism may have been successful. Meander was a necessary part of the process, but I had no role to play other than being an emotionally charged target for a jealous spirit's eternal vendetta.

I'm as troublesome as anyone else when it comes to certain spirits, and I want to minimize the risks of my talent. If any course will help me accomplish that, it's this one.

Our instructor, Professor Bhoula, is a spindly man of about fifty. A good portion of his scalp is bald, but there is a mass of frizzy hair on the back of his head. He is stern, and his tough teaching method means his course is not a popular one. In fact, there are only five of us—me, Reed, Isabis, and two other Entity campers. This year, I don't have any courses with Wraith or Revenant sector kids. If it weren't for the few glimpses I've caught of them in the library or at the houses, I'd think only two sectors even made it to Greenland for the summer.

Now, Professor Bhoula has split us into two teams to develop plans for how to escape a spiritual entrapment. We do these exercises every week, always in a different rotation of groups and with a different hostage scenario. I don't mind the mini-tasks, although I'd love to have one of my friends with me so we could brainstorm ridiculous methods for getting out of a ghost's clutches.

Unfortunately, I'm stuck with Reed as a partner today, while the three Entities work in the other group. Our scenario is that we're paralyzed with cold by a spirit encountered outdoors in a cool climate. I like the scenario, as I can see it happening to me back at home. I'd hate to be stuck outside on a January night in Ontario, knocked over by cold so numbing I can no longer force my limbs to move.

"Okay, five steps or less," I say, reiterating the professor's rule for planning an effective escape. "What should be step one?"

"I don't know… smelling salts?" Reed says, doodling something in his notebook.

I give him a pointed stare, wishing I was in the other group. "Smelling salts aren't going to do you any good if you can't move," I remind him.

"Oh yeah, right," Reed replies, sounding not at all enlightened.

Professor Bhoula has a rescue kit he supposedly keeps with him for spirit encounters. He says we should always have things like smelling salts on hand, so that if we're feeling faint—or we need a quick distraction from another awful scent—we can take a whiff to kick us back into action. His advice is practical, which I appreciate, even if I'm not sure I'll ever put it to use. The ideas I prefer are the ones that don't require my brain to be functioning well enough to pull salts from a nearby pack.

"We need warmth, real or imagined," I say, tapping my pen against the slip of paper that details our entrapment. "Heat packs could maybe work, but you'd need to be able to move in order to get them."

"A second person, that's the answer," Reed says. I start to glower at him again, and he shrugs. "It's true. A second person would help you get up."

"But what if you're alone, or the second person is as out of it as you are?" I ask.

Reed purses his lips and returns to doodling. "Then you're done for."

I roll my eyes and look back at the sheet. "You need to concentrate. Either on getting up, or getting to a heat source," I say, mostly to myself. "The key would be not to panic. To focus on something besides the spirit so you can keep your wits about you."

This technique is something I learned not in Hostage Arts, but in Meditative Communication. When the pain is tremendous, Ms. Lind suggests we focus on something else—something pleasant that can overpower the spirit's influence. At the time, the idea sounded stupid. But now that I reflect on it, she could be right. I've wanted to run away from ghosts many times. Usually, the desire wins out, and I get myself away as fast as I can. But on two occasions, I've pushed through, more eager to be finished with the business than to put off dealing with the spirit for another day.

I'm not sure what I'd think about to get me out from under the numbing cold of a wintry ghost. Or maybe I do. Despite everything that's gone on over the last year, there are still certain thoughts that send shivers of warmth skittering over my skin—old memories that make heat seep up through my core.

A couple of those thoughts flit unbidden through my mind, and I lower my head so no one notices the flush of my cheeks.

"Yeah, concentration would be the first step," I mutter. "Followed by slow movements like stretches to keep the blood flowing. Then you can either reason with the spirit—tell it you'll help if it goes away—or try to scare it off somehow."

Reed raises his head. "Ghosts don't get scared, do they?"

"Of course they do," I say, my eyes still low over the paper. "Not all of them, I guess. But that's the reason some spirits are still around... They're afraid."

"Huh." Reed puts his pencil down and folds his arms on the table. "Maybe that's what the Siren's problem is. Maybe she's scared." He leans close, and I glance up. "Hey, do you think if I, like, talk to her and tell her there's nothing to be scared of, she'll go away?"

How Reed has gotten through this many years of Camp Wanagi with such a total lack of comprehension of how unfinished business works, I'll never know. I'd pity his inexperience if he wasn't so irritating. I know he wants to feel like a proper Sender, but he pushes in the wrong places and fails to listen when he should. Meander must be going mad having him as a partner this summer. I'd feel bad for him too, if he hadn't initiated the partnership himself.

"It's not usually that simple," I say.

Reed is already lost in his own thoughts again, so I don't bother trying to repeat my explanation. Instead, my eyes drift to the other group. The three members are talking and writing in turns. At least these assignments aren't graded. I wouldn't want Reed Vodden responsible for helping me achieve a passing mark.

I write out my steps and sort them into order, starting with mindful concentration and ending with hightailing it somewhere warm. After a few minutes, the two groups share their scenarios and we discuss the steps we chose. Isabis and her group mates developed a similar process to mine, only without using internal thoughts to keep their minds off the chill. Their more practical step of surveying the surroundings to determine the quickest path to a heat source—or the natural tools needed to create heat from scratch—is sound. Still, I think warm memories might be more effective than relying on analytical decision-making and wilderness survival skills in the frozen moment.

When our discussion is complete, Professor Bhoula starts the topic of the day. I focus on taking notes, bolstered into providing my full attention by having Reed beside me not paying any attention at all. He wastes the entire course drawing pictures of mermaids and sirens. By the time class is over, I don't think he's taken in a word of Professor Bhoula's lecture on how to scrape your way up after a spirit has knocked you down.

26

Sefa is waiting in the living room.

"He had a girlfriend," he says as soon as we're inside.

"Who had a girlfriend?" Reed asks.

My jaw clenches at his interested tone, the enthusiasm he should have shown during class only appearing now that we're discussing something that doesn't concern him.

"Don't you have an assignment to work on or something?" Sefa asks.

Reed stretches his arms wide. "Nope. I've got the whole night free."

"Well then go and enjoy it *by yourself*," Sefa says.

Reed opens his mouth to argue, but Sefa doesn't give him the opportunity. He grabs Reed by the shoulder, shoving him towards the bedroom. When Shade's most annoying member is blissfully out of sight, Sefa returns his focus to me.

"Before he was married?" I ask, continuing the conversation he tried to start when I walked through the door.

Sefa nods. He waits for me to kick off my sneakers and peel off my coat before he heads to where he's laid out his latest interview transcript on the kitchen table.

"They dated until sometime in the mid-forties," he tells me. "Her name was Marlene Hempstock. Albert's sister said she only met the girl once or twice before they stopped seeing each other. She doesn't know what happened to her, but maybe we can find out."

I slump into a chair, and my head falls back as I groan.

"Does this mean another trip to the library?" I ask. "I haven't had dinner yet, you know."

Sefa studies his page. "We can do it tomorrow," he says. "If we get up in time. I'd like to organize these papers tonight, anyway."

"Fine," I agree, relieved to have a break before loading into another car.

I heat up leftover pasta and eat while Sefa works at the table. He sorts through all of his papers, arranging them first chronologically, then again by relevance to our case. His research process is as methodical as his stake out of Albert's home. I'm not blasé about the necessity of preparing for ghost-hunting. But I can't imagine ever being this thorough. I suppose that's the difference between people like me and Oracle lifers, as Dylan calls them. Sefa has been dedicated to his talents since his first day at Camp Wanagi. He'll be a good Sender when we've finished our training years.

Provided he can learn to stop discounting others

when their abilities don't perfectly align with his.

Once I've finished my food, I shower and turn in for an early night, headphones on and Erik Satie's "Gymnopédie" accompanying me to sleep. In the morning, Sefa calls us a car before I've had a chance to eat. I grumble about my lack of breakfast, but he's unrelenting as he ushers me out the door. We drive to the library, my stomach pinching with hunger and my eyes still tired from the early hour.

Inside the library, however, Sefa is quick to locate information that helps wake me up.

"She died," he says only minutes after logging back onto the genealogy site.

"When?" I ask, pausing my own search of "Clarinet Marmalade" and the possible venues where it was performed in New York.

"Nineteen forty-eight," Sefa says. "She was born in nineteen twenty-five. She was only twenty-three."

I glance away from my screen to peer at the record. "I thought you meant she died when she was an old lady… Given how young she was, do you think Albert knew about her death?"

"Maybe," Sefa says. "Didn't sound like it from his sister, but…"

He pauses, his eyes narrowed as he stares at Marlene's profile. She lived in New York City for the entirety of her short life. Which at least gives us confirmation of a time and a more precise part of the state Albert resided in.

Sefa scratches at his chin and clicks his mouse to open a new tab. He enters her name into a search engine, and scrolls through entries. The results are too numerous to get anywhere, and adding 'New York' to the query doesn't help.

"Try including the date of her death," I say after a moment.

With a small smile, Sefa nods, removing the city and adding the date to the search string instead. Three entries down, he stops on an article scanned from an old New York newspaper. He opens the link, and we read the headline together.

"Girl murdered outside of Manhattan nightclub."

My stomach twists, and my foot starts tapping an impatient rhythm.

"This is her," Sefa says, his voice confident.

We read through the article in silence. Marlene was mugged coming out of a performance. The crime was suspected to be an intended robbery, but she ended up getting stabbed in the stomach. She bled to death outside the Roseland Ballroom, but no witnesses were found and no suspects were ever arrested.

Roseland Ballroom. I reread the name of the club three times. Then, with a sharp intake of breath, I return to my own computer and search the name. Sure enough, the history of the club proves it was a popular place for jazz bands to play. I add "Clarinet Marmalade" to the search and, after a few dead-ends, I locate a collection of old performance posters from the venue. When I narrow in on our decade of interest, I find the connection I can't believe we've now made.

Albert Timmons was, at some point, dating Marlene Hempstock. And Marlene Hempstock met an untimely end in New York City after being mugged outside of the Roseland Ballroom—a club that showcased many popular swing bands of the time, including at least one band that played the song "Clarinet Marmalade".

"This is it," I say, turning my computer so Sefa can see.

"Why wouldn't he have told his sister what happened?" he asks as he reads over the page. "He has to know... You wouldn't have heard the song otherwise."

The newspaper said that Marlene's death was unwitnessed and without a suspect. But in some way, that paper was wrong. Albert Timmons knew what happened. If the music in my head is any indication, I'd say he was there the night she was murdered, the night a star-performer dazzled the audience with his fast-fingered clarinet solo while she was being stabbed to death on the pavement outside.

"I think we need to have another chat with Albert," I say with a hard swallow.

Sefa laughs. "For pretty much the first time all summer, you and I totally agree."

ROBBIE IS QUICK TO SCORE US ANOTHER VISIT WITH THE SPIRIT OF ALBERT Timmons, though the swift arrangement means we have hardly any time to prepare. The owners of Albert's home must be questioning their decision to work with the Oracle. The slot they allow us is again small, and they provide less than twenty-four hours notice of their consent.

"We'll drive over right from the airport," Robbie tells us the night before we're set to leave—only one night after we've made our request. "We've got a short frame to work with. Unfortunately, we're at the mercy of the property owners, so you won't have any time to prep for the event when we reach Kangerlussuaq. It's okay, though. Y'all can do this. Just means you need to have everything with you—notes, clothes, staffs…"

"It's a walking stick," Sefa mutters.

Robbie grins. "Whatever, just make sure you're ready to enter *that* house before you leave *this* one."

The morning of our departure, I expect my preparation for the spirit to be easy. Sefa's the one with all the notes, and this time we don't need to pack an overnight bag. Still, the few moments I have to gather my things is spent wrestling with indecision. I stand beside my bed, the duffel bag I almost completely unpacked during our first week now open on the comforter. Staring at the outfit inside feels no less idiotic than it did the first time I considered it. Even so, I can't shake the nagging thought that I shouldn't be dressed in the sweater and jeans I currently have on.

Last time I left Ilulissat, I didn't expect to see a spirit. This time, I *know* I'll see one. Apparently, that small fact makes a difference. Because for some stupid reason, I can't stop myself from reaching for the outfit still folded at the bottom of the bag.

With a deep breath exhaled as a huff, I lock the bedroom door and make quick work of changing. I exchange jeans for trousers I'm impressed are wrinkle-free—though there is a crease from where they've sat folded for weeks. Then I throw off my sweater and pull a white dress shirt over my tee, buttoning the front and smoothing out the collar before sliding the slim-fit suit jacket overtop.

I stuff my regular clothes in the dresser before crossing the room to stand before the mirror. With slow, careful strokes, I comb my hair and study the outfit I've finally worked up the nerve to put on— unsure if the sight is mortifying, or if it offers a curious satisfaction.

I don't get to control much. If I hadn't learned that lesson years ago, the last eleven months have certainly drilled it into my brain. But music is a dominion over which I do still reign. For months now, the only power I've felt is while playing my violin. And this suit—the outfit I selected for my recital performances—is the ensemble that brings that power to the surface.

The sleek, slate grey wool-blend is flattering in its color, and the slight sheen of the fabric adds a sophisticated touch. The modern cut of the jacket is stylish in its design, lending me the air of someone far more suave than I could ever hope to be. If I had my violin in hand, the costume would be complete, and I wouldn't feel so ludicrous standing in an outfit that has no place at a summer camp for ghost hunting. But even if the instrument is far too precious for me to ever consider bringing it on a spirit outing, I do feel a bit of the familiar confidence from my recital days seeping in. I only wish it wasn't buried under the uncertainty of whether I'll be laughed out of the house by anyone who sees me dressed in such a senseless getup.

I make a final, obsessive sweep of my hair then, with a nervous breath, I unlock the door. Throwing it open, I cross the threshold—and halt as Meander turns into the hallway.

He freezes when he sees me, his eyes widening as he takes in my appearance. I haven't seen more than a fleeting glance of him in the past seven days. He skipped his courses this week, both Wednesday's Sender Management and this afternoon's Meditative Communication. The fact that we share a room and have not even met in passing seems impossible, but I think he's been sleeping during the day and staying up throughout each night.

Now, he looks over my outfit several times before his eyes veer up to meet mine. I try to keep calm, to channel the confidence I partially felt while alone in the room. But the pretence is gone now that I'm not by myself. When he doesn't say anything, my shoulders slump in a pout.

"I look ridiculous, don't I?" I sulk.

Meander opens his mouth, then closes it with an unsteady breath as he shakes his head. "Ridiculous?" he repeats, eyeing the outfit again. "N-no. You don't. You look... um..." he scratches the back of his neck, his cheeks pink. The color makes my shoulders straighten again, and my pout brightens into a cautious smile.

"Okay?" I offer.

He drops his arm and gives me a begrudging smirk. "Fantastic," he says instead. His eyes linger on mine long enough to assure me of his honesty. When I can't avoid the wider grin spreading to my cheeks, he ducks his head and speaks again. "You're going to see that spirit... I heard Robbie talking about it."

"Yeah, we're leaving in a minute." I nod.

With his head bent, his eyes are obscured by curls that are getting too long in the front. But when he lifts his chin, I can see he's grown serious. "Be safe," he says. "And, um... good luck."

"Thanks." I take a step towards him, and his eyes slide to my chest. He studies the cut of the jacket, his gaze lingering on the white dress shirt underneath. With an amused breath, he smiles to himself like someone who's just understood the punchline of a long-past joke.

Then he looks at my face again, his smile turning hesitant. "Do you have a minute?"

The words are as uncertain as his stare, a look he's given me before this summer—like he's not positive he should be inviting me to spend time with him. Still, my body hums, the question filling me with anticipation.

"You ready, Cal?" Sefa calls from the living room. His ill-timing is impeccable, and I roll my eyes as Meander glances over his shoulder.

"Nevermind, you have to go," he says, shaking his head before I have time to assure him that Sefa can wait. He moves to step past me, but I reach for his arm.

"No—" I start, desperate not to let whatever he was going to say slip away. "I-I have time. Whatever you need. I'm here."

He smiles, his eyes flitting back to the shirt. "I know," he mumbles, so quiet the words are almost lost in the space between us. "I've been counting on it."

My fingers grip his arm more firmly. "What—"

"Go on," he mutters, cutting me off. "It can wait."

He twists out of my grasp and enters the bedroom. Inside the doorway, he pauses, turns back, and mouths another 'good luck' before he disappears behind the closed door.

With a reluctant, puzzled sigh, I turn and head in the opposite direction.

TWO HOURS LATER, SEFA AND I ARE BACK IN KANGERLUSSUAQ.

"All right, y'all ready?" Robbie asks as we drive to the small house along the coast.

"We don't know if we'll get anywhere," Sefa reminds him. His walking stick is poking out the window and laid over his lap, so long it's by default laid over mine as well.

"That doesn't mean you'll have an easy time of it," Robbie grins. He twists around in the front seat, his head bent as he looks at us—his mohawk too tall for him to keep upright.

"Don't worry," I say. "Easy is not at all what I'm expecting."

"Like last time, I'll be outside," Robbie assures us. "If I don't hear from you after a while, I'll come to check." He turns his gaze to me, his eyes glinting with amusement. "And try to keep all walls—and bones—intact, will ya?"

I sink in my seat, unable to keep the smile off my face. "Shut up," I mutter.

When we pull up to the house, Sefa and I take a moment to collect our thoughts and steel our nerves. Then we unload.

The first time I went to visit a spirit for a camp project, our group brought bags of equipment and record books. The second time, we carried tools and flashlights. But this year, the set-up is the simplest it's ever been. Sefa hefts his walking stick over one shoulder, his folder of notes tucked under his other arm. And I have nothing on me but my phone, the earbuds raveled up and the whole device stuffed into the pocket of my slacks.

"If it's too intense, you can leave," Sefa says as we approach the front door.

He means it as a supportive gesture, but his words make me determined not to wimp out again. Earlier this year, I didn't care about the spirit. He wasn't, after all, supposed to be mine. But now that we're both involved, I'm going to see it through. For as long as I can, at least. If it's between keeping pace with Sefa and keeping my eardrums intact, I'm happy to let him have the victory.

I grab hold of the doorknob and push my way into the house. "Let's just get inside," I say.

The front hall is warm, and I pause, happy the air is clear and my head still quiet. Sefa lowers his walking stick, his fingers tapping against its top.

"No activity out here," he says. He scoops the stick up, holding it like a ski pole and swinging it at his side as he continues down the hall. His steps are sure and heavy, his bulking frame squeezing down the narrow corridor. But when he hits the living room, the change is instantaneous. He halts, his step faltering and the walking stick landing hard as he plants it at his side. With a shuddering breath, he droops forward and staggers into the room.

The static switches on when I'm halfway down the hall. I wince, dread washing through me as I prepare for what's about to happen. My feet want to stop, but I don't let them. With another few steps, the smell wafts under my nose, sour and boozy enough to make me cough. I place a hand on the doorframe leading into the living room and continue forward. Stumbling into the room, I lose my balance as the temperature plummets and "Clarinet Marmalade" roars to life through the static.

Within two seconds I've failed to be useful and am once more on my knees, moaning in pain. How anyone does this for a living, I can't fathom. No matter how many times I face ghosts—even when I know exactly what I'll be feeling—it's never easier. Each new encounter is a fresh hell where I'm convinced I'll be crumpled by the pain and eaten alive by the sickness in my gut.

I plug my ears and bury my head, struggling to focus on my surroundings. The tune, now familiar but still mostly incomprehensible through its impossible volume, cracks into my brain with an upbeat swing of tempo. The drum pounds like a migraine, and each shriek of the clarinet pierces like a needle. The static is nothing compared to this chaos. The sensations of being tortured with sound are so intense they push the smell, cold, and sickness back, the discomfort still there but unimportant next to the screaming of the song.

Focus, Cal.

I struggle to think of something aside from the pain. *Anything* aside from the pain. And, as always, only one thought manages to worm its way through.

I want this to be over.

When we're finished here, the pain will go away. The sound will vanish, and I'll never be forced to withstand this vehement rendition of "Clarinet Marmalade" again. Once this spirit is dealt with, I can return to the house—where I can sit by the fire, play my violin, or sleep until this whole event seems like nothing more than one of my horrendous dreams.

I cry out, dropping my hands to the floor and pushing myself up far enough to see Sefa leaning against the nearby wall. His hands clasp the walking stick, his knees buckling under his own weight.

Focus.

I glance back down, staring at my suit and using it as a distraction. I haven't noticed the oddity of wearing such formal fabric here. The material is not designed for running or curling into a whimpering ball, but although it tugs where the jacket is strained with my position, I'm not uncomfortable.

Well, I *am* uncomfortable—leagues beyond simple discomfort now—but not because of my outfit. I cling to the peculiarity of it, studying the cut of the jacket and admiring how well-tailored it is. I don't think I've ever appreciated the quality of my clothing before. The thought makes a smile form—whether on my lips or only in my head, I'm not sure. Either way, the sliver of enjoyment is substantial enough to help me onto my knees.

Sefa is saying something to the spirit but, so far,

Albert hasn't responded. With a weak turn of the head, I view the ghost. He is more whole than last time I saw him. The gaps in his misty body have filled in and, as he looks between Sefa and me, I notice the definition now etched into the dark sockets—an impression of lined and deep-set eyes, the kind of piercing stare that cannot be dulled with age. His friends and family probably said he had eyes that were full of life, even to his dying day. But I think a more accurate description would be that Albert saw something in his life that couldn't be unseen, no matter how many years passed.

He went to war, so it's not a stretch to assume he witnessed life-altering moments. But maybe those eyes were affected by something else, a gruesome event located in a happier place.

"Marlene?" Albert asks through the music, his voice papery and wrapped in rhythm.

A thud vibrates through the floor, and I force my head to twist in the other direction. Sefa has fallen and now sits looking huge but frail. His muscles are wide with definition, but his skin is sickly and breaking out with what looks a hell of a lot like liver spots.

He mumbles something I cannot hear over the blazing brass.

"I just want to forget," Albert says in response to his question.

I wait for Sefa to continue, but his head is drooping and his eyes are struggling to stay focused. I don't know if he's on the verge of passing out or if he's only dealing with tired vision, but I can't afford to wait for him to continue his speech. With a long groan, I push myself up and make an awkward attempt to stand. The effort fails halfway through, and I sprawl forward, catching myself in time to stop from slamming my face against the ground.

My arms tremble and, for a moment, I slip under the music again, gasping for breath and thinking there's no way I can combat the pain. But then I struggle through it, reminding myself that the sooner I figure out this spirit's business, the sooner I can put him—and his incessant tune—to rest.

Rolling onto my side, I fold my unsteady legs and sit in a crooked, cross-legged position. I grab hold of my ears again, helping to support my head as I lift it in Albert's direction.

"Marlene Hempstock was murdered," I yell over the noise.

My own words ring in my head. Albert is the one who is supposed to be the murder victim. Which maybe means they were killed by the same person? Except, it makes no sense that these murders would have happened in different countries, over forty years apart.

Perhaps it's the music shaking my brain and turning my intuition on its head. Yet with a tug of certainty, it occurs to me that I'm seeing the wrong spirit. Albert witnessed a murder. But I don't think he was murdered.

Alcohol ferments under my nose and my vision swings, my senses lost in the confusion of what is going on. The music was one thing—something totally unexpected but, in hindsight, not entirely unexplainable. But this? I see the ghosts of murder victims. If Albert wasn't killed…

The big band falters for a beautiful second as clarity strikes, and I remember what I heatedly told Meander a week ago. Our abilities aren't just developing—they're changing. And while he's drawing not only anger but also sadness and who knows what else from spirits, I'm sitting now in front of the first ghost I've ever seen who didn't meet his end by murder. He died, like everyone suggested, in a fully natural way.

I stare wide-eyed at Albert. He wasn't murdered. But his girlfriend *was*. And Albert saw it.

"You never told anyone she died," I continue, the white space in my conscious filling with music again. I cringe as it pushes into my ears, but I don't take my eyes off the ghost. "You were there with her. You saw it happen, and you never told anyone. Why?"

"*I just want to forget,*" he repeats.

The clarinet trill shrieks, and I grit my teeth before words gush from my mouth. "You're dead and it's still on your mind, so I don't think trying to forget is working out for you!" I snap.

Three short thuds vibrate through the floor, and I look back to see Sefa tapping his stick against the ground. He tries to mumble something to me, but I can't read his lips. I stare back at him blankly, and he gives me a pained expression before yelling.

"He was afraid!"

"Afraid... of what he saw?" I turn to the ghost and raise a shaking hand to my mouth, working to piece his story together. "You saw her murdered, and you were afraid to speak up," I mumble, unable to hear any of my own speech. "Is that why you're still here? Because of guilt? Or because you're worried the killer was never caught?"

"*Yes,*" Albert admits, the word cutting sharply through the sound of horns.

I clutch my head again, desperation surging through me. I was hoping having his secret revealed would be enough to send him on his way. Instead, we've been given another target for a hunt I'm not interested in.

"Well… who killed her?" I ask. Albert doesn't respond and, with a pierce of pain, I rephrase the question in another frustrated yell. "Do you know who murdered Marlene?"

The wispy blue-white mass that was once Albert Timmons moves, tangled threads of smoke swaying back and forth as he shakes his head.

"You don't know," I say. My jaw aches from clenching my teeth between words. "Did you see anything? Do you have any clues?"

"*No,*" Albert says, the word quick and meek in my head. "*Too dark. Too dark.*"

"You saw *nothing*?"

"*Too dark,*" the ghost repeats. "*Too dark.*"

I pull myself up to my knees in fury. "Well, what the hell are we supposed to do with that?" I yell.

"Cal!" The sound comes from Sefa, but I don't risk the pain of checking what he wants. I keep my sights focused on Albert, my blood sloshing with the reverberations of the song.

"If you saw nothing—and the cops found nothing— you can't expect us to figure the damned thing out now," I growl.

In my peripheral vision, I see Sefa dragging himself along the floor to get closer to us. When he stops, Albert looks at him, and I make myself do the same. He's talking, but I can't understand his words. I try to read his lips, but my vision is swimming with sound and smell, and without the distraction of being annoyed, the icy cold is beginning to creep back into my bones.

"*I just want to forget,*" the spirit says again in response to whatever Sefa asked.

The answer goes beyond irritating me—it pisses me off. I round on the ghost, placing one shaky foot on the ground and struggling to stand up.

"You can't forget," I say, slipping back to my knees but making another go at forcing my legs to work. "And we can't solve this case for you. What do you want, some kind of absolution? Some way to get rid of your guilt?"

I plant my foot and manage to straighten into a standing position for about a second before my knees waver. Stumbling again, I throw my body towards the nearest wall to give me something to lean against.

Sefa mouths—or says—something I can't comprehend, so I ignore him in favor of continuing my rant.

"Sometimes we don't get an easy answer," I say, my shoulder landing hard against the edge of a framed photograph on the wall. "Not everything has a quick fix. But instead of dealing with that, you've spent so long wallowing in your secret that you went and botched your own death! You're a ghost, doomed to wander the earth forever because of a solution you can't have."

"Cal!" Sefa yells.

I don't acknowledge his aggravated tone. I'm too busy berating Albert.

"Maybe the person who killed Marlene got caught," I tell him in a howl that makes my throat burn the same way my shoulder does where it hit the picture frame.

"Maybe he or she is dead—there's a good probability of it. But it could be that person is still free today, killing other people for the hell of it because no one ever bothered to catch them all those years ago. I don't know, and you don't, either. So, you're just going to have to accept the fact that you were a coward who didn't stand up when he had the chance."

"*Coward?*" Albert asks. His smoky mass dissipates so much the music fades into static, and Sefa takes a coughing breath before standing up.

"What the hell is wrong with you?" he asks, but I don't answer.

"Yeah, a coward," I say to Albert instead.

The spirit doesn't fade further. When the second accusation comes, Albert lashes out, stealing Sefa's energy so fast my sector mate falls onto his back. My ears are assaulted with a new burst of music, the sound so immense I lose my balance and crash onto my side.

"*I'm no coward!*" Albert roars.

I fall onto my sore shoulder, wincing as a shock of pain flares across my collarbone. Albert's wartime training has come back. The trembling old man is gone. In his place, a solid, rigid military ghost now hovers across from me. The voice in my head is sturdy and demanding. Calling him a coward has offended something deep in his core.

"It sure seems like it to me," I say, my voice too weak for me to hear it over the music. "You can't accept what you did. So, you're trying to hide from it, even in death. That's something a coward would do."

"*No.*" Albert's mass fills in, his posture upright and his eyes pooling with dark smoke. "*Not a coward. Never.*" The music in my head is fading again, but

Albert's voice remains loud and clear as he yells at me. *"Not a coward. Never a coward!"*

His voice morphs into a hum, and his mass billows out like smoke filling the room. I try to look at Sefa but, as soon as I push onto my elbow, the room around me explodes in white and I'm not even conscious long enough to feel myself fall back against the floor.

29

LAST YEAR, RELEASING SPIRITS TOOK LESS OF A TOLL THAN IT HAD THE first two times I was a part of the process. I assumed that meant we were getting stronger as Senders and, as our talents progressed, so too would our ability to withstand the shock of being near when a spirit crossed. But when Albert Timmons pries away from our realm, he wipes me out so completely I'm mostly unconscious for a full five days.

I have no recollection of the remainder of Saturday, or of Sunday or Monday either. I can't recall even the slightest blurry vision of Robbie overseeing our removal from the house or our flight back to Ilulissat. The first thing I vaguely remember is sitting up as someone rubs my back and tips water into my mouth. Then—later—someone holding my wrist and shining a flashlight into my eyes. Next is shuffling to the bathroom, someone holding me by the waist and standing outside the door until I'm ready to return to bed. Then more water, me mumbling something about music I'm not sure made any sense, and the person sitting next to me—the person I *think* was Meander— laughing before helping me lay back down.

On Thursday, I blink awake to find Kornelía sitting on the floor beside my bunk, sketching.

"Keeping watch?" I ask, my voice scratched and dry.

She glances at me with a small smile. "I had a feeling you'd be up soon." Closing her sketchbook, she lifts a cup of orange juice from her side. The glass is still cool when she hands it to me, which means her intuitive accuracy is remarkable.

"Thanks," I mumble. I sit up to take the glass, noticing for the first time that my left arm is in a sling. With a groan, I hold the cup in my right hand. "I didn't break something again, did I?" I ask.

Kornelía laughs. "Just dislocated your shoulder," she says. "Doctor said you'd be good to take the sling off once you woke up."

I nod, the movement bringing pain with it. Every part of my body is heavy with sore exhaustion. But I'm also thirsty, and the juice is soothing against my parched throat.

"How long have I been out?" I ask when I've drunk half the glass.

"A while," Kornelía says. "You were brought back here Saturday afternoon. It's Thursday afternoon now."

"Thursday?" I balk. I hold the cup against my leg, panicked at the loss of time.

Kornelía nods. "Sefa's still out cold, so don't feel too bad."

"That *does* help a bit," I admit, downing the rest of the juice. Sefa's a hell of a lot stronger than me. If he's still wiped, it means I'm not a complete weakling.

Kornelía takes the empty glass as I rub my eyes and stretch my good arm through a yawn.

"You'll likely want to sleep again in a while," she says. "But if you're up to it, I can bring you something to eat first."

The idea of food makes my stomach pinch, though I can't tell if I'm recoiling at the thought or if I'm sick with hunger.

"Maybe in a bit," I offer. I try to recall the past five days and come up with only small spurts of memory. "The doctor... came to look at my shoulder?" I ask, latching onto the vision of someone shining light in my eyes.

"No," she says. "She only noticed your shoulder once she was here. Robbie and Alex didn't think a doctor was necessary... They didn't realize your shoulder had been hurt."

My brows furrow. "So, why was a doctor called?"

"That was Meander's doing." Kornelía grins. "He pestered them until they got someone to do a quick check. He wanted to make sure you were okay, on account of..."

She nods towards my face, like I have any idea what she's talking about. I reach my free hand up and rub it over my features, feeling for a broken nose, an open gash—something to explain her reaction. Everything seems to be in place, and I shake my head as she continues to stare.

"On account of what?" I ask.

Kornelía studies me, then glances to the mirror on the back of the door. She helps me out of bed, and I hobble on half-asleep legs until I can make out my haggard reflection. With a shock of fresh panic, I take in the sight of my hair. In particular, the front right portion of my head where a small patch about an inch wide and an inch thick has gone white—the color drained from root to tip. And it's not just my head that's been affected. The inner half of my right eyebrow—as well as the inner lashes of the same eye—have also turned a complete, stark white.

I finger the strands on my head and run a fingertip over my eyebrow and lashes. Leaning close, I check the rest of my hair to ensure no other white spots have appeared. Then I look back at Kornelía.

"What the hell happened?" I ask, my voice cracking on the last word.

She tries to look serious, but my worried expression and high-pitched tone bring an amused smile to her face. "I don't know," she says. Her voice is apologetic but nevertheless tinged with enjoyment. "From what the doctor found, there doesn't appear to be anything wrong with you. Of course, you have been unconscious. But so far, you seem all right awake as well."

"My hair is white!" I start, quieting when she shushes me with a glance at Sefa's bunk. "Clearly something is wrong," I add in a whisper.

"Dylan's *skin* is gray," Kornelía counters. "And I can barely see. I'd say a few discolored hairs are nothing to complain about."

I shut my mouth against a retort. Kornelía's point is valid, even though I don't totally agree. Dylan's skin and her eyesight are, arguably, far more problematic than this. But that doesn't mean I shouldn't be worried. Hair doesn't turn white in an instant. Nor does it usually lose its color at the age of sixteen. Besides, my eyelashes are affected, too. That is definitely not in the normal course of premature graying.

I give myself another pained once-over in the mirror, raking fingers through my hair to at least try and push the greasy strands into a semblance of order. Then I twist away from the mirror and focus instead on the first part of what Kornelía said a few moments ago.

"Is Meander here?" I ask. Despite the horrid nature of this newfound discovery, the fact that Meander bothered our leads so much they had a doctor come in to check me over is a pleasant surprise.

Kornelía shakes her head. "He's been waiting for you," she says. "But he and Reed are working on their own project. They're trying to make contact this afternoon. Which was most definitely Reed's choice, not his. He wanted to be here when you woke."

"They're making contact with the Siren?" I ask.

My concern must be obvious. Kornelía squeezes my good shoulder, her eyes bright.

"I wouldn't worry about it," she says with a laugh. "Reed's the only one who believes there's any contact to be made. They'll be back in a few hours. In the meantime, you should eat. Maybe shower? Then get some more rest."

I take Kornelía's advice, shoving food in my face, then washing the sleep from my body. My shoulder is sore, but it feels well enough that I take off the sling before getting undressed. The shower helps to energize me a little, though I have a mini-panic attack when I step out and see the white patches of hair reflected in the foggy mirror.

I'm thankful I'm alone when my eyes start to sting. The tears are stupid, brought on by fatigue and, I guess, vanity. Still, the sight is repugnant and, for a long while, I think I'm going to be sick. A couple of white hairs wouldn't be a big deal. But a full patch of white—not to mention my half-white eyebrow and lashes—is going to make me a greater oddity than I already am. People won't be able to help staring. I can only imagine what the kids at school and my violin recitals will think when they see the freak's newest addition.

With a deep, shaking breath, I wipe my eyes and clench my jaw against the roil in my gut. A good portion of my sector mates have it far worse than I do. And who knows? Maybe this bleaching is only temporary. As suddenly as it appeared, maybe it'll go away in a few days.

I cling to the hope as I turn from the mirror, undecided as to what I should do next. I want to go back to bed, but I'm afraid that if I fall asleep, I'll miss Meander's return. Knowing he's been waiting for me makes me anxious for him to get back. I'm nervous, too, to ensure he's okay after his outing with Reed.

Dylan is in the house when I step out of the bathroom dressed in clean pajamas, my altered hair at least combed into its usual neat side-sweep. His eyes are drawn to the hair immediately and, despite the nudge Kornelía gives him, he's quick to grin when I come into view.

"Sleeping well, Nancy?" he asks, but my brain is too muddled to recognize which movie reference I'm sure he's making. Kornelía's frown is reprimanding, but Dylan responds to her hard stare by kissing her cheek.

"You going to stay up?" she asks me, pushing him away despite the smile tugging at her lips.

"Yeah, I guess so," I say with a shrug. "I'm going to

try, at least."

I don't manage to keep entirely conscious. Curled up on the sofa adjacent to my friends, it doesn't take long before I slip into a doze. The fire is on, and I watch it flicker, picking up snippets of inane conversation as Kornelía resumes her sketching and Dylan snuggles into her side.

The couch is soft and the company congenial, but eventually Dylan grows bored with keeping so quiet and still.

"Want to go for a walk?" he asks Kornelía.

"A *walk*?" she asks, amused by the question.

Dylan grins again. "I promise I won't run off," he says, which makes me think he's done exactly that in the past.

Kornelía doesn't seem to believe him but, after first checking I'm not in desperate need of provisions, she agrees to leave. I'm happy to have the living room to myself. Once they're gone, I doze again until the front door swings open.

I sit up with a yawn, expecting Dylan and Kornelía back from their walk. But after a few footfalls thud through the entryway, Meander appears—shivering, damp, and staring into the living room with vacant eyes.

"Meander?" I pull myself up, my heart thudding hard against my ribs as I cross to him. "What's wrong?"

He blinks twice before realizing who's standing before him. When he does, he steps close, his head drooping onto my shoulder. I wrap my arms around his waist, shocked at how cold he is. His arms hang limp at his sides. After a pause, he stands upright again.

"Reed," he mutters, his lips dark with cold. "He's in the hospital."

"Wh-what… How?" I remember what Kornelía told me earlier, that Meander and Reed were trying to make spirit contact this afternoon. My chest constricts, and I tighten the grip Meander hasn't stepped out of. "Hell, was it the Siren?"

Meander nods. "Turns out he was right about there being a spirit."

"Is he okay?" I ask.

"Yeah, he's all right," Meander replies. "He almost wasn't. But he's fine now."

"What happ—" I start, but then I shake my head, Meander's shivering frame pulling my attention elsewhere. "You're freezing. You need to warm up."

He tugs the hem of his sweater outwards, peeling the wet fabric from his skin. "Yeah, okay," he agrees.

While Meander showers, I stand in the kitchen, boiling water and making tea as a million questions rampage through my mind. I want to know what happened. I want the full account of how Reed got hurt, and how Meander got so cold and wet. But when the primary subject of my thoughts appears in the kitchen changed and dry—save his hair, which retains some of its dampness despite the towel he continues to run over his head—the questions fade as I hand Meander his tea.

"Thanks." He takes a sip, then turns towards the living room. "I don't want to see anyone else yet. I don't want to be the one to explain. Can we sit outside? Just for a while."

"You need to stay warm," I protest. "It's cold out there."

"It's fine on the porch," Meander argues. He walks into the living room, grabbing throw blankets that are folded over the sofa backs. "We'll take these."

His pleading glance breaks my resolve, and I acquiesce to his wish. Meander gives me a small, grateful smile before he heads out to the porch. I move in the opposite direction, sneaking into our room to take a couple of additional blankets from the collection on his bed. Then I join him outside where he's sitting in the back corner of the porch, one throw spread over the wooden boards like a picnic blanket. He beckons me to him, and I rest with my back against the house's exterior. We drape the extra blankets over our laps, and Meander tucks his legs under their edges.

He watches the water as he drinks his tea, and I watch him as I sip mine. He doesn't speak, and I don't try to make him. When his beverage is finished, he pulls one of the blankets higher and curls into my side. I place my half-drunk mug on the porch floor, and slide one arm around his back as his head rests against my shoulder.

"Do you want to talk?" I ask at last.

Meander lets out a long, slow breath. "I want to sleep," he mumbles.

"Okay," I say.

A few minutes after we grow quiet, the front door opens and voices rumble low in the living room. But no one finds us. I listen, poised to shoo away anyone who might try to interrupt this dual solitude. When our sector mates scatter and the voices fade, I focus instead on the soft movement of Meander's breathing as it starts to even and slow. He's warm, his weight like one more blanket added to our nest. When my eyes grow heavy, I lean back a little, and he shifts so he's nuzzled into my chest.

"Cal?" he asks.

"Mmm?" I hum, my eyes slipping closed.

"You were right," Meander whispers. He wraps an arm around my stomach and hugs me to him. By the time my tired brain is able to formulate a response and ask exactly what it is I'm right about, Meander has already fallen asleep.

I WAKE AROUND TEN THE NEXT MORNING IN MY OWN BED. VAGUELY, I recall a muddled conversation with Robbie and Alex around three a.m., when the sun—dropped below the horizon but still not setting into total darkness—confused any remaining order clinging to my internal clock. The temptation to stay outside was strong, but the urging of our leads, combined with the ache of my shoulder and an insufficient mound of warm blankets for Meander, sent the two of us reluctantly trudging indoors to pass what was left of our sleeping hours.

My head is considerably clearer when I blink in the brightness of proper daylight streaming into our room. Rolling onto my side, I take in the empty bunk across from me, distracted enough I fail to keep from pressing weight on my sore shoulder. With groggy uncertainty, I sit up to stretch, staring at Meander's made bed and wondering if perhaps I dreamed the whole of yesterday. The pieces seem surreal. Like the episode with the mosquitos three and a half weeks ago, it's plausible that my continued exhaustion allowed the construction of such a disjointed fantasy.

Getting reacquainted with my patches of white hair in the bathroom mirror offers a surprising source of momentary relief. I'm not happy with the continuing permanence of this new aspect of my style. But if nothing else, it suggests the events of yesterday are at least partially true. The likelihood of me hallucinating last night's episode is unnerving. Yet the memory of Meander's shivering body—followed by the warm weight of his closeness outside—feels too real to be mere subconscious wish-fulfillment. *You were right.* The memory of those words is real too. It has to be—even if I never did get an explanation of what they meant.

I shower and dress before wandering through the living room to see if Meander is lounging on a sofa or back outside on the porch. I find Sabeena and Naasir playing a board game, and Alex watching something on her tablet. But Meander is nowhere in sight.

Confounded, I head into the empty kitchen and grab an orange from the fridge. Leaning against the counter, I peel its skin as I replay the quiet moments of last night, trying to figure out what happened—and wondering where the two of us will end up next. Meander let me get close, and he told me I was right. But if he's disappeared already, it might mean that yesterday was just another temporary lapse of his obstinate resolve.

The juice from my orange is still fresh on my tongue when the acidic probabilities of Meander's further retreat brings a soft ache to my stomach. But all my thoughts, defeated and otherwise, are cut short by

Meander's appearance in the kitchen doorway.

"Hey," he says.

I stop with a slice of orange halfway to my mouth, unsure what to make of the nervous way he watches me.

"Hi," I mumble.

"I, um… Can we talk?" He glances around the empty room, then points a thumb behind him. "In private?"

I lower the orange slice and place the rest of the fruit on the counter. Following him to the classroom, my head swarms with thoughts about what he might say, and how I'm going to respond.

Meander waits for me to enter the room before he closes the door and crosses to sit on one of the tables. Legs dangling and fists balled together in his lap, he stares at the floor before raising his head and fixing his eyes on me.

"After the séance," he begins, "what you said… I thought maybe you had a point. But I wasn't sure if that was an honest belief on my part, or just a hopeful one. Now I know… You were definitely right."

I falter, happy to hear the repetition of those sleepy words. But while I'm glad he's not ignoring yesterday's events, I'm not yet ready to get excited.

"Right about what, exactly?" I ask, repeating my part of last night's conversation. "Meander, what happened yesterday?"

He shifts, and his jaw tightens, the muscles straining with aggravation. "Reed dragged Alex and I to this place on the outskirts of town," he explains after a moment. "He thought he'd spotted a spirit in the water, and he got an idea that he might get her attention if he stood on an outcrop of rock near where she'd drowned."

"Couldn't get a boat then, eh?" I say in a quiet voice.

"No, couldn't convince either of us to let him have access to that," Meander agrees. "So, he came up with this new plan. He wanted to walk out onto the ledge and see if she would notice. He kept going on about sunken ships—I think he really believed she was some sort of mythical siren. I intended to stay in the car while he risked his neck alone. But he was eager to see if I could feel her, too. I shouldn't have agreed. I just wanted the whole thing to be over with. I said I would go, but only if he would wait near the car. He wanted to come onto the ledge with me, but I refused to move if he didn't first agree to stay back until I gave him the all clear."

"You went out on a rocky ledge overlooking the arctic sea… *by yourself?*" I ask, my pitch rising into a scold that catches him off-guard.

He considers me, something like a smile twitching briefly at his lips as he nods. "I was foolish, too," he says with a sigh. "I didn't think anything would be waiting for me. Obviously, I was wrong."

Numbness pricks at my skin, and I stagger to lean against one of the desks. I can envision far too clearly Meander teetering on a precarious ledge while a spirit pummeled him into danger. I've spent a lot of time trying to prevent nightmares about such things, when weeks went by without a word from him and I feared he wasn't responding because he couldn't.

Meander watches my movement, waiting until I've steadied myself before he continues. "There was a spirit," he says, his voice swelling with contempt. "A shrieking woman who devoted most of her energy to making a show of sloshing water about. As soon as I saw her drawing near, I began to retreat. But Reed—he didn't listen. He followed me and, when he saw the effect I was having, he tried to make me stay."

I shove off the desk, my heart hammering. "What did he do?"

"He pushed me back near the ledge," Meander says. "He wasn't so much forceful as stupid. He thought he needed me, so he tried to make me stay. But the rocks were wet from the splashing, and he slipped. If he'd fallen right off, there's no way he'd still be alive. As it is, he was submerged to his waist, and the water crashing over his head almost drowned him. He caught hold of an edge, and I held onto his other arm long enough for Alex and the driver to get close. They pulled him up and got us away, then took us to the hospital."

"Damn it, Reed," I mutter under my breath. Reed has been a pain this entire summer, but I never thought his irritating eagerness would result in such a drastic show of stupidity. I grit my teeth against an onslaught of additional curses, and instead focus on Meander. "I guess I'm a jerk for saying this, but I'm so glad he's the one who fell. I'm glad you're safe."

Meander breathes out a gentle sigh. "They were worried about hypothermia," he says. "So they kept him for observation. Mostly, he was unharmed. But shit, Cal. It could have gone so differently. He could be dead now. We both could be."

"Meander—" I start, but he doesn't give me the chance to soften the blow of his words.

"The whole ride over I wondered if I'd made a mistake by not listening to you," he admits. "When

Reed snuck up and blocked my path… You never would have done that. Even if we'd been caught unaware, you'd never have tried to make me stay on that ledge. Do you know what Reed said when he was forcing us back? He told me it was a ghost, that it couldn't do anything. He is so *bloody* clueless, Cal. I told him the risks, and he didn't listen because he still thinks this is all a game."

His gaze drops to his hands, his fingers wringing together as he talks.

"You were right. I should have partnered with someone who understands my ability. We could've… If I'd just finished the damned project in time—"

"What project?" I interject. I think of his sleepless nights spent in this room, his only company the books and notes now laid on the back desk. I remember what he let slip our first week of camp, that he had come to Greenland in search of information. "Meander, what the hell have you been working on all summer?"

His chin tilts up, but his eyes remain obscured under the fringe of curls. For a long beat, the room is swollen with silence. Then, slowly, the word falls from his lips.

"Mim."

"Mim?" I repeat, my voice crackling with bewildered confusion. This is his secret? This is the information he's been seeking? "Your project is about Mim?"

"Yes." Meander shrugs one shoulder, but the attempt to look casual is thwarted by the anxious fidgeting of his hands. "I've been trying to work out how to fix her."

"You've…" I stare at his makeshift workstation at the back of the room. The largest volume is there, the same book he's been carrying around since his arrival. I knew it was Latin, but I never made the connection between his reclusive behavior and Mim's obsession from last year. "How long have you been working on this?"

When I look back at Meander, his expression is reflective. His chin tilts further, lifting until his eyes steady on mine. Even his hands have stopped fidgeting—they grip the edges of his desk, taut and still.

"December," he says, this time without hesitation. My stomach drops as he offers me a small, solemn nod. "Christmas."

With a hard swallow, I clench my jaw against the sting of oncoming tears. Christmas Eve was the night I received the harshest words I've ever heard from Meander, when he told me to leave him alone and move on with my life. And Christmas morning was when I received the text that took those words back, when he apologized for what he'd said and ensured I wouldn't give him up.

"I spent months looking forward to your letters while telling myself I wanted you to stop writing them," Meander mumbles, nodding as he recognizes the shock in my stare. "I tried to be resolute with my decision when I wrote you that stupid note on the twenty-fourth. But as soon as I hit send, I knew it was a mistake. After a few desperate hours of wondering what the hell to do, I texted you—not knowing if you'd even bother to accept my apology. I wouldn't have blamed you if you didn't." He smiles, a hint of pink blooming in his cheeks. "But you did. And I knew I could no longer sit around waiting for you to forget I existed while secretly hoping you never would. So, I got to work."

He glances at the desk, appraising the materials he's collected over the past seven months.

"At first, I wasn't sure if I'd find anything to help Mim. But when a few ideas started to present a real possibility, I formed a vague sort of plan. It's taken longer than I expected. I thought I'd have it finished before the summer started. That's why I never answered when you asked if I was coming to camp. I was hoping I'd have more to reveal. And when I didn't, I thought coming here and having a whole library at my disposal would at least speed up the remainder of the process."

"Why didn't you tell me any of this?" I ask. No wonder he's been so drawn out, huddled in this classroom and avoiding everyone as much as possible. "I would have helped."

Meander's gaze drifts back to me. "I know you would have," he says. His tone is serious, though his smile is affectionate. "But that was the point. I was determined to do it without you."

"Why?"

I wanted this conversation to come, to know what Meander was hiding and the truth of why he came here this summer. But now I feel like I need a couple more nights' sleep in order to process what he's saying. The fact he's been trying to find a way to help Mim is incredible. And knowing this whole project somehow started because of me makes my head feel buoyant, as if it's been flooded with the warm waters of last summer's tropical beach. But I don't understand why he's trying to achieve something the entire Oracle has had no luck doing—and why he's been keeping it a secret.

I suspect he has an answer laid out, but Meander's shoulders slump in a helpless shrug.

"I'm not sure," he admits. He lowers his head, his

fingers still gripping tight to the edge of the desk. "I thought if I could do this *one* thing—complete this task on my own, without anyone else getting hurt—then maybe it would be proof that I have more to offer than my shitty talent."

"Offer?" I take a step forward while Meander keeps his head bowed. "Meander, the Oracle doesn't blame you…"

He glances up, and I'm frozen mid-step by the shy gleam in his eyes. I've seen that look before. A year ago, on a beach, when we argued about my safety and I realized Meander's worry wasn't that I couldn't handle myself in the face of danger—it was that he wanted to make sure I never needed to.

My lips part in surprise, and his cheeks brighten as his eyes drop again.

"Offer… to me?" I ask with timid hope. This whole summer, I suspected he was trying to keep out of my way until he could slide back into the ease of having an ocean between us. I knew he missed me. But I wondered, continually, if he could possibly miss me as much as I've missed him.

Meander nods, and my heart kicks into a wild, storming beat. All this time, all this work—he's been doing it because of me.

And I never even bothered to ask what his project was about.

I never bothered to do much of anything, and the truth of that fact lashes in time with the hard beat of my heart. Despite my determination to get my life under control this summer, all I've done is sit back, impatiently waiting for Mim to get better and for Meander to decide he still wants me. I've stood in the shadows, waiting. Waiting—but never doing a damned thing.

I put a hand to my mouth, shocked at my own ignorance. Then I cross to Meander's desk as I marvel at his. I've done nothing, while he's tried to do everything by himself. I never attempted to be a part of his project, and he never offered to let me in. I've wanted him close, and have given him nothing but space. He's wanted me close, and has continually shut me out.

Meander glances up as I approach his desk, and I think about all the times before this that our eyes have caught—times I wished he would come closer. Moments I waited for him to move without moving myself.

"Cal?" he asks, the word as uncertain as all my thoughts since he pulled away from me last summer.

"You are such an idiot," I mutter. I step between his knees, allowing a small smirk to curve my expression as I bring my hands up to his neck. Staring into his eyes, I wonder at the vast scope of our cluelessness as I pull him close. "And so am I."

My fingers graze his jawline, and I don't let myself think anymore as I press my lips to his.

31

MEANDER'S SHOULDERS TENSE AS I MOVE AGAINST HIM. BUT EVEN IN THE startled half-second of our abrupt subject change, he doesn't hesitate to kiss me back. As my thumb strokes the line of his jaw, his arms wrap low around my waist to close the remaining gap between us. The push of his lips is gentle, the first notes of the kiss a *dolce pianissimo*. But then he pulls back, his eyes searching for a few cautious seconds before he kisses me harder, his bottom lip slipping between mine as I meet him halfway.

I slide a hand onto his chest to steady my wobbling legs and feel that the quick tempo of his pounding heart matches my own. Sitting on the desk, he's a little above me, and I tilt my face farther up to reach more of his mouth. His hands roam over my back, but when I touch my tongue to his lip he shivers, gripping my waist tight. I move my hands from his chest back to his neck, my fingers dipping under the high collar of his sweater in a desperate attempt to feel more of his skin. When my fingertips are rewarded with the warmth of his bare neck, Meander sets one hand on the back of my head, holding me firm. He pauses, his eyes alighting on mine again. Then he moves in, and heat strikes through my body as he deepens the kiss.

Meander's tongue meets mine, and I'm overwhelmed by the human, salt, and flesh flavor laced with the indescribable spice I'm sure is simply *him*. But there's also a hint of cinnamon between his lips—from the toothpaste he uses, because he has a never-ending love of sweet things and also finds the taste of mint too strong. The realization is strange, mundane and extraordinary all at once. Not because I'm tingling with the flavor of his toothpaste. But because in all my fantasies of kissing Meander, it never occurred to me that this moment (if it ever came) would be without the taste of tea.

I don't believe Meander expected our talk this morning to end with us making out. Which means he got up, readied himself for the day, then waited for me. He wouldn't have had breakfast before brushing his teeth, which means he hasn't had anything to eat all morning. The lack of a meal is not surprising given his recent eating habits. But I'm shocked that this discussion was important enough he didn't first make a cup of tea to fill his stomach or calm his nerves.

Talking to me outweighed the simple task of making his staple beverage. And it turns out, I know Meander well enough that I can tell the rhythm of his day by a lingering taste of toothpaste on his tongue. Separately, the two facts are of little interest amidst the delirium of his mouth against mine. Together, however, they make the reality of this moment kick into full focus.

This is not simply a kiss. This is Meander. And we are now—*finally*—picking up where we left off a brutal year ago.

My skin buzzes as a tingling lick of flame sweeps from my head, engulfing my entire body in heat. Every muscle is tight as I push my hands into Meander's curls, and I let out an involuntary groan as I feel the soft, twisting hair I've wanted to grasp for such a long time. Meander chuckles, his breath hot as both hands return to my back. His teeth scrape against my bottom lip and, with a burst of ferocity, his tongue finds mine again.

Maybe we're awkward, our lips bumping and teeth clashing as we work to figure out how best to move in tandem. But it doesn't feel that way. The hesitant, cautious inching of last year has given way to hard-pressed exploration, as if that long-ago, would-be kiss had not been interrupted—as if this is not the first kiss we've shared, but only a continuation of something we've both been aching for.

Meander's hands drop long enough to push off the desk so we're on a more even level. When his arms envelope me again, we press against each other, fighting to see which of us can get closest. My hands stay in his hair, fisting the strands, while his reach up to my neck. His thumb strokes the edge of my ear, then his fingers glide over the fabric of my t-shirt to run along my spine.

The kiss continues, time muddling into a confusion of swimming warmth as each moment rages with the deep, endless hunger strumming through every part of me. Still, despite my best efforts to avoid anything more than small gasps in the heat-riddled seconds before our lips crash back together, at some point I'm forced to pull back to catch my breath. Panting hard, I untangle my fingers from Meander's hair and brush curls from his eyes. He smiles, drawing me forward and planting a softer kiss on my lips. Then he rests his forehead against mine, his arms still firmly wrapped around my waist.

I draw in a ragged breath, savoring the remnant sensation of his lips as I close my eyes. The room grows quiet, everything still except for his breathing and my own. We stay like that for a full minute before I'm rational enough to speak.

"No more secrets," I mumble.

Meander nods against my forehead. "No more secrets," he agrees, his arms tightening their hold.

I open my eyes and lift my head to look at him. In the sweeping crescendo of the last fifteen or twenty minutes, all of the strangeness between us has evaporated. The uncertainty, the questioning—the daunting distance unravelling between us. Our paths diverged when we left Tonga last summer. Time has not erased. But we have made it back to each other, and it's like tapping into a well-known rhythm as we once more fall into step.

"Okay," I smile, my thumb grazing the faint scar along his jaw. "Show me what you've been working on."

Meander keeps me close for another few lingering seconds before loosening his grip. When his arms drop from my waist, he takes my hand and leads me to the far table.

"On Christmas Day, I started researching exorcisms,"

he explains as I survey the assortment of notes laid across the tabletop. "I knew a bit from the summer, but this time, I looked for information about exorcisms gone wrong and how they were made right again."

I pick up a notebook and flip through pages of neat handwriting. The breadth of his research is obvious, and I have no words to express how impressed I am by his efforts—and how ignorant I feel having had no idea any of this was going on.

Meander stands behind me, his fingers grazing the small of my back. I lean into the touch, and his arms slide again around my waist.

"For the first month, the search seemed pretty hopeless," he admits, resting his chin on my shoulder as he speaks. "A lot of fake cases and dead ends. Too much demonology and not enough about ghosts. But then it occurred to me to stop looking at exorcisms and focus on possessions instead. Those results were a bit more promising. Particularly once I found *that*."

He points to the book, releasing me so I can put down the notes and pick up the bound volume instead. Then his arms resume their former position. When he kisses the spot behind my right ear, a warm thrum buzzes under my skin like the low vibration of strumming a violin's string.

I open the book at random to see pages marked with a vast array of colored sticky notes.

"This whole thing is written in Latin," I say, my voice awed. I tilt my head towards Meander. "How did you even find it?"

"By doing a fair number of online searches and skipping school to visit a used bookstore outside of London," he says.

The book is old, the pages full of footnotes and diagrams. It's laid out like a textbook.

"And understanding it? Did you really learn Latin just for this?" I ask.

He lets out a breath of laughter, and I bite the inside of my cheek, unable to stop the excited thud the sound brings to my heart.

"I thought I might have to," he admits. "But between Latin to English dictionaries and a decent online translator, I've managed to pick out what I need. I translated key phrases and wrote them down. The further I got, the more I started recognizing words, too... I'm good at remembering things I've read."

I recall the séance two weeks ago, the quick way he related part of a story to the spirit's unfinished business. His retention may be related to his talent. Regardless of its origin, I suspect it's a handy quality.

"So..." I flip through the book, thinking of what he said earlier about wanting to finish the project this summer. "What have you found?"

Meander stands up straight, letting go of my waist as he walks to his workstation.

"I never believed the Oracle couldn't do anything for Mim," he says, leaning over the table as he considers his notes. "It didn't seem possible that she was doomed to spend the rest of her life in a coma. When I started researching possession, I was thinking there might be some kind of ritual that could force the spirit out. But the more I've read, the simpler the solution has become. Don't get me wrong, it's not like we can snap our fingers and she'll be well again. There are uncertainties—and risks. One serious risk, which is why I think the Oracle's done so little with her case."

"I'm not surprised it's a risky venture," I say, painfully curious to know how much worse things could get. "What is it?"

Meander turns to face me. "It's possible I'm wrong," he says, his tone measured. "I'm not an expert, and this is not a normal situation. There's a real chance everything I'm about to say is total bollocks."

The conversation is serious, but nevertheless I smile, fixing him with a look of pathetic joy which— blissfully—he returns. His eyes are bright as he holds my gaze, his expression matching my own. Heat simmers at the back of my neck, and I have to remind myself why we're talking—why I'm not still wrapped in his embrace.

I clear my throat, willing myself to keep distance between us. "You were saying?" I press.

"Right." He smirks, licking his lips and dropping his eyes to my chest before he continues. "I might be wrong, but what I've discovered makes sense—to me, anyway. From what I can tell, there are two main components to getting that ghost out of Mim."

"Two? That seems really... reasonable." I quirk a brow. "Unless they involve blood magic or something."

Meander smirks again and shakes his head. "No goat sacrifices needed," he assures me. "The first thing—the easy thing—is that the exorcism Mim started can't be reversed. It has to be completed. The spirit of Anjelo Savou must be expelled from her."

"I take back what I said about this sounding reasonable," I say. Meander hasn't even explained the process yet, and it's already guaranteed to be complicated.

"I said simple—not easy," he reminds me. "The

problem is, we need to get the spirits' attention— Anjelo's *and* Mim's. If a Sender was beginning an exorcism from scratch, they could do it in whatever fashion they saw fit. But because Mim already started her exorcism, the best option is to continue it, mimicking her process and style. Hence all the Latin."

He glances at the thick book with a sigh. "I don't think it will take much to bring the exorcism to a close if I more or less replicate what Mim did. Basically, I need to use similar props and phrases, things Anjelo has witnessed and that Mim can cling to for strength."

"Okay, so far I think I understand," I say. "Theoretically, someone needs to say some words, brandish a cross, and bring the exorcism to an end. That doesn't sound like something the Oracle would be afraid to try. So, what's part two?"

Meander crosses his arms over his chest. He raises his eyes to fix me with a stare. "To bring the exorcism to its completion, Mim's spirit needs to force Anjelo's to cross over," he says. "But in order to do that, Mim needs to be... unaided. In January, I sent separate emails to Alex and Robbie asking if they could give me Mim's status. Their accounts matched up pretty well, so I think I have a good idea of her condition. She deteriorated fast after we got out of that cave. From what I gather, her life was at stake within a few hours. In order to keep her stable, they had to hook her up to life support. As far as I know, she's using it still."

"I had no idea," I mutter. My mind casts back to the night in Swallow's Cave and the blurry, hasty trip afterwards to the Tongan mainland. I wonder what would have happened if the Oracle took longer to react to our unplanned disaster.

"Anjelo's spirit cannot be pulled from Mim's body," Meander says. "She needs to get it out through the force of her own will. She can't do that if she's unable to even breathe on her own."

I try to link the pieces, to make a logical leap from what he told me to what he might say next. But the ideas don't connect. If Mim can't breathe on her own, I don't see any solution except to wait for her to heal before trying to finish the exorcism. Which, I take it, is not likely a viable option.

Meander must recognize the struggle in my eyes. He watches as I work—and fail—to figure out his plan for myself. Then he gives me another of his small, sad smiles.

"She needs to come off life support," he says. "She has to overcome this on her own."

"But if she can't breathe…" I start.

"Mim is not on life support because of an illness, or even a true accident," he explains. "Her body is fine, and—*I think*—her will is strong enough to do this."

"Well, I'll agree with that," I say. If anyone could force a foreign spirit out of her body, it's Mim. "But that's all there is to it? Take away the breathing machine?"

"Essentially, yeah," Meander nods. "She needs to be disconnected from aid. And the exorcism must continue in the fashion she believes will work—the way she started it a year ago. Anjelo is already in place. She needed to let him into her body to make him cross over. This is no different, except he's already inside. She just needs the strength to force him out again."

"Wow." I run a hand over my mouth and sit on the nearest tabletop. "Okay, so if this is how Mim can be fixed, then why hasn't the Oracle tried it? Do they just not know? Or..." I look at Meander's uneasy expression, and my lips press tight with worry.

"Remember that bit I said about this possibly being bollocks?" he asks. "If I'm wrong, or—what I think is the bigger likelihood—if Mim is not strong enough to finish the exorcism while off support, she could die."

"Die?" I stand again, my knees buckling as I take a step towards him. "Meander, if she dies..."

"Then her spirit will cross as well," he says with the decided air of someone who has given this a lot of thought. "And all things considered, I think she'd find that the better alternative."

He's right. Mim believes in angels, and she has faith that things are supposed to happen. I can't see that she'd ever choose to suffer in a coma, struggling against the angered spirit of a stranger long-since dead. Knowing for sure what she would have us do is impossible. But what Meander's proposing would at least give her a chance—an opportunity to free herself.

"Well... shit," I mutter.

Meander laughs, his hands reaching for me. I'm more than happy to oblige, stepping close and looping an arm around his back. I've missed touching him so much. The heat of his skin and the motion of his breath are a new thrills and familiar comforts in one.

"Yeah, that sums up the situation nicely," he says when I'm in his arms.

"In theory, if this plan was going to be put into action, how would it play out?" I ask.

His brain is sharper than mine, and he understands my meaning without so much as a pause for thought.

"I don't want to tell the Oracle," he says. "I know

that's how we got into this mess in the first place, but… I refuse to believe they don't know what I do. They have experts, people who have had longer to work and better resources to access. They know what to do, but they don't want to risk her death. I get it. But it's not an answer. Waiting around for another year, five years, maybe more for them to make a decision isn't helping anyone, least of all her."

I sweep again at his hair to get a clear view of his eyes.

"You want to do this yourself, don't you?" I ask, the certainty hitting hard.

Meander nods. "I played my part in getting her stuck," he says.

I start to protest, but he brings a hand up and uses it to cover my mouth.

"I know you don't think I'm to blame. But I am, at least a little. And I want to do this. I told you already… I need to prove I can offer something useful. Besides, I think I might stand a better chance of getting a successful result than other Senders."

I tilt my head under the silence of his hand. He smirks and drops it.

"You think your ability plays into this?" I ask when I'm free.

"Thankfully, I don't seem to make living people angry by simply being near them," he says. "So, it's possible my talent won't have an effect. But Anjelo is dead, even if he's in a living body. And I've made him angry before."

"Isn't that a bad thing, though? If he's angry, won't he be able to fight against Mim?"

"Yeah," Meander admits. "But if he's angry, Mim

might be mad, too. I think they're both in stasis right now. In this case, the anger could bring them out of their stupor."

"Okay…" The word trails into silence as I remember the other conversation I had about Mim this summer. "But you are wrong on one point," I add, thinking of the conclusions Kornelía drew about why Mim's plan failed. "You didn't make Anjelo angry… At least, not on your own. I believe I had a hand in that."

His eyes flit up to my hair, and it takes a moment before I realize he must be looking at the white patch I forgot was there.

"I need an assistant," he says vaguely. "Someone to hold things and distract anyone who might want to interrupt." He lowers his gaze to meet mine. "I was going to ask Kornelía. Thought you'd be safer here."

The declaration is not exactly a surprise, but it is a disappointment. My arms are heavy as I drop them to my sides. "You weren't even going to tell me, were you?"

Meander looks stricken by my movement, and he holds my waist tight, as if I'm liable to retreat.

"I wasn't sure," he confesses. "I figured it'd be better to keep you out of it so you wouldn't worry. But to be honest, I don't think I could have left without saying anything." His fingers press into my back, urging me closer. "I'm telling you now, yeah? And as much as I hate the idea of doing something so risky with you in tow, you make a valid point. If we want Anjelo to be mad, having you nearby might be a good idea."

A slow smile spreads across my face, and I'm tempted to seal the offer with a kiss. But another question begs to be asked before I lose myself in his lips again.

"We need to be with Mim in order to do this," I muse. "Does that mean you're planning to *go* to Guatemala?"

"Unless we can convince the hospital to transfer their patient to Greenland for a few days," he says in a dry voice.

"How…"

He cuts me off. "I have money. For both of us."

"Meander, I'm not letting you pay my way to *Guatemala*," I say.

He shrugs, his hands sliding to his sides. "I have to get there if I'm going to do this," he reasons. "And I'll have a much greater chance of success if I have help."

"Help?" I tease.

He kicks my foot, his eyes wide and serious. "I need you, Cal," he says. "I'm sorry I didn't ask before. I'm sorry for a lot more than just that. But I'm asking now. Will you help me?"

My smile is soft as I nod. "I will always help you," I promise.

Meander's cheeks are pink when he leans forward to grab the front of my shirt. He murmurs his thanks in a low voice tinged with quiet elation, and the resonance of his words shivers down my spine as I cut him off with another kiss.

DESPITE MEANDER'S EXPLANATION, THE REALITY OF HIS PLAN IS HARD TO believe. In order to reach Mim and finish the exorcism, we need to fly to Guatemala. The idea is ridiculous when I think of it, even if it sounds perfectly plausible coming from Meander's lips.

Clinging to whatever semblance of order I can, I promise to pay him back for the cost of our plane tickets. But for the moment, money seems like the least of our concerns.

"When do you want to do this?" I ask as he fills me in on the smaller details of his research.

"I have a few more phrases to translate, and one more supply to collect," Meander says. "But it's almost sorted. With your help, I think we can go before the end of camp."

"T-the end of camp?" I stammer. "We've got less than three weeks left!"

"You've finished your project, and Mrs. Buxley shut

down mine and Reed's yesterday at the hospital," he says. "Besides, I'd rather deal with getting in trouble here than trying to coordinate flights while we're both at home with people who will be far quicker to notice we've vanished."

The timeline is tight. But figuring out how we'll sneak away from camp is even more problematic. Meander plans to use his half-brother's credit card to purchase the tickets, and we at least have the advantage of camp being spread out. Getting to the airport shouldn't be a problem. But Robbie and Alex check nightly to see if all of Shade is accounted for, and that means someone will be fast on our trail. We might be able to board a plane in time. But even if we do, there's a very real chance someone from the Oracle will be running interference as soon as we land.

We talk through our options while Meander explains in more depth what he's found and what he thinks will be necessary to complete this outrageous task. If I were trying to sort through this alone, I would be consumed by the overwhelming uncertainty of the risks involved. I'm not sure how Meander's done as much as he has by himself. Having him here, always within touching distance, makes processing the impossibilities a hell of a lot easier.

Locked in the classroom, we skip Meditative Communication so we can continue to work. But early in the afternoon, a knock on the door interrupts us, and we find ourselves brought to the living room with the rest of our remaining sector so Alex and Robbie can fill us in on what happened to Reed.

The others are baffled by the news, which strikes me as odd until I remember it was only last night that

Meander came into the house damp with cold after the incident with the Siren. Only a couple of hours have gone by since he explained the full story. But a lot happened between his return and us getting called out of the classroom to meet with the rest of Shade.

"Reed is expected to leave the hospital today or tomorrow," Alex tells us. "But he won't come back here straight away. Mrs. Buxley has arranged a temporary room for him closer to her and the other instructors. They'll keep an eye on him for a few days before he rejoins us."

"And you're sure no damage has been done?" Sabeena asks.

"He's fine," Robbie says. "Y'all don't need to worry. We just wanted to make certain you knew."

"Are *you* okay, Meander?" Kornelía asks. I'm pleased she's given him some thought. Thus far, the only attention he's received is a glare from Dylan and a measured glance from a half-awake Sefa.

"Yeah, I'm all right," he says in a low voice. He gives her a small nod of thanks before shifting in his seat, looking uncomfortable with all eyes suddenly on him.

"Reed shouldn't have been out there alone," Sabeena says with a sigh.

"He wasn't. That's the problem," Dylan mutters.

Kornelía smacks his arm, and he rubs the spot, giving her a wounded look.

"No, I meant that he should have been with us," Sabeena amends. She glances at Naasir. "We could have kept him under control."

"He's not the one who's out of control!" Dylan protests.

"Dylan, be *quiet*," Kornelía hisses.

"The only one out of control here is you," I snap at the same time.

Meander leans his shoulder into mine, and I press my lips tight, trying to keep calm. I didn't defend Meander the last time the sector had a discussion like this. Knowing what he went through on that ledge, I refuse to let Dylan attack him now.

"Reed's ability is not what caused this," Sabeena says. Her voice is softer than usual. "His attitude is. Ever since last summer, he's been determined to be like the rest of us. But he's trying to dive into the deep end before he learns how to swim."

The metaphor is apt, given Reed's floundering attempt to tread water in Tonga last year. Despite his supposed talent for seeing drowning victims, I still don't think Reed's ever mastered the task of keeping himself afloat.

"That's true," Naasir says with a slow nod.

"Think how he must have felt, seeing the effect Meander had," Sabeena continues. "He shouldn't have partnered with someone so strong."

"But Reed's not a kid. And Meander can't help the fact he's powerful," Sefa says. He sits with one elbow propped on an arm rest, his head cradled in his palm and his eyes closed. "We can't be responsible for babysitting Reed any more than Robbie and Alex can watch the rest of us. That's not how it works."

"Sefa's right," Robbie says. His mohawk is down again, perhaps because he's been at the hospital since first thing this morning. The sight is still unsettling— it's as if he's missing part of his head. "We've tried keeping you on a leash this summer, but it hasn't done any good. Y'all are a wild bunch… We can't tame you."

He flashes us a grin, while Alex offers a gentler smile.

"The point is, Reed is okay," she says. "And he'll be back, just not for a few days. In the meantime, go about your routines as usual. When he returns, maybe don't pounce on him right away. Let him broach the subject first."

"Can we visit him?" Sabeena asks.

Alex shakes her head. "Mrs. Buxley doesn't want any visitors just yet," she says. "She wants to make sure he's stable, and then she wants to have some time to work through his issues."

"His *issues*?" Dylan scoffs.

"As Sabeena suggested, Reed has proven to be over-eager. He's not the first camper to have high ambitions here," Alex says. She gives Dylan a pointed stare, and he flinches at the reference to Mim. "I was there when it happened. And I can attest that Meander tried to keep Reed from entering into a dangerous situation. Reed didn't listen, and it could have cost two Shades their lives. Mrs. Buxley wants to ensure he understands that. She'll help develop a one-on-one program for him to explore his ability in a safer environment."

"The best thing you can do is to continue on with your day," Robbie suggests. "And when he's back, act normal. He made a mistake. Most of us have, myself included."

"*A* mistake?" Alex laughs. "I don't have fingers enough to count your mishaps."

Robbie gives her a playful shove. "Because you're a paragon of innocent obedience," he counters. Alex laughs again, and his grin returns as he glances back at us. "Anyway, y'all won't hear from Reed for a few days. For now, you're free to resume whatever you were doing."

"That mean I can go back to bed?" Sefa groans.

"That spirit really wiped you out, didn't he?" Robbie says.

Sefa nods, opening his eyes long enough to glance at me. "I don't know how you're awake," he mutters. "I'm pretty sure I could sleep another day or two."

"Maybe it's your ability," I say with a shrug. "You were drained before he crossed over."

"Yeah, I'm weak around ghosts," he admits through a tired bark of a laugh. He appraises me, yawning through the rest of his words. "But at least my hair's not white."

My neutral complacency falls, and I suddenly wish I had a hood to draw over my head. I settle for slumping lower on the sofa.

"What caused that?" Naasir asks, his penetrating eyes on me. "Your hair wasn't white before."

"Must have happened with the cross-over," Sefa mumbles through another yawn. "Like I said, I may be weak around ghosts, but at least I'm not white-haired and shouting everything like a lunatic. I've never worked with someone so annoying before." He laughs again at my horrified expression. "Hey, I'm not complaining. You managed to piss off a ghost to the point he crossed over. I'm just saying... Next year, let's partner with other people."

He gets up and heads back to bed, while I continue to wallow in dismay over this newest piece of unwanted information.

"I don't suppose anyone has any insight into why my hair turned white?" I ask, ignoring the accusation that I looked like a lunatic while yelling at a ghost. The past few hours have offered a wonderful distraction from lamenting about the state of my hair. I'm surprised Meander hasn't brought it up. Of course, he saw it long before I woke. He's probably also guessed how much it freaked me out.

"It was your first spirit release after turning sixteen," Kornelía offers. "That could be why."

"Makes sense, in a twisted sort of way. But why white?" I press, failing to keep the whining note out of my words. "And why is it so random? And... my eyelashes. Why the hell are my eyelashes affected?"

"There's a condition called Poliosis," Meander offers in a quiet voice, "where random patches of white appear because the hair loses its melatonin. There's no definitive known cause for it, but it's thought to be genetic and can onset at any age. Psychological stress can be a trigger, too. With the excessive noise from the music and the drain of the spirit crossing over... Might be you always had the potential to develop it, and the ghost brought it out."

I quirk the affected eyebrow, intrigued and amused by his easy answer. "How do you know all of this?"

"I—" he starts.

"Read it somewhere," I finish for him.

He nudges my shoulder, smirking as he surveys my hair. "I like it," he says, the words almost a whisper. His gaze lingers on the longer strands before lowering to my eyes, his smirk softening into a gentler, genuine smile.

"What if it gets worse?" I ask, suppressing the urge to kiss him—at least until we're alone.

"You can dye it," Dylan suggests, oblivious that the

question was not meant for him.

"I can give you some coloring tips," Robbie adds.

An image of trying to comb bright pink, neon-streaked hair into place makes me shudder.

"Or you can embrace it," Alex offers. "White hair has a bad reputation. It's the mark of maturity and wisdom, you know."

"It's the mark of being old," Dylan says. He gives me a sorry shake of the head. "How long do you think it'll take before you're officially known as Skunk?"

My head falls back against the sofa as I stare up at the ceiling, my nose scrunching in distaste. "Shut it, Sludge."

Dylan laughs. "Skunk, Sludge… I feel like there's a punk band in there somewhere. What do you think, Robbie?"

I raise my head as Robbie offers Dylan a helpless shrug. "Don't look at me," our lead exclaims. "I'm more of a bluegrass sort of fella."

Dylan stares at Robbie open-mouthed, like he can't even begin to form an adequate response to that unexpected revelation. Robbie gives him an overzealous smile before he returns his focus to me.

"I wouldn't worry about it too much just yet," he says. "I can't say for sure, but my guess is those strands are, as Korni suggested, a side-effect of your first post-sixteen release."

"Agreed." Alex nods. She looks around the room, her lips pursing with thought. "Come on. If you're up to it, we'll call a car and take you all out for lunch. You can debate the merits of Cal's hair then."

"Good. I'm starving," Dylan says. He gets up, pulling Kornelía with him as Sabeena asks Alex more questions about Reed.

As the others move and talk, I glance at Meander. His presence next to me is so familiar, I can almost forget I haven't seen much of him over the last seven weeks. He's rigid, still awkward being so near everyone after such a long time spent alone. But when his eyes meet mine, I know his contented smile is real—as is the apology swimming beneath it.

"I do like your hair," he says. And for a short sliver of time, I'm blessed with indifference, not caring if my entire head turns white, gray—or bright pink with neon streaks.

33

THE REMAINDER OF FRIDAY PASSES IN A MUDDLED BLUR OF LONG TALKS, complicated planning, and a few joyful moments of escape. By the time dinner rolls around, I'm so exhausted I can barely keep my eyes open. Before the clock has even struck nine, I crash into my bed, happy to surrender to deep and heavy sleep.

In the morning, I wake before Meander does. After my shower, when I put away my toiletries bag and see him still tucked under his mound of blankets, I take my phone out and head to the living room. Prepared to cloak myself in music until he wakes, I intend to sprawl on one of the sofas and spend a few moments with my thoughts. But when I notice the door to the screened porch propped open, I stick my head outside and find Kornelía seated cross-legged on the ground—sketches strewn around her and a pencil tapping against an empty sheet.

Her head turns in my direction, and I raise my

hands in quick surrender. "I won't look." I avert my gaze from her art, but Kornelía only sighs, dropping the pencil and leaning back on her hands.

"You might as well," she says.

"What?" I glance at her, stunned. "You're letting me see what you've drawn?"

She shrugs. "Someone might as well see them before I can't draw them any longer," she mutters, the quiet words laced with sadness.

I move to join her on the ground, curious and perplexed by this sudden change in attitude. The wooden boards of the porch are cold without blankets piled atop them. For a moment, the memory of sleeping out here with Meander makes me smile. But then I pick up one of Kornelía's drawings, and the weight of what she said pulls me back to the present.

The picture I've grabbed is of a spirit. But unlike the sketches I studied two years ago—when I first discovered Kornelía's ability to convert the ghosts she sees in her mind into incredible renderings on paper—this drawing is not like the spirits I see with the power of my twenty-twenty Sender vision.

The drawing of a woman in early twentieth century garb is less detailed, and more human, than the spirits Kornelía has drawn in the past. The lines of her dress are vague, but not because the impression of fabric has been twisted into wispy tendrils of smoke. Instead, I have a sad suspicion the line of the skirt is plain because the eye drawing it can no longer focus on the intricacies of hemlines and pleats. And the face, one that should be full of smoky impressions, has been portrayed instead with sloppy features—like someone trying to draw a living person but unable to take the time for more than a quick sketch of the eyes and ears.

I study the picture and pick up a few others at random before I turn to Kornelía.

"They're terrible, aren't they?" she says, her lips curved in a somber smile.

"No," I say with a firmness I hope she believes. "They're quite good. They're just... different. Not the same kind of thing you used to sketch."

"I don't think I'll be able to draw much longer," she admits.

I eye the thick lenses of her glasses. Beneath them, Kornelía looks miserable, and I wish I had some sort of peace to offer.

"It's getting that bad?" I ask in an utterly unhelpful fashion instead.

She nods, her hand reaching back to pull out the ponytail constraining her long, mousy hair.

"I keep trying to convince myself it isn't," she says. "But I see less and less all the time. My parents are looking into surgery, but I don't think it will help. The doctor believes I will be partially-sighted for the rest of my life. Which I suppose isn't the worst thing. But it's not the greatest, either."

"I'm sorry," I say. I look back at the sketches. "You could use that to your advantage, though. People love artists who can't see. It's like songs composed by a musician who can't hear. Makes the end product more original. You could be a star in the art world. A vision-impaired artist creating replicas of the dead."

Kornelía laughs. "Or maybe I could become a famous psychic who draws vague outlines of people's loved ones to prove they are ghosts."

"Tell Dylan. I'm sure he'll draw up the business

plans," I say.

"He'll want to make a movie about it too, won't he?" she groans.

I give her arm a push. "That's not a bad idea. Get a few of us together in a haunted house... You wouldn't have to fake the effects."

"No, but you'd have to keep a store of fresh batteries nearby," she reminds me.

"Mmm, good point," I muse. "I guess that's why no Senders have their own TV shows. Too bloody expensive to keep the cameras rolling."

Kornelía gives me an amused, knowing look. When I replay my words, I catch the descriptor I didn't realize I used, and my face warms as she pats my knee.

"I'm happy to see you in such a good mood," she says.

"Yeah, well..." I try to come up with a reasonable, concise explanation for what occurred over the past two days. But Kornelía knows enough already, I'm sure. So, I offer her a simple nod. "I am, too."

"Have you found out what he's working on, then?" she asks.

I'm surprised she hasn't already gleaned this information. Then again, Meander's kept to himself so much this summer, it's possible she simply hasn't had the chance to pry into his thoughts. That, or she's just not the kind of mind-reader who noses around.

"Uh, yeah, I have," I mumble, staring at the sketches in hope she won't pick out any *ideas* of Mim or our in-progress plans to somehow sneak off to Guatemala.

Kornelía watches me and I tense, waiting for her to ask more about it. But at length, she only lifts her pencil again, sweeping her hair over one shoulder before touching the graphite to her sketchpad.

My eyes shift to her drawing, and I watch her in silence, awed—and pained—that she's letting me see her work.

"Did you get to try out any channeling yet?" I ask.

Since Dylan completed his impromptu project a few weeks back, I haven't heard anything more about the couple's plan to explore channeling options. But the way Kornelía hunches lower against her notebook tells me she doesn't have much to share.

"No, I didn't." She erases something on the page and makes an almost furious attempt to re-draw it. "And I don't plan to. I don't communicate with spirits. That's not what my talent is. You know that."

Her bent pose and defensive tone remind me of our first summer at Camp Wanagi, when I failed to convince her she should share her ability to draw ghosts. I didn't know Kornelía very well back then. I understand her a little better now.

"Hey..." I want to get her attention and end up sounding snappish in the process. Her stare is severe when she looks up at me, but I don't back down from the challenging gaze. "If you don't want to explore channeling, don't." I motion towards her sketches. "But stop hiding your talents because you're afraid no one will think they're any good. Maybe you can't communicate with spirits. But what's the harm in trying?"

"There's a lot of harm in trying things around here," she mutters. It's a truthful stab, but it doesn't pierce my resolve.

"Yes, but you have something Mim and Reed don't," I argue. Her stern look glints with curious doubt, and I press on. "You've got the foresight not to keep things a secret or ignore whatever warnings come your way. If you don't want to try, then don't. But if you're afraid to…"

"I'm not afraid," she says, cutting me off. "Not of hurting myself. I just don't want to *disappoint* myself." She pauses, her long hair swaying as she shakes her head. "I mean, my talent has grown so strong. Why should I tempt fate by trying to do more? I'm not afraid of failing, only… of confirming an end to my ability. Of knowing it won't get any stronger, that my development has stopped."

"But if you don't try, your development has stopped anyway," I say with a quiet breath.

Kornelía considers that. Her cheeks flush, her eyes growing foggy as she mulls over my words. After a moment, she gives me a small, reluctant nod.

"Maybe," she whispers. Then she turns back to her drawing.

I watch her sketch, hoping she'll at least consider what I said. After a while, I fish out my phone and put on the grandiose sounds of Sibelius's "Symphony No. 3" to accompany the feathery strokes of her picture. For fifteen or twenty minutes, Kornelía draws and I listen. Then she tilts her head to one side, her lips twitching with amusement.

"He's looking for you," she says.

I smile, switching off my phone and leaving her alone on the porch. When I step into the house, Meander is entering the living room from the hall. We pause, staring at each other from opposite sides of the room.

"Morning," he says, his smirk equally suggestive and shy.

I cross the distance between us, my body thrumming as he takes my hand. "*Good* morning," I amend. "The first of its kind all summer."

34

ON MONDAY, MEANDER AND I VENTURE OUT OF THE HOUSE TO COLLECT THE
final necessity for the exorcism. I think we're headed
for the church, about to commit serious feats of
sacrilege by "borrowing" a few religious items. But
Meander planned ahead and procured a Bible and a
cross while still at home. Now, it's only holy water he
needs, which makes me doubly surprised when he
leads us not to the church but to the coast instead.

"I didn't want to do this by our house, in case anyone
saw," he explains as we look for a safe place for him to
dip a bottle into the ocean.

"Fair enough," I say with a nod. "But am I missing
something? You want holy water, right?"

He smiles at my confusion as we head down a small
embankment. "Holy water has existed longer than the
Catholic Church," he explains. "Elemental purification
is an ancient process, and ocean water in particular is
supposed to be great for exorcisms."

"That is disturbingly specific," I muse. I'm amazed by the amount of knowledge he possesses on random subjects like this. I wonder how many hours he's spent studying exorcism and its related accessories.

Meander nods, holding my arm as his sneaker slips on a steep stone decline. He waits until he's sure of his footing before stepping again.

"I have to do an… incantation," he admits, his voice full of disdain. "But it won't take long."

We find a stretch of flat rock, and Meander lays on his stomach to fill the glass bottle he took from the kitchen this morning. When it's full, I help him up, and we head on foot back into town until we reach the nearest Oracle-rented house.

Inside what is normally the Wraith's kitchen, Meander reveals the gold charm he bought from a jewelry store in England. The metal is pressed into the shape of an angel's wing, and seeing it makes my throat tight. I can imagine him buying this, feeling foolish in the jewelry store until he spotted the wing shining under the shop lights. I can almost feel it myself—the absurdity of "making" holy water tempered with the serious reason we're doing it.

He fills a bowl with ocean water and drops the charm into it. With an embarrassed sideways glance at me, he sighs before lowering his head close to the water's surface. I smirk, turning to watch the doorway for intrusive Wraiths as he mumbles words I can't make out. His speech is not long. He talks for less than a minute before he stands upright and informs me the homemade holy water is ready to go.

Once the water has been created, the bulk of our efforts are focused on organization and translation.

Meander wants to replicate Mim's exorcism as much as possible, which will include using both Spanish and Latin phrases mixed with English commands. He wasn't kidding when he said he was almost finished with the process. I've stepped in to help at about the ninety percent completion mark. Still, I'm glad I at least have the chance to offer him support and make sure he's taking regular breaks to eat and sleep.

For the next week, we split our time between course work, translations, and sneaking to empty houses whenever we want a break. Meander's a master at hiding, and it comes as no surprise he knows when each sector's house will be the quietest. The two of us have a lot of missed ground to cover, so we steal every sliver of privacy we can to focus on catching up.

Academic pursuits mingle with brilliant glimmers of uninterrupted alone time, the week flowing fast and proving productive in more ways than one. By the time Saturday rolls around again, we've even managed to put together a solid plan for the second attempt at Mim's exorcism.

"*Ipse venena bibas*—You drink the poison yourself," I read as we sit in the Shade house's classroom. "Wait, is that what the holy water is meant to represent... poison?" I glance up from the Latin phrase translated in Meander's neat handwriting.

"I think the poison is supposed to be temptation or, you know, *evil*," Meander clarifies. "But for our purposes, I'll say the phrase and douse Mim with the water afterwards. If that's how Anjelo wants to interpret it, let him. Now focus."

Meander has written each phrase and its translation. Now, he's practicing, relating the words in their correct order while I check his script for mistakes.

"Sorry, right." I sigh, glancing down at the sheet again. "After you douse him in poison, you've got another phrase."

"*Vade retro phasmatis*," he mutters.

"There's an exclamation point written here," I say. "I didn't hear your enthusiasm."

"Shut up. I'll be more exuberant when we're doing this for real."

"*Fine.*" I smile at him from my seat. Across from me, the room's window frames a stormy sky, and rain pelts into the icy sea outside our door. "Then you do another bout of holy water before your last phrase."

"*Hinc itur ad angelus*," Meander says with a frown. "It should be *ad astra*, but I feel like Mim would have changed it. I hope she did, anyway. I can't remember."

The translation reads: *from here the way leads to the angels*. I'm not sure what the original phrase meant, but this one sounds like something Mim would have said.

"It's great. You've got this." I place the pad of paper on the tabletop with a nod.

"I hope so," he breathes. "It's not the end, though. The last bit I'll have to improvise in person. I've got to say some words to Mim, remind her who she is and why she needs to fight Anjelo's spirit while also resisting the temptation to cross over herself."

I don't want to dwell on what those words might be. If I'm going to make it through this excursion without a panic attack, I have to avoid focusing on the many ways this plan could go horrifically wrong.

"Does that mean we're ready?" I ask, blocking all my visions of Mim's spirit following Anjelo's to the other side of life's swinging door.

Meander runs a hand through his curls and leans against the table next to me. "Almost," he says. His voice is smooth and steady, despite the nervous jitter of his leg. "We've got two things left to work on. Figuring out exactly what Mim's situation is will be impossible, but we need to do our best to guess what equipment she's hooked up to, so I can learn how to turn it off. We also need to plan when we're going to leave, and how we'll get to Guatemala. I've done some preliminary searching on that front. It'll be a messy schedule. We can't fly direct—which is worrisome, given the Oracle has scouts all over the world. As soon as they realize we're gone, they'll start searching for us."

"They won't have any idea where we've escaped, though," I offer. "For all they'll know, we just went home."

"Together?" Meander reasons. "And without telling anyone? They'll be suspicious of me, I'm sure. I've been asking questions and using the library's resources. As long as I'm here, there's no threat. But if they get a hold of my brother's card and figure out what flight we've taken, they'll be on our trail."

"So, maybe we should tell someone where we're going," I suggest. "Somebody who can make up excuses for as long as possible, to at least give us a head start."

Meander's leg stops moving, and his teeth scrape his bottom lip in thought. "Kornelía," he says, resolute.

I nod. "She knows you've been working on a project and, if we're thinking about sneaking off, she's likely to pick up on it."

"Do you think she'll let us go?" he asks.

"Yes," I say, confident in Kornelía's reaction. "She doesn't like Mim's condition any more than we do and, unlike some other Shades I can mention, she doesn't think you're to blame for what happened in that cave. She might not be thrilled by the idea of lying for us, but I think she'll do it. At the very least, I'm sure she won't keep us from leaving."

"Okay," he agrees. "We'll talk to her. And since I can research hospital equipment any time, our biggest challenge now is finding an opportunity to go."

"Should we do it soon?" I ask. "This week?"

"I'd like to," Meander says. "If we wait too long, we risk camp coming to an end. Of course, it'd be easier to switch our flights at the end of the summer. But then we run into another issue... for you at least. You'll have family waiting for your arrival."

"Your mom won't be there when you get back?" I ask, annoyance coiled around the question.

"She'll be at home," he shrugs. "But I'm on my own from London. It wouldn't be hard for me to say I spent a few days with Liam before I came back. But that doesn't work for you."

"I could lie," I offer. "Tell my parents the schedule's been changed and I'll be arriving a few days late."

Meander studies my white hair as he considers the proposal. Having his eyes so casually fixed on me is still—more than a week later—a relief. Being close to him again is like picking up where we left off, the months of near-silence erased. And the way he watches me, his gaze falling from my head to my face as he ponders how we can accomplish this task together, is like being seen after a year of invisibility.

"It's possible," he says at last. "Though not ideal.

I'm not sure how long we'll be in Guatemala. If we have to give your parents a firm date for your return, I suppose we could make a guess. If no better time presents itself, we'll have to make it work."

"So, we'll look up flight times and keep an eye out for the chance to escape," I say. "And in the meantime, we'll try to figure out what kind of life support Mim's on, and… That's it?"

"That's it," Meander says like we've been working through a simple math problem and not planning the riskiest venture of our lives.

"Well, do you want to go to the library now? Or…" I look at him, my expression a suggestion he is quick to pick up on.

"The library's open late," he says with a smile. "We've got time."

He reaches for my hands and pulls me up, drawing me against him. My arms slide around his neck, and his lips press to mine with an already familiar motion that makes every inch of me flush with heat.

We don't have time to get lost in the moment. A few seconds after our conversation stops, a knock on the door forces us apart.

"*What*," Meander calls, his voice so uninviting it makes me laugh.

Kornelía opens the door, not at all cautious about facing Meander's wrath. As she steps into the room, her mouth draws in a worried frown.

"Reed's not here," she says, a statement that makes Meander furrow his brows as he turns to me.

"Yeah, he's at the other house," he says, the uncertain words almost a question.

Kornelía shakes her head. "No, he was supposed

to come back today." As soon as she says it, I recall Robbie mentioning that last night over dinner. I've been so wrapped up in Meander's plan—not to mention his arms—the comment slipped mostly unnoticed through my ears.

"It's only four," I say with a glance at my phone. "Maybe he's coming after dinner."

"No." Kornelía bristles with impatience. "The car came to pick him up at the house half an hour ago. But he wasn't there. The driver even went inside, but she didn't find anybody." She sighs, appealing to Meander. "He's gone. And I don't know why, but I thought you might have some idea…"

"Oh, shit," Meander mutters. He places a hand on my shoulder, even while he keeps his eyes on Kornelía. "You don't think he's gone to—"

"Saaniluk Salliartaq," Kornelía finishes for him. She stares at the wall behind us, her expression pondering, as if the words came unbidden and she needs a moment to figure out what they mean. She slips her glasses off and pinches the bridge of her nose. "Yes, of course," she whispers after a pause as she pushes the spectacles back into place.

"Saaniluk…" I struggle through the first word before giving up and looking to Meander. "Is that the place where you saw the spirit?"

Kornelía ignores my remark. "But why would he choose today?" she asks. "The weather is awful. The storms here are dangerous, and he wouldn't make another attempt…"

She stares at Meander, her pupils wide under the myodiscs. It's not hard to understand the thought bouncing between them. If Reed disappeared, he's doing something he doesn't want anyone to know about. For the last week, he's been under lock and key, probably suffering through a series of lectures from Mrs. Buxley and the other instructors about the importance of responsibility. None of us believed he could see a ghost and, when he finally tried to connect with one, he was told to stay away. Reed has never been good at listening. If he's annoyed with the Oracle for disregarding his talent, it's not hard to imagine him responding with dangerous disobedience.

Meander starts for the door, his arm slipping off my shoulder and trailing in wait for my hand. "He might attempt something," he says, following as Kornelía leads the way to the living room.

"Even Reed can't be that foolish," I say. "Can he?"

"Maybe he's just going to take a look at where the spirit was," Meander offers, although he doesn't sound convinced. "Could be he's sitting in a car, watching the point and reflecting on what happened."

"Whatever the case, we need to get over there," Kornelía says.

Meander and I nod our agreement, and we drop hands in favor of bustling around the house. Everyone left in Shade is here, so we tell them what we think has happened as we struggle into our coats and shoes.

"We'll call a second car," Robbie says as everyone gathers in the front hall.

A current of panic ripples among the sector. I don't know if it's the bad weather or Reed's past behavior. Regardless, no one dismisses the idea that we need to get to the ledge. We need to reach Reed before it's too late to stop him doing something infinitely stupid.

35

OUTSIDE, RAIN HAMMERS THE COAST OF CHOPPY, FRIGID SEAS. THE CAR Reed was supposed to arrive in is still waiting, and as many of us as will fit cram inside it. Alex rides up front while Kornelía, Sabeena, Meander, and I squish in the backseat. Dylan tries to join us, getting soaked as he waits for more room to magically appear, but Kornelía shoos him away as Alex tells the driver where to take us.

The ride is bumpy, the rain heavy, and our visibility seriously impaired. I watch the front windshield for a while, trying to make sense of our surroundings. But after twice being convinced we're about to careen off the coast, I stare at my hands instead.

"Mrs. Buxley wouldn't have left him alone," Sabeena half-yells next to my ear as she tries to talk with Alex.

"The instructors aren't here to watch campers all day," Alex says from up front. Her worry is obvious as she twists to face us. "One of *many* controversial aspects of Camp Wanagi is that campers have always been given a lot of space for exploration. Mrs. Buxley has other duties to attend. Besides, she's been looking after Reed all week. She thought he was fit to be on his own again. That's why he was being sent back to us."

"Why would he go off alone on a day like this?" Sabeena asks, her voice wild with concern.

"Maybe this was the first chance he had to get away by himself," Meander suggests. "He likely figured everyone would stay inside because of the rain."

"That's one thing you've got right," the driver says. I wonder if she knows anything about Reed and his accident last week. I haven't been chatty with the various drivers we've had this summer. I don't know if they're all Oracle affiliates, or if they're only locals who are clueless about why we're here. "No one should be out in weather like this."

"Thank you for taking us," Alex says, turning back towards the front. "Hopefully we'll be in time to stop anything from going wrong."

The words may be intended to reassure us, but the waver of her voice as we turn onto a muddy hill—the car's wheels spin for a frightful moment before the tires catch—does nothing to ease our anxiety.

We curve until the coastline runs to our right and drive for another five minutes before Meander sits forward. "This is it," he says.

The driver brakes, and the car slides a few feet before it grinds to a stop. The raging storm is deafening as she cuts the engine. The noise more than makes up for our silence as we stare out to the near-distance where, shadowed by a huge, far off rock formation and cloaked in the mist of the harsh rain, a narrow ledge juts over the sea.

"You all stay here," Alex says. She throws open her door, apparently expecting we'll remain huddled in the backseat.

None of us listen. Our doors fly open and we scramble out, the rain freezing and hard as it greets us. Sabeena and Kornelía huddle together, and Meander pulls me in against him as we hunch forward and press into the wind.

"Where is he?" Sabeena yells as we reach the edge of the crooked precipice.

The ledge is uneven, full of puddled pockets and dotted with wet grass. The wind is harsher out here too. I grab hold of Meander's sweater, worried a gust will pry us apart.

"Somewhere over there!" Meander calls back.

On a calm, sunny day, it would be an exhilarating experience to skirt the edges of this stone, peering at the close waters or the distant, taller rock faces that veer further over the ocean. But now the ledge is a dismal, gray trap. As our feet near the rain-slicked sheet of stone, my stomach is tight with fear at the reality of how fast one of us could plunge into the water—and of how close Meander and Reed came to doing just that when they were here last week.

"I see him!" Sabeena exclaims. She heads forward, but Kornelía and I grip her arms to hold her back. Her feet slip as we halt her momentum, and she shrieks as she stumbles to her knees before we drag her onto the grass.

"No one go any farther!" Alex says, her voice far more severe now. "It's too dangerous. Sabeena, where did you see him?"

"Just there… Look!" She points forward and, when I peer through the heavy rain, I can just make out a blurred figure at the far end of the rock. Behind us, the second car arrives, and the rest of our sector spills out onto the grass. Hunched low and bundled under coats, they rush to meet us.

"I called Buxley," Robbie says as he joins us. "Where's Reed?"

"He's there," Sabeena says. "Reed!"

He doesn't appear to hear her, which isn't surprising given the heaviness of the rain.

"What are we supposed to do?" Alex asks. "It's too dangerous for us to approach him."

"Can we get a boat?" Dylan asks.

"Who would take a boat out in a storm like this?" Sefa retorts.

"I don't know, a *rescue* team?" Dylan shoots back.

"Reed!" Robbie yells, his hands cupped around his mouth.

This time the figure stops and turns. A hand raises, waving to us.

"What are you doing?" Sabeena yells. "Come back here!"

A low, muffled noise is all that makes it to our ears. We peer at each other for a moment, trying to gauge if anyone understood. Then Robbie ventures a cautious step forward.

"Reed, we can't hear ya, buddy!" he tries, his feet shuffling onto the wet rock. "You need to come back here so we can talk!"

"…can't!" Reed says, his voice almost washed away by the storm. "I… ren!"

"What did he say?" Alex asks.

"Siren," Meander mutters. "He's trying to communicate with the ghost."

Alex moans. "Oh no."

"I'll go and get him," Robbie says. He takes another small step. His foot slips, and he teeters off balance until Sefa swoops in to steady him from behind.

"It's too dangerous!" Alex repeats.

"We have to do something," Sefa says. He looks back at us. "Can anyone reason with him?"

"I can, I'm sure I can," Sabeena says. She stares at the rock but doesn't move. Her eyes cast out to the figure, and she mimics Robbie's style of holding her hands by her mouth. "Reed! It's Sabeena. I want to talk to you!"

"Look!" Reed says from far off. "Look!"

"Look at what?" Sabeena asks.

"Shit," Meander mumbles. "The water."

I follow his gaze and, even through the rain, it's easy to see the swell of sea foam crashing over the rock.

Meander takes a step back, an automatic motion to put more distance between himself and the ghost that must be close. I grab his arm, holding him in place.

"Hey, this isn't you," I say, while the others continue calling for Reed. "Do you see the spirit?"

His eyes narrow as he peers at the ledge in search of Reed's siren. After a moment, he shakes his head. "No, I don't see her. I didn't last time until I was pretty near the water."

"Right, so this isn't you, okay?" I tell him.

Meander nods but stays back anyway. I stand beside him and take up the call with everyone else.

Reed yells something I can't hear. He raises his arms to the sky, and something like a broken, wispy remnant of laughter whistles through the wind.

"Is he… laughing?" Sabeena asks, her lips lifting in an unsure smile.

"He must see the spirit," Meander says. "He wasn't getting this kind of reaction before."

"Hey…" Sefa turns to us with sudden intensity. "What's the date today?"

"August fifth," Alex says. "Why?"

Sefa eyes Sabeena and, after a few seconds, both of their frowns lift into expressions of confounded amusement.

"It's his birthday." Sabeena smiles. She giggles, clapping her hands. "Today Reed's sixteen."

"What a birthday present," Sefa says.

A birthday present, indeed. From what I gather, most Senders don't come into the full extent of their power just because they've survived living long enough to mark their sixteenth year. But Reed's proven to be a special case. He said he could feel it coming. Maybe he was right. After all, he got what he wanted. He's sixteen and, like a bolt of lightning, his talent has crackled into existence. He's seeing his much sought after ghost. And he's thrilled.

The realization crackles between us as well, the tension of the last moments loosening as the mood of the moment alters. Sabeena leans into Sefa's side and, with a deep breath, I lace my fingers with Meander's—glad for the happy turn this desperate outing has made.

"Happy birthday, Reed!" Sabeena yells with a heartier laugh. "Now, come back here so we can celebrate!"

Reed turns around, his arms still upraised. Behind him, another wave of icy water crashes up, knocking him off his feet.

36

REED'S FACE HITS THE LEDGE. EVEN FROM WHERE I'M STANDING, THE bounce of his cheek against sheet rock is visible—and while the cracking thud can't possibly permeate the storm, I seem to hear it all the same.

"Someone needs to help him!" Sabeena cries. Her hands fly to her mouth in horrified awe, her eyes wide under the black hair plastered across her forehead. Her fear, along with the way she hunches forward against the blowing rain, gives her the appearance of someone small and delicate. She's older than half the sector and not at all timid or shy. But among the rest of us standing here now, Sabeena looks like a frightened child.

"I'll run back to the cars, see if anyone has a rope," Robbie says, already bounding away.

Alex resumes the earlier call. "Reed!" she yells. "Can you hear us?"

For an anxious moment, no one moves. The rain rages around us, but we stay still, watching the slumped figure at the edge of the rock. When he shifts, there's an audible sigh of relief from the group. Reed rises onto his hands and knees, but then one hand gives way and he slips back onto his stomach.

Sefa tries to go onto the ledge. "He needs help," he snaps when we protest his attempt.

"You'll slip and fall yourself," Alex replies.

Naasir holds him back. I'm sure Sefa could tear away from anything trying to retain him, but with a string of curses he turns from the rock.

"Where's Robbie?" he says. "I'll go when I've got the rope."

Out on the ledge, more waves swell. The crests crash over Reed, soaking his body with the same frigid waters that landed him in the hospital a week ago.

"They don't have any rope!" Robbie calls, running up behind us. "But one of the drivers is going to find some... She'll call the rescue service in town, too."

"What are we going to do until then?" Sefa asks. "We can't just leave him there."

"If we can get him to move halfway up the ledge, someone can meet him," Kornelía offers.

"Reed, can you come towards us?" Sefa calls.

Reed's shoulders rise and slump as he struggles to move. He pushes up, wobbling before he falls onto his side. Rolling onto his stomach, his head twists towards the water, his stare fixed over the ledge. His second attempt to rise is more successful, and he sits upright, his chin lolling onto his chest. I wonder if he's on the verge of passing out until, with great effort, he fumbles onto his knees. For a moment, his body points towards the ledge like he's about to crawl to where the water is splashing in dangerous waves against the rock's tip. He shifts forward and sways close to the rock's edge. Then he halts before carefully turning around and creeping towards us.

"He's coming," Sabeena says with a relieved breath. "Someone needs to meet him."

"I'll go," Sefa says.

Robbie is quick to shake his head, his mohawk crumbling under the force of the driving rain. "You stay, and I'll go," he insists.

"Why don't you both go, one after the other," Alex suggests. "Sefa first, and Robbie—you can stand behind, keeping a hand on him to make sure he doesn't fall."

"We'll all do that," Kornelía says. "We'll make a chain. That way everyone will remain safe."

"That might not be necessary," Meander says.

He stares behind us, up to the road where another car has appeared. Before the vehicle has time to come to a complete stop, the door opens and Mrs. Buxley steps out. Her usual high heels have been replaced with thick hiking boots, and cradled in one arm is a florescent red emergency bag.

"Mrs. Buxley!" Alex cries.

Our instructor approaches with swift, sure steps, her hands already working the bag's zipper. I'm not sure if this is a general collection of safety gear or something meant for Senders in trouble. Judging by the length of rope she retrieves from within the bag, I'm guessing she had at least a little foresight into what she might face this afternoon.

"He's on the ledge—just there." Robbie points as she nears us.

Mrs. Buxley doesn't speak. Her expression is hard

as she drops the bag and secures the rope around her waist. She knots the nylon with expert ease, handing it to Robbie once it's tight. He mimics her action, fastening the other end around his middle so he can act as her anchor. Alex is already holding onto his arm, ready to help keep him in place. Sefa hovers behind them, and the rest of us crowd close to offer our assistance if need be.

Our instructor surveys the rock, her slender form steady but immensely small amidst the gushing rain and distant formations. I can't help thinking a bulkier Sender, like my research and gadgets instructor, Mr. Olenev, or last year's fitness instructor, Althea, would be better suited for this task. But Mrs. Buxley doesn't falter. Once she has an idea of the landscape, she gives Robbie a nod and heads onto the stone.

"Do you think she knows what she's doing?" Kornelía asks.

"She must," I say, wishing I believed my own words.

Mrs. Buxley takes a surefooted step onto the ledge. But the steady movement is undone when a fierce gust of wind forces her to stagger two steps back. Our instructor braces against the burst of wind. But instead of dying down, it grows in volume, like a hurricane taking shape before us.

"What's happening?" Sabeena asks, as Mrs. Buxley is dragged back by the force of the gale.

Out on the rock, Reed slips, his head bouncing unnaturally as another swell of water covers him. My stomach plunges as I watch the waves subside, and blood-pinked foam draws back into the sea— dragging Reed along with it.

"Shit," Meander and I mutter at the same time.

"He's going under," Naasir says, the low resonance of his voice almost inaudible over the rain.

"We need to move—fast," Mrs. Buxley orders. She steps back onto the stone as Reed's body slips over its edge.

"He's in the water!" Sabeena cries as his crumpled form disappears from view.

Mrs. Buxley jolts forward, and Alex and Sefa grab Robbie's arms, ready to hold him back when she reaches the end of the rope. She hurries, her feet slipping but her balance incredible. She keeps a good pace, crossing half the length of the precipice before a fiercer gust of ice-chilled wind gushes from the water.

This time, it's not only our instructor who rocks back. The wind rips along the ledge and out to the grass, blasting the meadow— toppling everyone in it. I latch onto Meander, and both of us fall in a heap. We roll sideways, barreling twice before I dig a heel into the grass while he bears down on top of me, pressing hard into the ground to keep us still.

The cold of the air seeps into every one of my already drenched pores. I'm wracked with shivers, and I bury my face in Meander's neck, though the dampness of his turtleneck does nothing to keep the chill away.

"What the hell is that!" someone—Dylan, I think—shouts.

A wash of sickness enters my gut, but I force my head back far enough to look at the water. Just past the edge of the rock, a wispy, blue-white mass hovers above the surface. For a second, I think it must be the Siren. But although the presence is obvious—the white and blue colors vivid against the bleary gray of the stormy landscape—the mass is unformed. No facial features or body parts are visible, nor are there any pockets of faded mist or impressions of old clothing. And unlike every other spirit I've ever seen, this one has no accompanying static, music, or smell.

"It's a ghost," Sefa offers.

He's wrong though. I'm positive this is what Dylan is looking at. And that means this can't be a spirit—at least not the typical kind.

"Is it… Oh no, it's Reed!" Sabeena shrieks.

"No, it's not. Look," Naasir says.

Out in the water, something—someone—is flailing. Reed's hands splash among the frigid foam as he tries to paddle his way to shore.

"He's still alive!" Sabeena sighs.

Sefa and Naasir scramble up and start for the shoreline to our left, where a short slope drops down to the water.

"Then what *is* that thing?" Dylan asks.

"You see it," Kornelía says. "And I do, too. That shouldn't be. That shouldn't…"

"It's a wraith."

Everyone freezes when Mrs. Buxley speaks. The wind has died down, and her somber voice is clear even though she faces the sea. Her eyes are fixed on Reed, but she's not making a quick dash to the water's edge to try and pull him out. Her posture is stiff and motionless as she watches him struggle. When that registers, my body goes rigid with a different sort of cold.

Alex's voice is tearful. "Please don't let it be so."

"What do you mean, a wraith?" Sefa asks from where he and Naasir have halted a few steps away. "Isn't that like—"

"A ghost," Robbie explains in a subdued voice.

"One that appears right before... someone dies."

"*No*," Sabeena sobs. "You can't mean..."

Reed is still struggling in the water, but not even Sabeena or Sefa make any further move to rescue him. He's too far out, his shape growing smaller as the waves carry him farther out to sea. I study the unformed mass trailing the frantic figure bobbing in the waves. When the mist starts to evaporate like fog burning in the sun, I see the wind rippling before it hits us on land.

Meander sat up while Mrs. Buxley spoke, and he reaches for my hand to pull me off the ground as the wraith disappears. But his effort is pointless. Before his fingers even meet mine, the second gust of wind reaches the meadow, this one as cold and nauseating as the first. Sabeena screams while Naasir utters a low string of unfamiliar words that, even spoken a foreign tongue, are obviously threaded with fear.

Despite only my head hitting the ground—the rest of me still down from the first gale—the second impact is harder. The blue-white mass fades, and the water once again swells. But this time, it's not the storm raging or the Siren leaving chaos in her wake.

This time, the wraith is reconnecting with its body— at the moment of its death.

Reed's death.

When the wind dies off again, the absence of its resounding power makes the storm feel almost like a gentle pattering of rain. Climbing to our feet, everyone is silent as we collect at the grassy edge of the stone precipice. The waves are choppy from the storm but, even from our distance, it's easy to see how much calmer the water has become. How void the ocean is of anyone splashing in the frozen tide or floating atop the foam-topped crests.

The wraith is nowhere in sight. Neither is Reed.

"I didn't feel it," Naasir says, his heavy voice wavering with emotion, "not until the end."

Sabeena wraps herself around his side. "Didn't feel what?"

"His—" A soft sob interrupts his words, and he halts, unable to say the rest.

"His unfinished business," Kornelía answers for him.

I look at my friend, and I'm shaken by the way she stands. Her long, wet hair streams back in the wind. Her glasses are off, her eyes are closed, and tears drip from beneath her lashes. "He's here," she says in a breath high and pinched. "Reed's dead, but he didn't move on. He's still in the water."

The ten of us stare out at the unforgiving sea. Behind us, the emergency crew appears on the road, far too late to be of any use.

37

THEY DON'T TAKE US BACK TO THE SHADE HOUSE. AS THE CREWS SWEEP in, boots stomping and commands flying with mechanical swiftness, we're piled into cars. Orders are given in a language I don't understand, then we're driven a short distance to another home we eventually discover belongs to one of the drivers.

After drying off and getting preliminary once-overs by a medical team, we're loaded with hot beverages and pushed before a blazing fire. People come and go, talking in hushed tones and sneaking us sorry glances. Sabeena, Naasir, and Sefa cry as they huddle together. The rest of us sit in stunned silence as the next hour or two passes by.

Everything is numb as people bustle around us. But after the initial flurry dims and we've settled by the hearth, my mind becomes a spinning reel. I can't get the image of the wraith out of my mind, nor can I shake the disturbing pictures playing on a loop behind it.

Reed hitting his face, Reed slipping over the rock. Reed thrashing in the water while all I could do was watch.

When Sabeena breaks, her quiet sobs working themselves into frenzied accusations that all of us should have done more, it feels like she's been watching the scene by my side—reliving the moment and feeling the same weight of uselessness that I do.

"We should have saved him," she seethes.

"Nobody could have saved him," Kornelía replies, her tone so full of conviction it's almost unemotional.

"We pushed him away," Sabeena says. "We didn't listen when he needed us, and look what happened."

"He didn't ask for our help," Kornelía reasons. "He didn't want it. Not really. He didn't care what any of us were doing. He just wanted to do something for himself."

The girls argue, both of their points valid. I brace myself, waiting for the others to chime in and for the fight to get heated. But after a few minutes of back and forth, Naasir folds Sabeena into a hug, soothing her with whispered words the rest of us can't hear. She lets out a final shrieking sob, then she nods against his shoulder, her small frame shuddering with quieter cries.

Every twenty minutes or so someone comes inside to grab supplies or make a phone call. But despite this being a stranger's home, after a while, we're mostly left to ourselves. We don't see any familiar faces, no instructors or leads to explain what is going on. Eventually, the stillness proves too much for Sefa and Dylan. When the rain stops late in the evening, the two go out for a run with a promise to stay far inland and close to the house.

At some point I fish out my phone, slipping in one

earbud and offering the other to Meander. He takes it and, once Tchaikovsky's "None but the Lonely Heart" has started, he plays around on my phone while I lean my head on his shoulder and stare at the fire.

Unlike the scene of the accident, which I'm sure is teeming with discussions, interviews, and plans for what to do next, in here the world is full of a peaceful hush that makes it hard to grasp what happened. We're used to weird things occurring around ghosts. And in our own peculiar way, we're used to being around the dead. But for me, it doesn't quite click that a member of our sector has died—that he's now one of the spirits we're supposed to release.

I try to repeat the facts in my head until they cement into the heart-wrenching reality that one of my friends is gone. But each attempt is detoured, my mind slipping into tangents of muddled thought. I think about how Reed's absence will now stretch into eternity, and I wonder what it will be like to no longer have him nearby. Then, with a hard pang of guilt, I recall how much his recent absence has been appreciated—everyone annoyed by his complaints of our night terrors and tired of his constant talk of the Siren.

Stupidly, I consider how Mim will react to the news. As far as I know, she and Reed were not close, except that at the end of last summer, I could tell there was *something* between them. Even if that was only Sender camaraderie or the bond between tutor and mentee, I imagine her grief will be great—until it dawns on me that she's still in a coma, not too far from suffering the same terrible fate.

When I picture the ledge again, see Reed slipping and being dragged into the ocean's folds, a bite of fear makes me grab Meander's leg. His hand rests on mine, his fingers squeezing tight as the memory of last week returns. And then the fear subsides, swept into another source of guilt that Meander's still here, and I should feel more pained by what I have lost than relieved at what I haven't.

A few hours into our bated wait, a rough-looking guy appears with a dinner of fish that a couple of us pick and the rest ignore. Then, around ten, the woman who lives in the house walks in and stares at us like she wasn't expecting to see seven teenagers crammed onto her sofas. With a tired smile, she beckons us to her car and drives us back to our house. No one is there to greet us so, instead of heading to bed, we resume our places in the living room.

I don't expect any true rest to loom on the horizon. But the fire Kornelía builds upon our arrival does eventually lull me to sleep. Around two in the morning, I'm surprised to blink out of a murky dream as Meander rouses me.

"You okay?" I ask with a sleepy start as I sit up. The room around us is quiet. We're the only two left out here.

"I'm fine," Meander says in a low, gentle voice. He strokes my cheek. "How are you doing?"

I almost meet the soothing motion of his thumb with a swooning smile, until I remember what happened before I fell asleep.

"Okay," I admit as the memories snap back into focus. "It's just... weird, you know? Like, I *do* feel okay. But everything is a bit off-kilter. His stuff is in the room still. And he's been gone all week, and it's no different. Except that it's *completely* different. And it makes me... I don't know, sick? Not sad, so much as confused—and a bit ill."

Meander nods. "I know what you mean." He continues to stroke my cheek, his expression morose. After a minute, he takes a deep breath and catches me in his stare. "Fancy getting away for a while?"

My brows furrow with uncertainty. "To an empty house?" I ask. "I don't think we'll be able to get a car this late."

"That's not what I meant," he says. He sits back, his hand dropping to his knee as he considers me. "This is going to make me sound like an utter bastard," he starts, his words low and cautious. "But what happened tonight... It may have created the perfect chance for us to get to Mim."

I blink, caught off-guard and having no idea how to react to what he just said. "You want to leave *now*?"

"You've seen what it's been like tonight," Meander says. "No one even remembered us. That'll continue. There are a lot of things to deal with. Paperwork, phone calls, meetings. We're not important in all of that. It's the only chance we've got of not being missed."

"Won't they want to talk with us, though?" I ask.

"Yeah," Meander agrees. "But not right away. And given the circumstances, I don't think they'd be too shocked to find we'd gone off on our own. Not if we disappear together. Mrs. Buxley's sharp. I'm quite sure she noticed our changed behavior in Sender Management last week."

He makes a good point. Our instructor would definitely have caught the fact that, after a summer of sitting apart, Meander and I were once again next to each other, whispering throughout her discussion on sleep handling and taking full advantage of our mid-afternoon break to sneak off for a few minutes alone. Plus, if we have Kornelía to spread the story that we went off to process what happened by ourselves, it'd be an easy lie to pull off—at least for a while.

Meander watches as I weigh the options, giving me a moment to work through my thoughts before he continues. "Earlier, when we were at the other house, I used your phone to check for flights. We could leave tomorrow… er, today. This evening."

"That's what you were doing earlier?" I ask, my brain focusing on the least overwhelming part of that sentence.

Meander gives me a sad smile. "I'm a horrible person, I know."

"You're not horrible," I say. "Just… methodical. You've been waiting for an opportunity. I'm impressed you were able to think clearly enough to make sense of all of this."

"I was thinking about the cave," he admits. "The rocks and the waves… It reminded me too much of when we went into the water during the exorcism. And that made me think of Mim." He pauses, his eyes unfocused as he recalls last year's catastrophe. "If anything even *remotely* good can come out of this, it's saving her."

"Unless we're not successful," I counter.

"Yeah…" Meander rubs his neck, a guilty expression crossing his face. "But if that goes wrong, I might well end up in jail, which I'm sure would make at least a few people happy."

I balk. "That's the reason you've chosen to convince me this is a good idea?"

"Figured I'd better mention the possibility at some point," he says with a shrug far too casual for the declaration.

I lean against the sofa with a groan, my eyes closed and my palms pressed against them as I try to work this out. If we leave now, we'll be adding extra stress to the camp officials. If we're successful in Guatemala, some of the gloom will lift, and everyone will have something good to cling to in the wake of this tragedy. But if we're not successful, Mim could wind up the second victim of our third summer at Camp Wanagi.

The question seems impossible to answer. If we go, we'll be hated by some of our sector mates for abandoning the group and not sparing more than a few hours' thought to Reed. If we achieve what we're after, part of the sector will be ecstatic while the rest might remain indifferent as they continue to mourn a better friend they've lost. But Reed's dead, regardless of whether Meander and I leave. The thought is callous but true. And as much as I wish no one had died—that none of us had *ever* been physically injured or emotionally battered because of ghosts—I'm still wading in the quiet wash of relief that Meander wasn't killed. Which is selfish, I guess. But also true.

"Hey," he murmurs, his hand on my knee. "We don't have to do this. We can wait. I know it's asking a lot."

I lower my hands from my face and blink through the dancing spots of light to focus on him. A lot *is* at stake, and there's no guarantee this isn't going to be a dismal failure. But I'm good at hoping for the best. And recently, I've come to realize that the best won't ever come if all I'm doing is sitting around waiting for it to arrive.

"Let's leave," I say at last. I nod, and offer Meander a smile I hope doesn't look too forced. "Let's go and save Mim."

38

WE SLEEP FOR A FEW BROKEN HOURS BEFORE WAKING KORNELÍA TO TELL her about our plan. She's wide-eyed and silent as Meander talks and, for a moment, I worry she'll react badly given what happened less than twelve hours ago. But when he finishes asking if she'll cover for us—at least as long as she can—she doesn't hesitate to nod. She spends a long moment looking between us, then nods a second time, pulling us into a tight hug before she shoos us away so we can get more rest.

I pack before crawling back into bed, sleeping heavily until Meander wakes me around ten. He's already showered and dressed, and I make quick work of doing the same so we can leave the house.

We take a car into town, stopping at a café with an internet connection so Meander can order our tickets— an undertaking in itself for such a last minute trip. Then we return to the house. Our first plane doesn't take off until five, and we want to make sure we're seen as close to our departure time as possible to divert suspicion. For a couple hours, we camp out in the classroom, Meander reading while I play my violin. Around three in the afternoon, we head to the airport.

I'm sure we're going to be caught, and I manage to look entirely too suspicious by checking over my shoulder every few minutes as we wait at the gate. When our tickets are scanned and we step onto the plane, I'm halfway stunned we've managed to board without incident.

Ignoring the unease of knowing my violin has been left unattended under my bunk, I marvel at the weightless bounce of the ground dropping away from us as the plane veers down the runway and lifts into the sky. Out of habit, I glance out the window to watch our ascent. But the vast landscape of blue water serves as an instant reminder that, somewhere below us, crews have dragged Reed from the sea. I picture him lying on a steel table—his body cold and his spirit stuck among the waves—before I close my eyes against the crystalline view.

"You all right?" Meander asks as Greenland fades into the world beneath our feet.

"I'm fine," I say. With a hard swallow, I grab his hand. "You?"

"Yeah, I'm okay." He nods.

The first leg of our trip is over three hours in length, but the distance only takes us back to Iceland. We may be a country away, but the break between connecting flights is filled with as much unease as our initial wait to board the plane in Ilulissat. Meander is quiet on the subject, but I know he feels it too. He's tense, full of more concerns than I am. As much as I'm worried about everything we're going to face *if* we make it to Mim, I have to keep reminding myself that I'm only a bystander—he's the one about to enter a supernatural fray.

The wait in Iceland is a long one. We arrive shortly after eight p.m. our time, and we have to overnight it before our morning flight. We take turns trying to sleep between rounds of walking through the airport, switching gates and keeping a constant lookout for familiar faces. When morning arrives, I'm more than happy to board the next plane. When we make it out of the gate without being caught, it's a relief to know we're now on an eight-hour trek south to Texas. We'll have to be careful when we land as, by that time, our cover may well be blown. But until we reach Dallas, we're free to pretend our trip is a happier one.

"Are you heading out or heading home?" the middle-aged woman next to us asks fifteen minutes into our second flight.

"Somewhere between," I say with an almost convincing smile of excitement. "Just finished a tour of Europe. Now, we're visiting my grandmother for a few days before going home."

I don't know why I lie, except that a made-up trip to visit relatives seems better than explaining our real plans to perform an exorcism when we land. Meander glances up from his book when I start babbling about my rodeo-loving grandma, his head shaking with a soft breath of laughter. But the lady believes my story. Nodding patiently as I prattle on, she gives my hair a curious once-over and tells me how nice it is to see young people spending time with their elders. Then she relates her own reason for being on board as

Meander returns to his book with another gentle scoff.

The pretence of our make-believe works for short spans of time. Once the lady has discovered her magazine is more interesting than I am, I listen to music as Meander switches between reading his book and reviewing his notes. For a couple hours, we share a screen and watch an in-flight movie, our armrest up and our heads leaned together. In Reykjavik, I converted money, so I buy us lunch as we fly over Canada, and I wonder what my family's doing on the ground below.

Every now and again, the reality of what we've left behind and the unreal truth of what we're heading toward creeps in, forming visions like dense clouds behind our eyes. In those moments, we're silent, lost in thought but keeping close with our fingers laced together.

A two-hour layover in Dallas promises to be the trickiest stop along our path. We've been absent from camp overnight now, and it's hard to believe Robbie and Alex haven't figured out we're missing. With any luck, Kornelía's story still has them convinced we're only hiding somewhere in town. But Ilulissat is small, and it won't take them long to figure out we're not still there. I have no idea how many hours it will be before they connect our disappearance with our destination, and that is a very troublesome uncertainty.

Meander fires up my laptop in the airport, worrying the battery's going to die until I remind him I've got a charger with the correct type of plug for an American outlet. Once he's assured of continuing power, I leave him huddled in a boarding area for a flight not our own as I convert money *again* before getting us more food.

Despite it being dinnertime for us, it's mid-afternoon in Texas. I try to channel Mim's process from last year as I hunt for a meal, purchasing sandwiches and pasta salad to ensure we won't be hungry when facing Anjelo. When I bring our mediocre feast back to the terminal, we snack on carb-loaded fuel as Meander researches medical equipment and does a virtual tour of the hospital where Mim's a patient—while I keep a lookout for any unusual people watching us. The idea we may be persons of interest is weird, like it's a game we're playing and, in truth, no one could care less about our presence here. Still, my nerves coil whenever someone meets my eye or travels past wearing a particular shade of metallic blue.

"This is impossible," Meander says after a while, glancing up with eyes strained from exhaustion. He needs to sleep before he reaches Mim. I can't fathom how he'll pull this off if he's so tired he's barely able to stand.

"Little late for impossible now," I say. I tilt my head so I can see the computer screen. "What are you looking at?"

"Ventilators," he mutters. He rests his head on my shoulder, and I wrap an arm around his back, breathing the scent of sandalwood and trying to make myself as soft a resting place as possible. "There are too many systems, and too many variables. I don't know enough to guess what her specific set-up will be."

"There's not just, you know… a plug you can pull?" I ask. I wish I wasn't such a useless companion. My knowledge of medical equipment is even less than someone who binge watches a grossly inaccurate hospital drama.

Meander lets out a small laugh. "If I have to resort to plug pulling, we'll be in big trouble," he says. "Life support systems come with battery backups, you know. And that's my problem. Figuring out how to get her unhooked without triggering any alarms is not going to be easy. If I *could* just pull a plug, it'd make this whole excursion a hell of a lot simpler."

"We'll figure it out," I assure him in what I hope is at least a semi-confident tone. "If we need to reconfigure her machine so it won't alert the staff, well... I'm sure it's not difficult. It's not like you need an education to care for patients or anything."

Meander sighs, snuggling against my side as he clicks another link. "You may end up an accomplice if you start fiddling with equipment," he informs me.

"I'm going to be hopelessly optimistic and keep faith the Oracle won't leave us to rot in a Guatemalan prison."

"I'm not one for pegging my hopes on other people," Meander says. "But in this case, I'm going to agree." He's quiet for a minute, his breath so steady I think he may have drifted to sleep. But then he shifts, one hand coming to rest on my knee. "Hey, Cal?" he says, his voice quiet.

"Yes?"

"I'm happy you're here," he says. "I'm terrified of what's going to happen, but... I'm glad I'm doing this with you."

I nod into his hair and pull my arm tighter around his side. We stay like that for a while until he sits upright to continue his search.

No one catches up to us before we board the flight to Guatemala. Without the computer at his command in-flight, Meander's unable to research, so I snatch away his books and tell him to sleep before leaving him next to an elderly couple on route to my separate seat seven rows further back. He grumbles that he's not tired but, when we're free to roam the cabin and I wander back to check how he's faring, he's already out cold.

I doze myself, waking when the plane is about to descend in Guatemala City. With a sharp intake of breath, I open the window shade and watch the ground coming up beneath us, my fists clenched with nerves as the plane arrives in Mim's homeland.

39

THE HOSPITAL IS UNINTERESTING. AS WE CLIMB OUT OF THE PRIVATE TAXI and cross the crowded parking lot, I stare at the winged Rod of Asclepius shining white over an entrance that is remarkably similar to one I'd see at home. Despite being in a strange country, the familiarity of the setting puts me relatively at ease as we approach the care facility.

"We made it," I say as we step up to the main doors.

Meander nods, looking taut with displeasure. "And now our next feat of magic—getting in."

Over thirty hours of travel is enough to make this a weary venture. But our inflexible timeline also means we've arrived at the hospital around nine p.m. I'd envisioned strolling in, claiming to be visitors and hoping no one would suspect our motives. I don't know what the hospital's official visiting hours are, but I'd be shocked if they let us walk in now without question. If need be, we'll spend the night in a waiting room. But each passing hour increases the likelihood of getting stopped by the Oracle.

"If anyone can do it, it's you," I say, eyeing Meander with a smirk. "And if you're secretly hiding powers of invisibility, now's the perfect time to let me know."

He hitches his backpack further up his shoulder, a quick smile flitting onto his lips before it fades into a frown of concern. "Trouble with my powers of invisibility," he says, "is that they don't work on spirits. Hospitals are bloody awful when you see ghosts."

The only spirit I was counting on communicating with tonight is Anjelo Savou. I hadn't considered the possibility of other ghosts getting in our way, and the thought makes me swallow through a throat now dry with apprehension.

"Okay. So, in and out of rooms until we know they're safe," I suggest. "No hanging about, waiting to see what any spirits have to tell us."

"And if you suddenly insist we head to the morgue, should I pick you up and carry you out?" he teases.

I nod. "This *is* the kind of place I'd be guided by a ghost, isn't it? Probably a gunshot victim roaming the halls, convinced the surgeon will still be able to save him."

"I'll do the navigating, then, yeah?" he says.

"Sounds like a plan," I agree.

Meander stares at the glowing light of the entrance sign, his shoulder pressed to mine. "Then what are we still standing out here for?" he asks.

I give his profile another small nod, and together we head into the hospital.

Inside the green-walled building, we focus on getting to the right floor and correct wing, trying to figure out how best to locate Mim's room. Yet even with our thoughts on Mim, the reality of our friend being so close takes a while to sink in. She is our destination, but we're so preoccupied, I don't let the idea of her presence settle into firm fact. Even when it does finally dawn on me that she's nearby, it's strange to think of her lying in wait, totally unaware we've flown in from Greenland to attempt to set her free.

Meander has an incredible aptitude for getting around unnoticed, at least. We don't do any actual sneaking—no darting around corners or waiting for people to pass before we tiptoe behind them. We keep a normal pace, Meander wearing a bored expression that would, to most people, pass as genuine. I can see the anxiety as his eyes sweep every bit of signage we pass. But his manner retains a disinterested but purposeful air, casual enough no one pays us heed as we make our way through the corridors.

Only when we approach the locked doors of the Intensive Care Unit does his calm demeanor fade.

"I didn't even think about getting into the unit," he mutters. He stands against a wall, head back and eyes trained on the ceiling. "I knew it would be locked, but I didn't bother to plan a way in. *Shit.* What the hell are we going to do now?"

"Ask someone?" I suggest.

His eyes are wary as he lowers his head. "We don't have permission to be here," he reminds me. "They're not just going to let us in."

"You don't know that," I retort. "If we pretend we are supposed to be here, maybe they'll buy it. We can say we're a relative. My grandmother could just as easily live here as in Texas."

The corner of Meander's lips lift, and I take a deep breath, steeling my nerves in preparation for my own half-baked idea. Lying our way into Mim's room is a weak plan, and we both know it. But I'm not sure we have any other option at this point. Sizing up the unit doors, I beckon Meander to follow me. With a heavy breath, he pushes off the wall. We step forwards, my hand reaching out to press the buzzer that will call the ICU desk. But before I can complete the task, Meander halts me.

"Wait." Tugging on my arm, he pulls me to the side as a family rushes up the hallway. I'm not sure where they came from, but their appearance—harried as it is—is a blessing. Two women and a man hurry to the door, and one of two women slams her whole palm against the buzzer. She's crying, as are the other two. The man whispers something tearful, and the second woman nods, grasping his arm.

The door clicks open, and the family pushes inside. Before the door has time to shut behind them, Meander ushers me forward and we slide into the unit.

I brace myself, expecting we'll be caught as soon as we're inside. But the unit is busy, and Meander keeps us close enough to the family that no one else even bothers to glance our way. The woman who pressed the buzzer talks to the nurse behind the main desk. When the nurse lowers her head to the computer screen, Meander tugs my arm again.

"Over there," he whispers, nodding his head in the direction of the unattended doors around the side of the information desk.

My heart pounds as Meander walks towards the patient rooms, his casual stance returning as he rounds the desk. With as little movement as possible, I glance around, waiting for suspicious eyes to land on mine. But no one is looking at us. The nurse is still typing something into the computer while the distraught family block a good portion of her sight line as they press close to the desk. An orderly wheels a cart down the hallway, his back to us. And even as I turn in their direction, two other staff members disappear into one of the rooms.

People are all around us, but no one notices as Meander ambles past doors, peering through small windows to catch glimpses of the patients inside. Breathless with the panicked rush of our unbelievable break, I catch up with him as he stops by the third door.

The room is occupied, and I'm quick to avert my gaze upon seeing someone inside. But when I've taken two steps farther down the hall, my wits kick in and I slide back to the window. Inside, a girl is tucked under the covers of the bed, equipment beeping at her side. Her black hair lays beneath her shoulders, the bangs cut neatly above her closed eyes.

"Mim," I say, my voice strangled as I recognize the friend I haven't seen in a year.

Meander opens the door, nudging me forward so we can slip inside. Mim is by herself and, when we close the door behind us, it seems like a too-lucky break that we've ended up in a private space with no staff noticing we're here.

"She looks… different," I muse as we approach the bed. The pink has faded from her hair, and she's lost weight. Her sunken cheeks make her closed eyes look huge in her otherwise small face.

Meander closes the blinds of the door's small

window before he looks at Mim. His eyes linger for a few seconds, then he swings his backpack onto the bed. Unzipping the bag, his shoulders heave with a shaky breath as he reaches into the pack and glances at me with a nod.

"Okay. Let's get started."

I HELP MEANDER RETRIEVE THE SUPPLIES WE WEREN'T ABLE TO BRING with us without first checking his bag for the flights. We take out the Latin tome, a Bible, a wooden cross, and the bottle of homemade holy water. Meander opens his notes to the Spanish prayer Mim used last year in Swallow's Cave, while I lay the angel wing charm on the exposed skin of her neck next to the tracheostomy tube protruding from her throat. My fingers glide over the small piece of gold, then I step out of the way.

When all our supplies are laid out, Meander appraises the equipment Mim's attached to.

"I think I understand the set-up," he says after a moment. "She has a feeding tube, and any medicines she needs are given there." He points to the small tube hanging out of Mim's right arm on the far side of the bed. "Then there's a catheter, and the trachea hooked up to the ventilation machine. That's the big part. The rest of the tubes don't matter… It's the ventilation we need to cut off." His steps closer to the breathing machine that fills the room with a hushed rhythm of suction and hiss. I listen to its mechanical melody until Meander pushes up his sleeves and moves back to the bed. "Yeah, all right. I think we're ready."

I don't know whether to assure him he can do this, wish him good luck, or keep my mouth shut so he can concentrate. I settle on standing next to him, ready to hand over the first accessory.

"I'm here for whatever you need," I say.

He nods and, with a quavering breath, he begins.

Placing an unsteady hand on Mim's arm, he says the prayer. The words are awkward on his tongue, and it reminds me of Mim's trouble with the Latin phrases last summer. Her pronunciation didn't have any negative effect on the power of her exorcism. I hope Meander's non-native speech works the same way.

When the prayer is over, he grasps Mim's arm and repeats the sentiment she expressed a year ago in the cave, his words altered to fit the changed situation.

"Anjelo Savou," he utters in a low, angry voice, "we are here tonight to force you to cross over, to push out your spirit and make you leave. You have stayed too long. You are not meant to be here, and I *will not* let you remain. Go to the light, Anjelo. Let the angels take you. If you don't—if you will not leave of your own accord, I will *make* you myself."

His voice and his hand are steadier now. Already, I can see a bruise starting to spread on his arm. But unlike last year, he doesn't flinch with pain.

"*Et hoc incipere*," he says.

I hand him the cross, and he says another Spanish

prayer, the words losing their intensity as his voice grows hoarse. When he's finished, he coughs, one hand holding his throat. I take the cross and lay it on Mim's chest before opening the bottle of holy water and handing it over. My muscles are tight, my anxiety spiking with the knowledge Meander's struggling to breathe. But while I itch to grab his arm and drag him from the room, I stay rooted, the bottle outstretched as if I don't even notice.

The sooner this is finished, the better. I'm glad *something* is happening. And I know Meander won't quit until the process is complete—or he loses consciousness from lack of air. I won't try to stop him. But I hate not being able to offer more than petty assistance.

"With this water, I destroy your strength." He holds a thumb over the bottle's top as he splashes Mim's face. The water hits and Meander winces, doubling-over as Mim's chest rises in a jerky motion.

"Meander..." I say, caught between wanting to soothe his pain and congratulate him on having such an impressive effect. I hold his arm, pulling him until he leans against the bedside. Beyond the door, voices mumble as hospital staff pass by. Poised to run and barricade the door if need be, I get Meander steady and push at his arm until he remembers what he needs to do next.

"*Ipse venena bibas,*" he says through another cough. "With this water, I crush your defenses."

The room's low lights flicker and Meander cries out, wheezing as Mim jerks again like a body pulsing with electric shock. He braces one hand against the bed, and his head droops with a strangled groan before he forces it up.

"*Vade retro phasmatis,*" he hisses, the words reduced to a harsh whisper. "With this water, I drown you all over again, Anjelo."

I stare at Meander, intrigued by words I'm sure are not a copy of anything Mim said last year. His eyes are dark, his breath ragged and shallow. He empties the rest of the water over Mim's face. She convulses, and he staggers back, crashing into the machine at the bed's side.

"Damn it," I mutter. The sound is likely to draw attention, and we're not finished. Rushing to Meander's side, I try to pull him back to his feet. He grips my arm, struggling to stand before his strength gives way and he drops to his knees. I lower myself, my skinning buzzing with panic. We are going to be caught. I can feel it coming, and we've progressed too far to fail now.

"Hey, look at me." I hold Meander's face in my hands, but he can't manage to keep eye contact. He blinks, his vision seeming to sway as his head lolls to one side.

"I—I can't—" he coughs, his focus lost in a daze of pain.

His skin is drained of color, and his breath is coming in shallow rasps that hurt my ears. I can't imagine how awful the spirit's grip must feel. But if he doesn't push through the agony, he's going to lose the fight against this ghost. I can't let that happen. Not now. Not after every horrible thing that's led to this moment.

"You need to finish this," I say with sharp resolve. His head droops, and I lift it up, holding it tight. His eyes are barely managing to stay open, so I do the only thing I can think of to keep his attention. I press my lips to his, the kiss a hard, desperate reminder. Of who I am. Of where he is. "Anjelo's pissed off," I mumble against his mouth. "Let's make him so angry he leaves Mim's body to attack you, all right?"

Meander's eyes remain blank for a moment, before a hint of a smirk twitches at the corners of his lips. I smile, kissing him again and urging him to his feet. He keeps a hold of my waist, and we struggle up and stumble back to the bed together. When I move to step away from him, he shakes his head. Grabbing my hand, he keeps me pressed to his side.

"*Hinc... itur... ad angelus,*" Meander growls, squeezing my fingers as he fights to stay on his feet. "Get out of here, Anjelo. Your sweetheart abandoned you. Leave the world for lovers who stand a chance."

He takes the hand that's still holding mine and places both over Mim's heart. With a sudden burst of strength, he presses down so hard, I'm afraid we're going to do damage. She convulses under the contact and, with his free hand, Meander reaches for the ventilator. He doesn't even hesitate. He presses a button, opens a plastic covering on the machine's underside, and flips the switch to shut off Mim's support system.

"Okay, Mim," he says. His whole body is shaking now. "This part's up to you. Get that damned spirit out." He coughs, leaning hard into my side. "Where are your angels now? They've failed you. You're an idiot if you think you can rely on anyone other than yourself to get you out of this hell."

Meander presses our hands harder into Mim's chest. When she jerks again, he offers her body a grimacing smile.

"Want to argue with that?" he asks, his voice almost lost to the short, scraping breaths tinting his face a terrifying shade of blue. "I'm telling you that everything you believe in is wrong, and... I'm positive that, right now, you just... want to give me a good bashing. Sounds satisfying, yeah? Well... I'm afraid... the only way you can manage that... is if you do it in person—*Maria*."

He pushes our hands down one final time, the movement like a deranged attempt at CPR. The jolt hurts the shoulder I injured back in Greenland, but the minor pain is insignificant next to the momentous sight on the bed. Mim starts to seize, and Meander's thrown back, his hand falling from mine as he loses his footing and crashes once more to the floor. The lights dim, flicker, then go out completely, throwing the room into darkness. Outside, questioning voices murmur in the hall, the sound growing louder as they near us. I try to ignore the looming disaster as I watch Mim. Her body writhes on the bed, the tubes still attached to her swinging with the force of her movements. Her chest heaves, and the veins of her neck strain against her skin. Her back arches, the pose lasting a breathless beat before a final jerk sends her falling back against the bed.

The convulsions stop. Mim lies motionless against the sheets.

"Oh no," Meander croaks from his spot on the floor. He pushes onto his knees and crawls across the room. "No, no, no."

I approach the bed, yearning to catch a glimpse of movement from the shadowed outline before me. The tubes continue swaying, but the body they are attached to does not. I reach forward, push through my hesitation, and press a hand to Mim's neck. I wait one, two, three seconds—and don't feel any hint of a pulse.

My stomach drops, and my eyes sting with furious tears. I turn back to Meander and, even in the darkness, I know his expression matches mine.

"She's—"

White light bursts behind me, the sudden brightness sending me reeling. I stagger, tripping on Meander's foot and sprawling on top of him as my senses are overloaded with sight, scent, and sound. A thick smell of salt water passes through the air, twisting with the faint drumming beats of an old Tongan song.

On the bed, Mim flings forward, the tracheostomy tube gargling with a sound like the half-drowned gasp of someone finally pulled to shore.

"Qué ocurre aquí?"

The door opens, and an older woman stares at us in astonished silence as Mim begins retching on the bed. While the nurse is still stunned to stillness, I scramble to my feet and haul Meander to his.

"Let's go," I say.

I grab his hand and snatch our bags on route to the door. With a final look at Mim—a split second in which her eyes, wide and wild, stare back at us—we barrel past the nurse and run into the hall.

41

WE DON'T MAKE IT FAR. SOMEONE YELLS, AND AN ALERT BLARES OVER THE intercom. Rushing down corridors and crashing into the stairwell, I nearly trip down the steps as we hurry to reach ground level. But when we push into the first-floor corridor, there are no hospital personnel ready to restrain us. Instead, two blue-suited individuals wait near the entrance—one an elderly man I've never met and the other Miss Kappel, one of my instructors from our first year at Camp Wanagi.

"Busy night?" Miss Kappel says when she sees us.

Her expression is neutral though, to be honest, even a furious countenance wouldn't diminish my relief right now. I'm wired with the exhilaration of what just happened, an oddity given the usual exhaustion that accompanies a release. And, trouble or not, I'm glad we're being apprehended by the Oracle rather than the local police. I don't know any Spanish, and even if we got an English-speaking officer, we'd be hard-pressed to explain what the hell we just did.

"A tad," Meander says as we slide to a stop. He leans against the nearest wall, eyeing me with a smile that is overwhelmed and, I imagine, slightly disbelieving. I return the look, and by the way his cheeks turn pink, I suspect the beaming pride I also feel shows through in my gaze. Meander's accomplished something the Oracle hasn't dared to attempt. He's toiled for months, determined to find a solution to a situation apparently impossible to fix. And he's done it.

If we get a single moment alone in the midst of all the chaos that's about to ensue, I'll make damned sure he knows how brilliant he is.

"Would either of you care to explain what's going on?" Miss Kappel says, breaking our increasingly intimate stare.

I blink, taking a moment to tame my thoughts as Meander answers the instructor's stern question.

"Your patient's awake."

Miss Kappel's eyes snap to him as she considers what he said. Then she looks at the man next to her and, with a nod, he heads farther into the hospital. My former instructor leads the two of us to the nearest waiting room before ordering us to sit. She stands guard, and we stay silent as the other Sender investigates.

Half an hour passes before he returns, addled but pleased as he talks to Miss Kappel in a low voice and a language I can't decipher. She listens and nods, her eyes sliding to us every other sentence or so. When they've finished conferring, the man takes over watching us while Miss Kappel makes a phone call. Once another half hour has passed, more members of the Oracle appear to look after Mim and remove Meander and me from the hospital.

We're shuttled to a nearby apartment and, for the next three hours, we're questioned about what happened. Aside from Miss Kappel, I don't recognize any of the Senders we talk to. They range in many respects, including the way they treat the two of us. Some of them are kind while others fail to keep from yelling. A few even seem amused. But no one tells us what will happen next and, after the interrogation is over, we're sent to a hotel and instructed to get some rest before being escorted back to the airport the next morning.

We don't sleep right away. When we're alone, we talk, discussing what occurred and speculating about what's to come. The exorcism left us both alive with frenzied energy, and Meander's best guess is that the force of Mim's spirit was enough to make Anjelo cross without stealing reserves from us. But whatever the cause, the unusual experience of being wide awake after a release doesn't last. After the wait at the hospital and the lengthy period of questioning, the fatigue from our travel once more seeps in. Still, even after we're done talking, we push our strength, staying awake as long as possible to make the most of our time alone before the solemn journey back to Greenland begins.

The return trip takes a more leisurely route than the way we took here, with more lengthy stopovers that spark in me a growing hatred of being on a plane. Miss Kappel escorts us to Florida, then the three of us cross the large distance to Copenhagan before we fly to Kangerlussuaq and take a final short flight back to Ilulissat. If nothing else, the Oracle has paid our fares for the return trip. And, I suppose as a token of thanks, Miss Kappel hints that Meander's initial purchase will be reimbursed as well.

All things considered, we can't complain about our treatment. Still, our arrival in Ilulissat is nerve-wracking. I'm prepared to deal with Mrs. Buxley and the consequences of taking off. But I'm not sure if anyone in Shade—aside from Kornelía—knows where we went, and I can't fathom how we'll explain.

Mrs. Buxley is not waiting for us when we land. Robbie is and, despite a somewhat severe glance from Miss Kappel, he grins when we come into view.

"What the hell are we gonna do with you two now?" he asks. His voice is cheerful, his fanned, spiked hair like the rays of a black and green sun.

"Hey, at least I didn't break any bones this time," I offer.

"Broken arm, international escape and hospital break-in..." Robbie holds out both palms as if weighing the situations. Then he looks at Miss Kappel. "How is she?"

We haven't heard anything about Mim's condition since we left the hospital room. I glance at my old instructor, and she gives me a dubious look before deciding to answer Robbie's question.

"She's stable," she says, the statement sending another wave of enthusiastic relief washing over me. "We're still working with her to determine what, if anything, she remembers. But she is awake, and appears to be in a healthy, stable condition."

Robbie's smile is one of pure, genuine joy as he nods. "That's what I was hoping to hear," he says. He eyes Meander, then looks back at Miss Kappel. "I'll take these two. Buxley's awaiting your arrival. There's a car to bring you to her."

We walk together out to the parking lot before Miss Kappel separates as we load into different vehicles.

"We're not seeing Mrs. Buxley, too?" I ask as our car leaves the airport's parking lot.

"You will," Robbie says from the front seat. "But first we thought we'd take you back to the house. The others are waiting."

"To lynch us?" Meander asks.

Robbie laughs. "I don't think anyone's baking you a welcome home cake." He shrugs, his words a close echo of what he told me after the disaster in Swallow's Cave. "But I suspect it's not quite as bad as you think." His happy expression falters, the pain of the last few days sneaking through his cheerful exterior. "Mainly, they're just confused."

When we do arrive back at the house, it's to find the remaining five members of our sector—plus Alex—in the living room. Kornelía stands as we step in front of the fireplace but, for a moment, no one speaks. Then Dylan looks around, his expression one of utter incomprehension.

"Where the hell did you go?" he asks, and the casual way he says it makes me smile despite the weary and grave faces of the others.

"Guatemala," Meander answers.

Dylan does a double-take before looking to Kornelía like she might have some sort of explanation. I, on the other hand, turn to Robbie.

"Can we tell them?" I ask.

He shrugs. "Don't see why not."

I glance at Meander. This is his achievement, but

I know he's not one for group discussions. When he gives me a subtle nod, I step onto the soft rug, prepared to face whatever reaction might come.

"We went to see Mim," I say.

"What? Why?" Dylan asks, his voice no longer nonchalant.

Kornelía comes closer, her eyes searching. I figured she'd already grasped the truth. When she nears me, I realize she's waiting for my confirmation.

"Meander did it," I say, to her and no one else. "Anjelo is gone, and Mim is awake."

Eyes wide, Kornelía throws her arms around me before remembering it's not me she should be thanking. With a gasp of laughter, she pushes away to embrace Meander instead. He gives me a panicked look from under her surprisingly forceful weight, and I smile.

"Mim's... *awake*," Dylan repeats to himself in a breathless whisper.

"What are you talking about?" Sabeena asks. "What is going on here?"

I look back at the rest of my sector. "I'll start at the beginning. I guess there's a lot to tell."

42

I TALK, ALLOWING MEANDER TO ADDRESS WHATEVER BITS REQUIRE FURTHER explanation. The list of points is quicker to relate than I expected, but my shortened version of events is overshadowed by the onslaught of questions we're asked once I'm finished.

The reactions of our sector mates bring a wide array of emotions to the room. Sefa is impressed we pulled off such a big task, while Sabeena is angry—saying what we did was idiotic and, when we did it, cruel. Naasir stays quiet, his opinion buried under the contemplative mask of his expression. But Kornelía is thrilled, her enthusiasm filling the space left by his silence.

Dylan can't seem to make up his mind. I omit talking about the risks we gambled with, but he must sense the danger we put Mim in. He glares at Meander, shaking his head while I talk and looking at times like he might burst into a rage. But then something shifts and, more than anything, he looks overwhelmed by the fact Mim is awake. And perhaps by the knowledge that, while I joined Meander and Kornelía kept our guard, he played no part in helping her recover.

"You two are crazy," Sefa says with a smile when the conversation comes to its end.

"I want to know more," Kornelía insists. "The whole process, from the initial planning steps."

"Well, we've got the next week to fill you in," Meander says with a look of tired hope that maybe they'll lay off for a day or two so he can finally get some proper rest.

"Yeah... About that..." Robbie scratches his chin, sharing a look with Alex that sweeps away my energy.

"I think maybe we'd better get you to Mrs. Buxley," Alex finishes for him.

The others look confused, but Meander understands—and so do I. We knew serious trouble was a possibility when we left for Guatemala. For a brief moment, those fears disappeared when we came back to a familiar setting and a feeling of near-normalcy amongst our sector mates. But now Meander's expression is apologetic, as if this is entirely his fault and not something I willingly went along with. My stare is pointed as our eyes meet and, after a hard, lingering moment, I turn back to our leads.

"Should we go now, then?" I say. "No sense delaying the inevitable any longer, is there?"

"No, there's not," Robbie agrees.

He calls a car and, once more, we load into a vehicle and drive across the town of Ilulissat. We don't say anything for the duration of the drive. Meander is tense, less like he's worried about what Mrs. Buxley is going to say and more like he's trying to figure out how he can take the fall for us both. But even if he had a sure-fire lie to convince the Oracle I was somehow duped into aiding him, he has to know I won't allow him to use it. He is not to blame for what we're about to face. He's to be commended for having the bravery—and perhaps the recklessness—to attempt the exorcism that saved Mim's life.

Miss Kappel is still talking to Mrs. Buxley when we arrive at the instructor's house, but she says goodbye when we step into the room. Robbie tries to hang around, but Mrs. Buxley sends him on his way as well.

Meander and I sit on the room's l-shaped sofa while Mrs. Buxley stands a few paces away. She fixes us with a steady gaze. For a long moment, no one says a word. When he can't be bothered with the silence anymore, Meander sits forward, his hands on his knees as he sighs.

"We getting kicked out?"

Mrs. Buxley gives him a wry smile. "I believe you've asked me that question before, Mr. Rhoades." She appraises him, her purple-heeled shoe tapping against the dark hardwood. "You left camp unattended, travelled internationally, broke into a private hospital room, and performed a dangerous maneuver that put a camper's life at risk. Yes, Mr. Rhoades. You and Mr. Silver are, indeed, getting *kicked out*."

The news is not unexpected, yet it still manages to hit me like a brick. Sinking back in my seat to stare at the ceiling while Meander puts his head in his hands, I tell myself it was worth it—and know at some point I'll believe that. But right now, I'm stuck with the misery of losing months of time to hone my skills and be with my friends, not to mention an entire summer I won't have with Meander. Nine weeks ago, I didn't think I'd want to return for my final year with the Oracle. Now, hearing I can't is like a punch to the gut.

"You will be leaving here tomorrow," Mrs. Buxley continues. "And your suspension from Camp Wanagi will be active until this year's session is complete."

I blink at the ceiling for several seconds before looking back at our instructor. "This year's session..." I repeat. "You mean, like, until next week?"

Meander sits up, glancing at me before we both stare at Mrs. Buxley—taut with anticipation until she at last graces us with a nod.

"And next year?" Meander asks in a cautious voice.

"You will be reinstated as members of the Shade sector at the beginning of the summer term," she says.

Meander shakes his head. "So... you're kicking us out... for a *week*."

Amusement glints in Mrs. Buxley's eyes as she wanders the room like she's teaching one of her lessons.

"You did immense research on the subjects of exorcism and possession," she begins. "You also used the full extent of your mental, emotional, and financial means to attempt a complex and daring venture you believed would work. You did the job of a dedicated Sender, all for the sake of helping your fellow Shade. Your foolishness cannot go unpunished. But your incredible achievement cannot go unrewarded either. So, yes, Mr. Rhoades. You both are being removed from Camp Wanagi. For a week."

A soft smile tugs at Mrs. Buxley lips while a laugh of disbelief escapes my throat. Of all the outcomes I imagined, this is not the sort of ending I thought our adventure would receive. Given the alternatives, however, I can't believe our absolute luck—and the sheer generosity of the Oracle.

Meander turns to me, his eyes wide under his brim of curls. I want to kiss him. If we were alone, I'd send us both crashing to the floor in a tackling embrace. But our instructor is still watching us, so I settle for a look of enthusiasm that—after a pause—he returns.

"I should, however, warn you," Mrs. Buxley says, her firm voice cutting into our joy. "There is a chance Camp Wanagi will not resume next summer."

"What?" I ask. "Why wouldn't it resume?"

"The death of a camper is monumental," she explains, and the sudden reminder of why we escaped grounds me further. With a guilty pang, the smile falls from my lips. "Many complications arise from a tragedy, and there will be a vast number of discussions over the immediate future of our camp."

"This can't be the first time something like this has occurred," Meander says. "Even regular summer camps have deaths. It happens."

"Unfortunately, it does," Mrs. Buxley agrees. "And it has for us. This will not be the end of Camp Wanagi, I assure you. But it is possible there will be a delay in resuming normal camp activities after this summer is over. If these issues are resolved by next June, you can be assured you will both receive your invitations. But I'm sure you've figured out by now that life—and death—are complex. For the moment, all I'm able to offer are uncertain hopes."

The news is not great but, after the certainty of being banished from next year's camp, the *possibility* that we'll be able to complete our time at Camp Wanagi is enough to keep me going.

"Thank you," I tell her.

Meander nods his agreement and offers a few thankful words of his own. Then Mrs. Buxley smiles, a rare, wholehearted expression.

"This afternoon," she says, "you should return to your sector and enjoy your remaining hours. Rest, eat, and spend time with your fellow Shades. There is one final event you will be part of before your flights home tomorrow."

"What event?" I ask.

Mrs. Buxley only shakes her head. "You will find out tonight."

THE SKY IS CLEAR, THE MIDNIGHT SUN FADED TO A PINK DUSK THAT shines over the calm water of Disko Bay. An hour ago, students and instructors lit candles and placed them in small glass jars, whispering farewells over the open flames before dropping the jars into the sea. Now, dozens of lights bob in the gentle waves like floating fireflies while, across an expanse of rocky hills, clusters of Wanagi campers wait for the next part of the ceremony to begin.

On the grass of a high mound, Shade sits together— the seven of us huddled close.

"They released the Siren while you were gone," Kornelía says. She sits next to Dylan, her legs outstretched before her. His knees are tucked into his chest, and his wild hair drapes over his eyes as he nods in absent agreement.

"They brought someone to communicate with her," Sabeena adds. "She only needed to relate a message.

After all of that, she just wanted her family to know she had been taken by the sea. She was easy to release when the right Sender found her. But she's been here for hundreds of years because the correct one never came close. Until Reed."

"All he wanted was to release a ghost," Naasir says. "Mrs. Buxley told us that's why he stayed. He wanted to be a true Sender."

"Mrs. Buxley can communicate with him?" I ask in surprise. We've never been told what our instructor's ability is.

Kornelía smiles. "She can speak with spirits who are new. They're different from other ghosts. More confused and fragile. But more fixed on their purpose for hanging about."

I shake my head with mild incredulity. "That's really why he stayed? Because he wanted to release a spirit?"

Sabeena clicks her tongue in disapproval. "Yes," she mutters. "And you'd already know that, if you hadn't left."

"So, if the Siren's gone, why isn't he?" Meander asks, ignoring her obvious contempt.

"He doesn't know... or doesn't quite understand. I don't know if ghosts can see each other," Kornelia muses. "He may not have any idea she's been released."

"Mrs. Buxley's going to tell him tonight," Sabeena says. Her voice is softer now, her momentary anger sliding back into resigned melancholy. "She was waiting for his parents to arrive."

Out on the water, close to the jutting rock where Reed fell, our instructor stands aboard a small boat.

In addition to the captain and Althea acting as Mrs. Buxley's assistant, two other people are present—a man with dark blond hair and a woman with a head of rusty orange-red.

Reed's parents hold one another tight as Mrs. Buxley starts to talk.

"It's beginning," Kornelía whispers, her eyes closed and her chin tilted towards the water.

What little conversation was bouncing between us stops when Mrs. Buxley raises one hand to signal for us to be silent. All human sounds fall away as Shades, Revenants, Wraiths, and Entities turn their attention to the coastline. The whole of Camp Wanagi is here to witness tonight's event. At this time of summer, various campers should be away completing their final projects. But I don't think anyone is. I see Daniel and Isabis standing among the Entity sector, and even the oldest Revenant campers have returned. All of the camp's current instructors are here as well, along with Miss Kappel who hasn't yet returned to Guatemala— or wherever she usually considers home.

I can't hear what Mrs. Buxley is saying, but it doesn't matter. She speaks and, every so often, she pauses to listen. Occasionally, she flinches, but otherwise she shows no sign of distress. Her composure is incredible. She's had years to perfect her stance while being around a spirit. Still, her solid footing and mostly neutral face makes my inability to keep my head around a ghost that much more pathetic.

After a few minutes have passed, Mrs. Buxley takes the hands of Reed's parents so they can each say a few words to their son. The scene is heart-wrenching. We're close enough to watch the pain and anguish rolling in waves across their faces. But at the same time, I think everyone here recognizes that what we're witnessing is amazing. Reed's parents speak, and Mrs. Buxley translates. The knowledge they are communicating with their dead child for the last time must be an impossible weight for them to bear. But the fact they get the opportunity to say these farewells is astonishing—what I suspect many people would consider a miracle.

When each of Reed's parents has spoken, they fold into one another as our instructor bows her head and mutters a final few words.

"He's going," Kornelía says, her voice happy even though tears streak her cheeks.

Out on the water, the boat begins to rock with a sudden sway of waves, as do the lanterns floating near the shore. Like the sun peeking under the cover of cloud, a bright spot collides with the icy water surrounding the boat. Mrs. Buxley holds her hands over her mouth, staggering into the waiting cradle of Althea's powerful arms. Reed's parents stare around them, their expressions pained and confused. But then something shifts, and they look up at the sky in disbelieving awe.

Light sweeps over the coast, accompanied by a strong, cold wind and the smell of stale water. The scent triggers memory, and I envision the stagnated lake outside the French château from our first summer as Senders-in-training. There are many reasons a person becomes a ghost when they die. This is the first time I've ever been so well acquainted with a spirit's unfinished business.

As the white light spreads, so does a resounding

cheer. The other sectors yell and clap, as if they've been dazzled by a conjurer's grand finale. For a moment, their noises seem disrespectful. But then I remember where we are, and why. Reed's death was tragic. But his release is something to celebrate. His parents will always have the painful burden of missing and mourning their son. But while we'll miss and mourn him too, much of our pain has been lifted. The worst part of Reed's death was that he did not move on. We know how awful it is to see desperate spirits clinging to our world. And most of us are now familiar with how astounding it is to help a spirit cross to the other side.

So when the wind of release blows back my hair, I find myself laughing. Sefa makes a loud *whoop*, and Sabeena calls a goodbye. Kornelía's head leans back, her eyes still closed but her arms open to the sky. Naasir smiles, Dylan grins, and Meander smirks. And when the wind starts to fade away, the whole of Camp Wanagi raises their hands as if the spirit of Reed Vodden can see us saluting him as he goes.

AFTER THE RELEASE, THE OTHER SECTORS HEAD INTO TOWN FOR THE YEAR-end party so they can reminisce about the camper hardly any of them knew.

"You want to come?" Isabis asks on her way back to one of the waiting vans.

"No, you go," Sabeena says. "We've got something else planned."

We return to the Shade house together. Alex starts the fire, and most of us find somewhere to sit while Sabeena, Naasir, and Sefa go into the boys' room to look through Reed's things. I suppose, with his parents here, the clothes and accessories will soon be packed and shipped to his home. But for now, everything is still in place as if awaiting its owner's return.

When they come back to the living room, Sefa's carrying a dark green sweater made of thick, ribbed cotton. I'm sure I've seen Reed wear it a few times during the course of the summer, but there is nothing special about this particular article of clothing. Which is the point. This isn't something his parents are likely to notice missing from his collection of items. Which means they won't mind if we keep it for ourselves.

Sefa grabs a pair of scissors from the kitchen, and the nine of us—seven Shades plus two Shade leads—sit together in the living room as he prepares to cut.

"We're all agreed?" he says, scissors poised to snip. "Everyone gets a piece."

A chorus of assent ripples through the room, mixing with the crackling of the fire. Sefa nods and begins.

The first piece, a rectangle of fabric from the front hemline, goes to Naasir. Kornelía and Alex each take a long, thin strip, while Robbie asks for a thicker length. Sefa rolls his eyes and says he won't comply with Sabeena's insistence her piece be shaped like a heart but, in the end, he does it—even going so far as to cut the fabric from the section of the sweater that would have rested over its wearer's heart.

The rest of the pieces are cut into squares. Kornelía takes two.

"I'll mail one to Mim," she says, stacking the two shapes on top of each other. "Lu, too. She is still a Shade, even if she's not here."

I haven't given any thought to what I'll do with my piece but, when it's handed over, I realize I don't have to. As soon I have the square of sweater, I fold it into thirds and immediately envision it tucked into the breast pocket of my suit in place of the handkerchief I've never placed there. I don't expect I'll be wearing it to my next violin recital. But the next time I know I'll face a spirit? I'm quite sure this small memory of Reed will make its appearance.

Sefa cuts the sweater, and when everyone has their piece, we burn what fabric remains. As the cotton is engulfed by flame, Sabeena starts talking about the first project she worked on with Reed, the ghost her group released during our first summer of camp. The stories continue, anecdotes and memories shared between us. When the sweater has burnt into ash, the remnants of our conversation flake away. For the last little while before I can no longer keep my eyes open, I curl next to Meander on the sofa and sit in silence as what's left of the Shade Sector watches the dancing flames.

45

I DON'T INTEND TO SLEEP LATE, BUT TRAVEL AND EMOTION KNOCK ME OUT.
Around eight the next morning, I blearily raise my
head. Upon seeing Meander still in his bunk, I fall
back into a heavy sleep that lasts until almost noon.

When I do finally drag myself up, I have a quick
lunchtime breakfast and a short shower before
returning to our room to pack. The bedroom is empty
when I reach it, but as I approach my bunk I notice
something sitting on the rumpled sheets. I drop my
toiletries bag and pajamas on the bed, wondering at
the thin package neatly wrapped in white tissue paper.

"I skipped school on your birthday," Meander says
from behind me.

The words take me by complete surprise, and I start
before turning to see him standing in the doorway. He
smiles at my reaction and nods at the package.

"I couldn't stop thinking about you so, instead of
going to school, I boarded a bus and went to London,"

he continues. "I'm not sure why. I think I just wanted to be somewhere busy... somewhere I could get lost in the crowds."

He pushes off the doorframe and steps into the room, one hand raking through his curls.

"I wandered for a while and ended up in a market. I wasn't paying attention to anything around me. Not until I saw that." He glances at the slim package and smiles again. "It was ridiculous, and I walked through that bloody market at least five times trying to convince myself to leave it. In the end, I couldn't. So, I bought it as a birthday present for you. And when I got home, I stuffed it under my bed with no plan to ever deliver it."

I open my mouth to interject with questions but stop before I start prying into his story. Motioning for him to continue, I press my lips to keep them shut.

"I wasn't going to bring it," Meander says with a smirk at my suppressed curiosity. "But when I pulled out my bag to pack for the summer, I dragged it out too. Couldn't help wrapping it up then, even if I figured it'd stay zipped away until I got back home. And then I saw you before you left to release that spirit." He lets out a chuckling breath. "The whole thing is still barmy, and if you don't like it I won't blame you. But..."

He closes the door behind him before crossing the room to the bed. With a hesitant, almost incredulous shake of his head, he picks up the package and holds it out to me.

"Happy birthday, Cal. Five and a half months late."

I don't quite know what to say. So for a moment, I don't speak at all. Taking the present, I peel back the tissue, my fingers grazing the soft fabric nestled beneath the crease of paper. Curiosity gives way to confusion as I separate packaging from present, and Meander snatches the loose paper away. One eyebrow arched, I glance at him as I reveal the back of a heavy, white cotton dress shirt.

I turn the shirt over to view its front, the arms falling to its sides in the process. My eyes widen, and I bite the inside of my cheek as the full details of the shirt come into view. This is not an ordinary piece of clothing. Its design is decorative—bordering on outlandish. The arms have a loose pleat, and the cuffs are sewn with flowing fabric and lace that billow at the wrists. The collar is high, and a rectangle of ruffled layers run down to the middle of the chest.

The style is like something from the Regency era. I know, because I've seen drawings of people wearing similar fashions—people like Haydn, Mozart, and Beethoven.

Meander watches me, uncertainty in his gaze. He's nervous, and I understand why. Most people would look at something like this and laugh. But my reaction is different. My feet tingle as if I've started walking on half-asleep legs. My heart races too, the patter a flutter of bewildered excitement.

"I'm collecting, aren't I?" I say at last.

Meander's lips curve in a smile, though his eyes remain unsure. "What did you tell me Robbie said?" he asks. "Senders collect. Perhaps he was right?"

I stare at the shirt, knowing it will fit—that it will align with the cut of my modern suit and look ludicrous and perfect all in one. I used to believe the notion of collections preposterous. Honestly, I think I still do. But I have my suit, the small piece of Reed's sweater, and now this fantastically absurd shirt. Turns out, I'm a collector after all.

Hell, maybe it means I'm a proper Sender too.

I lower the fabric and step forward, the shirt hanging behind Meander's back as I drape my arms over his shoulders. His smile is relieved when he pulls me close, his thumb stroking my ear as my free hand resumes its increasingly frequent position tangled in his hair.

"Thank you," I murmur. "I feel bad I didn't get you anything for your birthday."

Meander draws me closer until his forehead is touching mine. "You were there when I didn't deserve to have you," he whispers. "You stayed, you waited— and then you forgave. I've got you, Callum. That's the best birthday present I could receive, even if I didn't unwrap it until the wrong side of the year."

Taken as a whole, the fact that we're being forced out of camp one week early isn't a big deal. Although it hurts that we're losing that time together, I don't regret what we did. Mim is awake. And while I already knew Meander was useful, I think after what he achieved, a part of him might believe it now as well. He still has his doubts, and I'm sure there will be times he still worries his talent is putting me at risk. But I made it through the second exorcism without injury. And my presence—the way our hands were laced together as Meander demanded Anjelo go—had an effect.

I'm not nearly clever enough to have figured out what Meander did in order to save Mim. But I helped in a few small ways. And I'm hoping he's realized how much easier being a Sender is when he's got someone by his side. Of course, I've learned a few things this summer too. If he ever shuts down again, I'll be quick to tell him how stupid he's acting. Then I'll distract him with kisses until he's forgotten everything else.

I distract him with kisses now. Or more accurately, he distracts me. Packing is forgotten as we get lost in the heat of each other's mouths, until attempting to sit on my bed reminds us both of the mound of clothes sprawled overtop the mattress. Only then, with a frustrated sigh and a few muttering curses, do I fold my new shirt and get back to the task at hand.

"So, what will you do with your extra week of summer?" Meander asks when most of my items have been put away.

I stuff my Wanagi hoodie into my duffel bag as I shrug my shoulders. "Get an early start on my music studies, I guess."

Meander gives me a questioning look. "Music studies?"

"Dealing with the ghost of Albert Timmons would have been a lot easier if I'd known more about that damned song," I sigh. "If I'm going to start hearing music whenever I see spirits, I should probably expand my knowledge beyond the works of classical composers."

Meander hands me my hiking boots, an appraising glint in his eye. "Want me to send you some Bee Gees?" he asks, his tone deadpan.

A bubble of laughter rises from my throat, escaping through a smile wide with affectionate amusement. "Absolutely."

Meander's arms slide around my waist, and his chin rests on my shoulder as I zip my duffle bag. I tilt my head back, my eyes falling closed and my hands resting overtop his where they meet on my stomach.

The summer is officially cut short, but there's been no shortage of activity. New ability has come with new pain. An injury led to a reunion, and a death led to life. The balance is odd, and I suspect it will take a while to process it all. For the moment, I'm content to revel in the warmth of Meander's weight against my back. I'll have plenty of time to ponder how my ability has changed and what that means for my uncertain future with the Oracle when I'm on my own.

"Shall we say goodbye to the others?" I ask after a long moment of easy quiet.

Meander smirks, his grip on my waist tightening. "Or maybe we should wait a little bit longer. If we've got time?"

"I already told you." I twist in his arms so we're standing face to face. "I've always got time. Whatever you need. I'm here."

He nods, his eyes catching mine. "From here on, so am I," he promises.

"Well, according to Sefa, I'm as good at pissing off ghosts as you are." I smile. "So, I guess that means we're going to make one hell of a team."

"I think we already do," Meander says. "And if we get to come back next year, we'll make sure the bloody spirits know it too."

I nod my agreement. Then I grab the front of his shirt and pull him close for one of the last kisses we'll get before we have to leave.

THE STORY CONTINUES
IN BOOK 3.5 OF THE ORACLE OF SENDERS SERIES

PRESENCE

ABOUT THE AUTHOR

MERE JOYCE is a Canadian author of books for young adults. Her writing includes contemporary tales, high-action mysteries, and her personal favorite—ghost stories. When she's not writing, Mere can be found recommending books as a librarian, or spending time at home with her husband and two sons. She's also been known to be a selective, yet highly enthusiastic fangirl.

Find her online at:

MEREJOYCE.COM